PARKS PAT MYSTERIES

PARKS PAT MYSTERIES

BOOKS 4-6

P.D. WORKMAN

ISBN: 9781774683484 (Lulu Direct)

ISBN: 9781774683453 (KDP Paperback)

ISBN: 9781774683477 (Kindle)

ISBN: 9781774683460 (ePub)

pdworkman

ALSO BY P.D. WORKMAN

MYSTERY/SUSPENSE:

Parks Pat Mysteries

Out with the Sunset

Long Climb to the Top

Dark Water Under the Bridge

Immersed in the View

Skimming Over the Lake

Hazard of the Hills

Auntie Clem's Bakery

Gluten-Free Murder

Dairy-Free Death

Allergen-Free Assignation

Witch-Free Halloween (Halloween Short)

Dog-Free Dinner (Christmas Short)

Stirring Up Murder

Brewing Death

Coup de Glace

Sour Cherry Turnover

Apple-achian Treasure

Vegan Baked Alaska

Muffins Masks Murder

Tai Chi and Chai Tea

Santa Shortbread

Cold as Ice Cream

Changing Fortune Cookies

Hot on the Trail Mix

Fateful Plateful

Cut Out Cookie (Coming Soon)

On the Slab Pie (Coming Soon)

Recipes from Auntie Clem's Bakery

Reg Rawlins, Psychic Detective

What the Cat Knew

A Psychic with Catitude

A Catastrophic Theft

Night of Nine Tails

Telepathy of Gardens

Delusions of the Past

Fairy Blade Unmade

Web of Nightmares

A Whisker's Breadth

Skunk Man Swamp

Magic Ain't A Game

Without Foresight

Careful of Thy Wishes

Time to Your Elf

Undiscovered Tomb

Missing Powers (Coming Soon)

Thrice Spared (Coming Soon)

Zachary Goldman Mysteries

She Wore Mourning

His Hands Were Quiet

She Was Dying Anyway

He Was Walking Alone

They Thought He was Safe

He Was Not There

Her Work Was Everything

She Told a Lie

He Never Forgot

She Was At Risk

He Drowned in Memory (Coming Soon)

Their Walls Were Empty (Coming Soon)

They Came for Him (Coming Soon)

Kenzie Kirsch Medical Thrillers

Unlawful Harvest

Doctored Death

Dosed to Death

Gentle Angel

High-Tech Crime Solvers Series

Virtually Harmless

Cowritten with D. D. VanDyke

California Corwin P. I. Mystery Series

The Girl in the Morgue

Stand Alone Suspense Novels

Looking Over Your Shoulder

Lion Within

Pursued by the Past

In the Tick of Time

Loose the Dogs

YOUNG ADULT FICTION:

Medical Kidnap Files:

Mito

EDS

Proxy

Toxo

Pain

Fail (Coming Soon)

Between the Cracks:

Ruby

June and Justin

Michelle

Chloe

Ronnie

June, Into the Light

Tamara's Teardrops:

Tattooed Teardrops

Two Teardrops

Tortured Teardrops

Vanishing Teardrops

Breaking the Pattern:

Henry

Sandy

Bobby

Stand Alone YA novels

Stand Alone

Don't Forget Steven

Those Who Believe

Cynthia has a Secret

Questing for a Dream

Darkness before the Dream (prequel story)

Once Brothers

Intersexion

Making Her Mark

Endless Change

Gem, Himself, Alone

AND MORE AT PDWORKMAN.COM

STYLE NOTE

Since my largest readership is in the USA, I have chosen to use US spellings throughout this series. That includes the Americanization of centre to center, even where it is an actual place name, just for consistency's sake. I apologize to my Canadian readers for this.

I have chosen, however, to use Canadian grammar, particularly for Canadian voices. If you see what you think is a grammar error, it may just be Canadian, eh?

IMMERSED IN THE VIEW

A PARKS PAT MYSTERY #4

To the survivors

CHAPTER ONE

Margie was puffing by the time she got to the park. She was getting into better shape. She could go farther than she had been able to when she started, but she was still in pretty sad shape compared to what she had been as a beat cop, getting plenty of exercise walking the streets. Sitting at a desk was not good for her, and she had not been getting as much exercise as she had thought she would once she arrived in Calgary.

She still hadn't started cycling in to work, using the new pathway over Deerfoot and under Blackfoot, then through Pearce Estate Park and continuing downtown. She had followed it a couple of times on Google Maps to make sure she knew the way, but hadn't yet tried it in real life. She was working her way up to it and wanted to make sure she knew the route really well before she tried it, not wanting to get turned around and lost.

She had promised herself that once she reached Valleyview Park, she would give herself a break. Walk around the pond, have a drink of water, take a few pictures, and get her breath back before returning home. The whole route was only about three kilometers and, once she was comfortable with that, she intended to increase the distance by adding a loop through the pathways by the Max Bell Arena. Calgary had a lot of green space and pathways; she might as well make use of them.

Margie slowed to a walk. It was a clear morning, the sun shining brightly and the greens of the trees and blue of the pond looked like a painted picture. Despite the early hour, it was already 18 degrees Celsius. Actually, it hadn't gotten below 18 the night before. The last few days had had 36-38 degree highs, almost unheard of in Calgary. Most homes—the ones in Margie's neighborhood, anyway—did not have central air conditioning. She had been lucky enough to find a window AC unit a month before when the first heat wave had hit at the beginning of June. It was *never* 30 above the first week in June, she was told. There had been a few flakes of snow on Victoria Day, just a week before that. Calgary didn't normally hit 30 until August.

With the AC unit in Margie's bedroom, they could at least sleep. Christina had said at first that she would be fine in her own room, she didn't need to come sleep with Margie like a little kid who'd had a bad dream. But that didn't even last a full night. With the house heating up and holding on to the heat, Margie's bedroom and the unfinished basement were the only tolerable spaces.

Now it was already Canada Day. July first. Margie didn't have to go in to work, and Christina was out of school, so they had stayed up a bit late the night before to watch a movie while they waited for the house to cool. But Margie had promised herself she would still go for a run, and knew that she would need to head out by six if she wanted to beat the heat. She was glad that she had.

She nodded and said good morning to an elderly man walking around the pond with a cane. She had seen him there before. And she could see a couple with a pair of dogs approaching that she recognized as well. A lot of people wanted to get out and enjoy a bit of fresh air before it got too hot.

Margie sipped her water, then put it back into the holder on her running belt and took out her phone for a few pictures. She walked by the little waterfall, bubbling happily away. Even just this little slice of nature, listening to the trickle of the water and the whistles of the red-winged black-birds, helped to restore her peace and serenity after all the recent news. Down below that, there was a marshy area with cattails and some scum and plant matter floating on top of the water.

There was something in there. She had seen a muskrat a couple of times in the pond and figured that was probably what it was. He was remarkably brave about all the people and dogs who walked around the pond. Most of the time, he just ignored them unless they got right to the edge of the water, and then he would dive, disappearing below the surface.

But as she got closer, she could see that whatever was in the water was much larger than that. It was obscured by the weeds, but it looked as though someone had dumped a dark blue suitcase into the water. A short distance away, she could see the bottom of a shoe floating on the surface of the pond, which confirmed to her that it must be luggage. Why would somebody throw that into the water?

Margie left the pathway to get close to the water's edge where she would be able to see better. The closer she got, the more clearly she could see that it was not a suitcase and random assortment of clothing that had been dumped into the water.

What she had initially taken for the fabric side of a suitcase was the broad back of a man in a denim shirt. The shoe she could see floating a few feet away was still on the foot of its owner.

CHAPTER TWO

*H*ey! Some help over here!" Margie shouted to the man and the woman walking their dogs.

She scrambled out onto the large sandstone rocks at the edge of the pond and tried to reach the man. Facedown in the water. Not a good sign. Floating just a little too far away for her to grab his shoulder or shirt. She shuffled toward his feet, her knees protesting at the hardness of the rocks. She would end up with bruises just from kneeling there. Margie reached out again, overbalanced, and nearly toppled into the water.

She drew back, breathing hard, her heart racing. She hated the water. She couldn't swim. She couldn't even wade, not without going into full-blown panic mode. But she forced herself to try again. She was a police detective. She had a responsibility to the public. She was a first responder, and it didn't matter whether the emergency was on land in the water; she was expected to take action.

There were concerned questions from the dog walkers as they approached, not yet sure what was going on.

Margie caught the corner of a pant-leg. She hooked her fingers around it to pull it tightly into her palm, then tugged the entire leg toward her. The body was heavier than it looked, dragging on something as she tried to pull it to the edge.

The man handed his girlfriend the second dog's leash and hurried to Margie.

"What happened? Did you see?"

Margie shook her head. "No. I just got here. Saw him." She continued to tug the body closer, wondering whether she would be able to break the water tension and get it out of the water. The victim was not a small man.

The dog walker knelt down at her side, closer to the head. Because Margie had already pulled the body closer to shore, it was easily within the man's reach. He grabbed an arm and the cloth of the denim shirt and pulled hard, bringing the body to the shore and partially out of the water. Margie got her hands around both of the legs and hauled on them, trying to bring them up onto the rocks she knelt on.

"Let's try it together," her helper suggested. "One, two, three!"

On three, they both tried again, and managed to pull the body out of the water and drag it up onto the rocks. Margie was out of breath—not from running anymore, but the exertion and the adrenaline rush.

"What do we do?" the man asked. "Is he breathing?" He called over to his girlfriend. "Did you call 9-1-1?"

The woman nodded impatiently, still talking to the dispatcher on her phone, answering the series of questions that Margie knew the operator would be asking her. *Name? Location? Phone number? Nature of the emergency? Are there any weapons present? Is everyone safe?*

Margie looked down at the bloated face turned to the side and knew that it was way too late to be attempting any lifesaving measures. She shook her head at the dog walker. "He's dead."

"We should do something. Should we do CPR?" her helper asked.

"No. It's too late."

"Sometimes you can't tell," he objected. "On TV, sometimes they think someone is dead, but they can be revived. If we keep his blood pumping until they can shock him…"

"No," Margie told him again. "I'm a police detective. I'm an experienced first responder. It's too late."

He looked around. "Where is your police car? Don't you carry those v-fib machines?"

"I was just out for a run." Margie went through the motions of checking for pulse and respiration, in order to reassure him that they were doing everything they could, even though she knew it was far too late.

A siren whooped. The fire station was only a few blocks away. First responders must have been dispatched from there. With just a few blares of the horn, the firetruck came into view. It pulled into the parking lot and a couple of firefighters climbed out.

Margie stayed where she was. The man looked around, not sure what he should do. He stood up as the firefighters with black masks approached, giving them room to get in and see to the victim.

"Sorry," Margie told them. "Too late to do anything for him. I'm Detective Patenaude." She repeated it, pronouncing it clearly for them, "PAT-en-ode. I came upon the body by chance. I will take control of the scene until it is assigned to someone."

"Parks Pat?" one of the firefighters asked, the skin beside his eyes crinkling in a smile. So the name had spread further than just the homicide department.

"Yes, that's me," she agreed, her face warm.

"Well, lucky us." The firefighter also checked for any signs of life but, like Margie, he knew there was no point in it. "Have you called it in?"

"Not yet. The young lady called 9-1-1. I was busy getting him out of the water."

Becoming suddenly more aware of the water, Margie backed away from the edge of the pond, her throat constricting.

"You need a radio?" the second firefighter, a redhead, offered, indicating his shoulder mike.

"No, I've got my phone and I know the numbers." Margie got to her feet and stepped back from the body. "There's nothing we can do until the crime scene techs and medical examiner's office get here. Let's make sure there is no more contamination of the scene."

The two firefighters agreed and also took several steps back. Margie had nothing with her but her running belt. No yellow tape. She didn't even have her police ID. Luckily, everyone had taken her at her word that she was in law enforcement.

"Thank you," Margie told the man who had helped pull the body out of the water. She nodded to his girlfriend, standing farther away. The young woman looked both anxious and excited, her skin very pale in the bright morning sun. Margie pulled out her phone and dialed Staff Sergeant MacDonald.

"Detective Pat," Mac greeted. "You're off duty today. I thought you were going to be spending the day with your daughter. Get off the phone and go enjoy your holiday."

It wasn't actually a day of celebration for Margie and her daughter, but it wasn't the right time to point this out. "Actually, I was out for a run this morning... and I found... a body in the pond." She was aware that her voice squeaked up slightly at the end of her statement, making it sound like a question.

There was silence from MacDonald for a few seconds. Margie pictured him running his fingers through his silver hair, eyebrows raised, trying to process what she had just told him.

"You *found* a body," he repeated.

"Yes, sir."

"Is this some kind of a joke?"

"No, sir. Sorry."

"Well, that's going above and beyond, don't you think?"

Margie chuckled. "Yes, sir. It wasn't exactly planned."

"Where exactly is this body? Am I your first call?"

"A bystander called 9-1-1. We have first responders on the scene. We're all in agreement that there is nothing we can do for him. You're my first call."

"You're supposed to be off today, but I'm going to make you primary since you're already there. There isn't any point in calling someone else to take over. Are you able to handle the preliminaries?" He sounded suddenly uncertain. "Your daughter isn't there with you, is she?"

She appreciated his concern. "No. She's still at home asleep. I just went out for a quick run. The body is in Valleyview Park. I can get things started on this end. I can't spend all day, but I've got a couple of hours. I don't think there will be much for the forensic team to do. The scene is pretty small."

"Any sign of violence? Cause of death?"

"I haven't made any kind of examination of the body. No blood or trauma that I can see."

"Okay. Valleyview... I think we had a drowning there a few years ago. Is this a drowning?"

Margie looked back toward the body. "A definite possibility. I don't imagine it will take the medical examiner long to find out."

"Give them a call."

"Yes, sir. Will do. Can you send me a couple of units? I was just out on foot, so I don't have crime scene tape or anything. We'll need a little crowd control and to canvass the houses around here to see if we can narrow down time of death and if anyone saw or heard anything last night or this morning."

"I'll send you some backup. Could the body have been there longer? A few days? Sometimes it's hard to be sure. If the body sank or was hidden…?"

"No, I don't think so. It's a very small park. Nothing like Fish Creek or Glenbow. Just a little pond with a pathway around it. And lots of foot traffic. Runners, walkers, dog people. I don't think it could have been here any longer than last night or early this morning."

CHAPTER THREE

a couple of police units rolled up within a few minutes. Margie was more relaxed once they could cordon off the pond and the pathway that looped around it to prevent anyone from getting too close to the scene. They covered the body until they could get screens up to shield it from view.

At that point, it became a waiting game. Margie supposed she should have guessed that there would be only a skeleton crew on in the forensics department and medical examiner's office due to the statutory holiday. There were people on call, but it would take time for them to get out to the scene, especially if they had been planning to spend the day with family, as Margie had.

She stood watching the various walkers rubbernecking to see what was going on, gathering in little clumps to speculate with each other. She didn't see anyone who looked concerned, as if they might be missing a family member and worried about some misadventure. At least she didn't have to deal with trying to keep a mother, brother, or best friend away from the body.

The crows were cawing loudly and the magpies screaming, drowning out the sounds of the blackbirds she had been listening to earlier. Margie had noticed that the magpies had become much more vocal since their babies had left the nest, frequently calling warnings of predators or other perceived dangers. The black and white magpie fledglings were so large that it was hard to tell them apart from the parents, other than by the fluffiness of their baby feathers or their behavior if she watched them for long enough.

"There they are," one of the constables commented.

Margie blinked her eyes and looked around, realizing that she had zoned out listening to the birds. Not a good idea. As a detective, she needed to have her head on a swivel, always looking around for possible dangers, clues, people she needed to talk to, behaviors that might give people away. It wouldn't do to let herself be distracted.

The medical examiner's van and the forensic techs both rolled up, nudging their way into the now-crowded parking lot, then rolling through the opening for the pathway to drive over the grass and stop beside the body. No point in trying to carry a body and the equipment back and forth to the parking lot. Much more efficient to have everything right at hand.

Margie nodded to each of the techs. She recognized them from earlier cases but wasn't sure enough of names to address them with certainty.

"What's this I hear?" one of them asked, a tall fellow with a goofy grin that he covered with a mask as he approached, "You're providing your own bodies now?"

Margie's smile felt stretched thin, like her emotions over the past few weeks. It was taut and uncomfortable. But he didn't know how she was feeling. The nature of their business often led to morbid humor.

"I didn't plan it that way, believe me. I was supposed to have the day off."

He chuckled and went to work, scouting around the area, getting equipment out of the truck, working in tandem with his partner. Margie recognized the death investigator who got out of the medical examiner's van.

"Dr. Galt. Nice to see you again."

Dr. Galt nodded. He had white hair and a small white beard and appeared to have missed a spot shaving that morning. He probably had not been planning to go out anywhere and had shaven quickly when he got the call. But he was calm and unhurried in his approach. Everyone worked together to set up privacy screens so that they could uncover the body again without spectators. Dr. Galt looked the man over very slowly, not touching him.

"Who discovered the body?"

"That was me."

By his lack of reaction, she suspected he already knew that and was simply asking as a matter of course. "In the water or out?"

"In. Face down. I could see his back and one shoe, to start with."

Dr. Galt nodded. He gave the techs various instructions, making sure that all visible evidence was retrieved. They stretched a white body bag out next to him and then, together, turned him over, setting him into it, so that for the first time Margie was viewing his chest instead of his back. She saw his long black hair, brown skin, and the Indigenous cast apparent in his features, even with how bloated his face was. Margie sighed.

"Does he have any identification on him?"

They looked in her direction, but ignored the question, going over the body in their own methodical procedure. It was a few minutes before they pulled out a slim wallet protruding from his pocket.

"Bruce Hungry Bear, according to his identification."

"Thirsty Bear, more likely," one of the techs intoned. The other, the tall one, punched him in the shoulder.

"Hey! What was that for?"

"Shut up. Look at her."

The tech who had commented turned and looked at Margie not-so-surreptitiously. It was a moment before everything apparently clicked into place and he realized his mistake. Making racist remarks about a victim in front of an Indigenous detective was not a particularly smart thing to do.

"Sorry," he muttered. "Didn't see you."

Margie was counting off each intake and exhale of breath, trying to keep herself from breaking into a tirade. He was going to make *drunk Indian* jokes about a victim? In the current political climate?

Hundreds of unmarked graves had been revealed at residential schools in the last six weeks. The entire Indigenous population of the country was in mourning, many calling for the cancellation of Canada Day celebrations altogether, and he thought it was appropriate to voice his racist biases out loud? In front of Margie?

There were going to be fireworks all right, and they wouldn't be the ones that would be going off at midnight.

"What is your name?" she demanded.

The man swallowed and pretended to be occupied with carefully rechecking all the evidence that had been bagged so far. He looked away from Margie, out at the glass-smooth surface of the pond. There might be more evidence out there. Might have to drain the pond to check.

"Your name," Margie repeated. "Now."

"Oliver Symons. But it was just a joke. I didn't mean anything by it. Just trying to lighten the mood. Morgue humor."

Margie didn't have her duty notepad on her, but she had her phone. She woke it up, tapped out his name below the notes she had already made about the investigation, and slid it back into her running belt. "Your comment was not funny," she told him flatly.

She could see it was a struggle for him not to respond. He wanted to justify himself. Maybe to call *her* a few choice names. But he'd already dug himself deep enough, and he was clearly fighting the urge not to dig himself any deeper. He pressed his lips together and continued to work the scene. There were no more comments about the race of their victim.

Margie stayed out of the way, fielding inquiries on her phone from MacDonald and the constables who were canvassing the nearby houses. They each had a job to do there and, while she was the primary and was there to supervise the gathering of forensic evidence, she believed that, as a rule, the techs were better when left to do the job the way they had been trained than for her to micromanage the process.

"Detective Pat!"

Margie turned at the familiar voice. It was Detective Cruz, one of the other detectives on the homicide squad. A good cop and a good man. Filipino. Her smile of greeting was not as plastic as the others had been.

"Cruz. You didn't need to come out."

"You aren't even supposed to be on today. I am."

"I can take care of this. Didn't you want to take the day off with your kids?"

He was older than Margie, near the age when she expected him to retire from homicide, but his children were younger than Christina. Margie wasn't sure how many kids he had. She had seen them at the department Christmas party, but they had all looked so much alike that she had lost track of how many there were and which was which.

"No. We are going to wait until the heat breaks, and then take them out for some fun. In this weather… about all they want to do is paddle in the wading pool. The heat doesn't bother me so much. But they were all born here in Canada and they are not used to it."

"So maybe Saturday you can do something with them."

Cruz nodded. "And until then, I'm at your service. Where do you need me?"

Margie removed her hat and wiped the sweat collecting along her forehead. The day had warmed very quickly, and everyone was moving slowly and looking uncomfortable. "You know what? I need to move around a bit. I ran here, and then I've been standing around and my legs are seizing up. I'm going to scout a wider perimeter, just to make sure that there's nothing we've missed, then I'm going to run home, shower off, and come back in my car."

"You're that close?"

"Just about a kilometer from here." Margie swallowed a couple of gulps of water to replace what she had already sweated out. "So I'll be back in a few minutes. Probably before the techs are done."

She looked back toward the men around the body. When she looked back at Cruz, he gave her a puzzled look. "What's going on?"

"What?"

"You're looking kinda ticked off, there. Is it just the heat?"

"Symons there… making racist comments."

Cruz's brows went up. "Really? That doesn't sound right. Never heard anything from him before."

"Maybe he's okay with Filipinos."

"But not you? You're about as Canadian as they get."

"Too Canadian. Doesn't have much respect for Indigenous peoples, I guess."

"Do you want me to say something to him?"

Margie laughed. "No. I'll make a report. Let his department deal with it. I was here and saw and heard what he had to say. You didn't."

"You just say the word, and I'll take him in the back alley," Cruz teased. "Or we could do it right here. I could help him look under the water to see whether there's any evidence to be gathered there."

"Don't beat anyone up before I get back."

He grinned and nodded.

CHAPTER FOUR

*M*argie made a large loop around the park, crossing over Twenty-Sixth Street to the hill overlooking the irrigation canal and Deerfoot Trail. There was a lookout point there that she and Christina often stopped at when they were taking Stella out for a walk. Margie looked for anything that was out of place. There was no litter, and there were no breaks in the foliage or tracks through the grass that she could see. Nothing out of the ordinary. It was a high-traffic area, lots of people through there with their dogs, plenty of wildlife, including foxes and coyotes right there in the middle of the city. And skunks, of course. Stella had recently had a close encounter with one of the little black and white stinkers.

She returned through the parking lot where the police vehicles were parked, along the longer loop that got closer to the houses, looking into the back yards for anything that might have been thrown over the fence in an attempt to get rid of evidence. Bystanders watched her curiously, but didn't approach to ask any questions. When she reached Twenty-Eighth Street on the other side of the splash park and volleyball courts, Margie stopped and gazed at the chain link fence by West Dover School. Someone had tied orange ribbons through the links.

There were no signs explaining the memorial, but Margie didn't need one. Orange ribbons for the children who had died at the residential schools. Currently at the forefront of the minds of the public because ground-penetrating radar was being used at some of the old residential school properties to seek out the Indigenous children who had been buried there, victims of abuse, neglect, and disease, their resting places and identities obscured during the intervening years.

Her chest was tight. She had listened to the stories. She could imagine having Christina ripped from her arms to be sent away to a school designed to "beat the Indian out of her." Having her stolen away, knowing full well that she was going to be abused and might never return home.

Margie breathed deeply, trying to loosen the tension in her shoulders. She crossed the street to touch a couple of the ribbons. She took a few pictures from her phone and then put it back away.

She completed her circuit around the park, back past the church with the cross on top, through the playground, and to the parking lot again. She called Cruz's number as she crossed Twenty-Sixth Street again to run the pathway home.

"Detective Cruz," he answered.

"Pat here. There are a number of garbage cans and bins in the area. The school, the church, the playgrounds, and the park itself. We'll want to at least have a cursory look to see whether anything was thrown away."

"On it. See you after your shower."

❦

MARGIE WAS REALLY SWEATING. The weather pattern was extreme compared to what she had been accustomed to in Winnipeg, and she wasn't used to running in the heat. She slowed to a walk for the last block and chugged the rest of her water.

Stella barked excitedly and ran around when Margie walked in the door, clearly wanting to be taken out herself. Margie glanced around, not expecting Christina to be awake.

But Christina was in the kitchen, leaning against the counter, eyes partially closed, waiting for the coffee maker to finish its duties.

"Hi, Mom." Christina yawned and rubbed her eyes. "What time did you get up? I thought you would be up really early for your run. You said you wanted to beat the heat." She looked Margie over accusingly. "You'll get heatstroke."

"I'm fine, thanks." Margie laughed. Christina had taken on the role of mother lately, repeating back all the things that Margie had taught her about eating properly, cleaning up after herself, getting enough sleep, and all of the other things that Margie had assumed Christina hadn't been listening to over the years. "I'm going to have a quick shower and then I'll tell you about it."

Christina was still in the kitchen when Margie got out, sitting in one of the kitchen chairs with her feet on the seat and her knees to her chest while she sipped her coffee. Too hot for a day that was so warm. Margie was craving one of the cold cans of Coke in the fridge but didn't want a lecture on healthy eating from Christina too. She got herself a cold bottle of water instead.

"So, something happened?" Christina asked, trailing her fingers through Stella's thick fur.

Stella had been spending most of the week sprawled out on the floor, using as little energy as possible. But she did have occasional bursts of activity when she was hungry or wanted outside.

"Yes… something happened in the park today."

"In the park? What?"

"In Valleyview, where we go to play Frisbee and they have that splash park?" Margie suggested, not sure Christina knew which park she was talking about.

"Yeah?"

"There was… something in the water when I went by it today."

"Did you see the muskrat? Or the ducklings?"

"Well… I'm sure they were there. But there was actually… a man died there today."

Christina's eyes widened. "What? Were you there when it happened? I saw on the internet that lots of people are dying from the heat. Old people."

"He didn't die in front of me. His body was in the water when I got there. Maybe drowned, we'll have to wait for the autopsy."

"I can't believe it." Christina shook her head. "Parks Pat strikes again. Detective Patenaude investigating another park murder."

"I wasn't *trying* to find a body. And I certainly didn't have anything to do with it being there."

"That's crazy." Christina ran her fingers through her long, black hair. "It wasn't anyone we know, was it?"

"No. No one we know." Margie decided to pour herself a little bit of coffee. It smelled so good. She took a sip, looking down into the depths of her cup with sadness welling up inside. "One of our brothers. A Siksiká man, I think. But not one I've ever met before."

"Oh." Christina too dropped her eyes, considering. It had been a difficult month for everyone in the Indigenous communities, opening old wounds and bringing fresh trauma. "That's sad."

Margie nodded her agreement. "I have to go back. I just came home to shower and change. Will you take Stella out for a bit? Not for too long, I don't want either of you to get overheated…"

Christina nodded. "Sure. We'll go for a walk."

"Thanks, sweetie." Margie leaned forward and kissed Christina on the forehead and scratched Stella's ears. "*Maarsii.*"

⁋

WHEN MARGIE GOT BACK to the park, things had quieted considerably. Most of the police vehicles were gone. The forensic techs and Dr. Galt were gone. Which of course meant that the body had been removed. Margie took a deep breath in and blew it out again. She joined Detective Cruz once more.

"Looks like things are moving along."

Cruz nodded. "There is nothing suspicious, probably just an accident. We'll have the scene cleared pretty soon."

"Good. Run into any trouble?" Margie didn't specify whether she was talking about more comments by the tech, bystanders, or any one of a hundred other things that could go wrong at a scene. Let him interpret it as he saw fit.

"No. Everything has been quiet. We'll check the rest of the garbages," Cruz took a quick look around. "Then, I think we'll be done."

"All right."

Cruz pulled his phone out to look at the screen. "We have the address from his driver's license. Are you up for a death notification?"

Not Margie's favorite part of the job. Not any homicide detective's favorite part of the job. "Yes. Of course. Is it close by?"

21

"He lived in the neighborhood."

"Do we know who he lived with?"

"Jones ran down the address. Looks like friends or roommates. She'll check social media too, and we'll get a look at his personal effects, talk to the friends, see whether he had family who need to be notified."

CHAPTER FIVE

*L*et's take my car," Cruz suggested. "Yours can stay here for now. I'll drop you back here when we're done. No point in wasting gas taking two vehicles."

Margie was just fine with that. It meant that she wouldn't have to use her GPS or follow Cruz. Her sense of direction was bad enough to make her ancestors turn over in their graves.

Cruz didn't even bother looking up the address on his phone, he just drove directly to it. Calgary was a big city and it amazed Margie how well he knew his way around. Hungry Bear's house was only a few blocks away, but it wasn't Cruz's neighborhood. Maybe he had looked it up on his phone map before Margie's return. But even then, he'd been able to remember what he had seen on the map and to translate it to real life in order to find the house without any wrong turns, which, in Margie's mind, was still pretty impressive.

Cruz checked the time as he called in to let the team know where they were. "Should be late enough for people to be up, don't you think?"

"My teenager was up, if that's any indication. And I don't know how anyone could sleep once it's this hot out."

"If they have an air conditioner or basement room. Teens, young adults, night shift workers, plenty of people *could* still be asleep now. But I'm going to assume that they're up. If not… I guess we're their wake-up call today."

Margie was on board with that. They got out of the car and walked up to the door of the bungalow. No children's toys on the lawn or sidewalk. Grass that had been mown at least once during June and was now burning in the summer sun. No gardens. Some shrubbery around the front door and windows, which really wasn't a good idea if they wanted to prevent a burglary. The cars on the street in front of the house were a combination of nondescript leases and older vehicles that were probably paid for. She didn't hear any voices from inside the house as they approached. Windows were open and box fans were running as the residents tried to keep the house cool.

Cruz rang the doorbell and knocked hard on the door. They both stood slightly to the side, always watching for anything that might be off. Anything that might indicate that they were about to walk into a meth house or a domestic situation or anything else that could be dangerous for them.

A few minutes passed with no answer. Cruz knocked again, hard, his knock undoubtedly echoing through the house and audible to all the residents. Unless they were downstairs. Or wearing headphones. Or asleep.

This time, Margie could make out voices. Complaining, arguing over who was going to get the door, tired and frustrated.

Cruz knocked again.

A minute later, the door was opened by a skinny blond woman, her hair stringy and tangled. She was swearing before she even opened the door all the way.

"What's your problem? People are trying to sleep!"

"Calgary Police, ma'am," Cruz cut her off. "Can we come in?"

"Police?" She stopped complaining and just stood there scowling at him.

"Yes, ma'am. If we could have a few minutes with you..."

She pushed a hank of hair back behind her ear. "What's this about?" She looked out the door, craning her neck to see around them. "Did someone hit my car? Or steal it?" She could apparently see it sitting there unharmed and withdrew back into the house again. "What is this?"

Cruz stepped toward the door, turning his shoulder as if to push his way past her. She stepped back and let him in. Margie followed. They all walked into the small living room, hot and still, sealed windows preventing any air from circulating through the room. It had to be almost 40 degrees. Margie took a deep breath. Hopefully, they wouldn't be there for too long. Cruz invited the woman to sit down.

"What did you say your name is, ma'am?"

"Samantha." She looked toward the hallway. "Jonathan? Come out here."

There was grumbling and groaning from a nearby bedroom and, eventually, the padding of bare feet as the owner of the grumbles made his way in their direction.

Jonathan was a tall man with a full bushy beard, a painful-looking red sunburn around white skin in the shape of the tank top he had been wearing when he'd apparently fallen asleep in the sun. He rubbed his eyes and looked at them, surprised to find visitors in his living room. He hitched up his Sponge Bob boxers and leaned an elbow against the wall.

"What's this, then?"

"Police," Samantha said.

"About what?"

"They were just gonna tell me." She sounded aggrieved, as if he had done something wrong instead of just coming out when she'd asked him to.

"Would you like to sit down?" Cruz suggested to Jonathan.

"No, I'd like to stand. What's up?"

"Do you have a roommate in the house, a Bruce Hungry Bear?"

"Is that who you're looking for? Bruce!" Jonathan went into the kitchen, calling down to the basement. "Bruce! The cops are here!" He returned to the living room, shaking his head in amusement. "That should bring him up here."

Margie and Cruz looked at each other.

"Actually, I don't think it will," Margie said in a soft, measured voice. "We're here *about* Bruce, not to see him."

"Oh." The roommates looked at each other. "Is he in some kind of trouble? Did he get arrested?"

Samantha blinked, looking around, reaching back into her memory. "They were talking about setting off some fireworks. I told them they're not supposed to do it within city limits, you know, 'cause of the by-laws. And it's so dry with all of this heat. But I didn't think you'd arrest someone for something like that…"

"Bruce hasn't been arrested, ma'am," Cruz said gently. "I'm afraid that this morning, his body was discovered in a nearby pond. He was dead."

Cruz had done enough notifications to know not to leave any doubt in the recipient's mind that the person was actually dead. Not gone away. Not hurt or sick in hospital. Unequivocally dead. Leaving room for misunderstanding was not a kindness.

"Dead?" Jonathan swore. "Are you kidding me?"

"No, sir. I'm afraid not. Were you and Bruce close?"

"We were friendly... I mean, we didn't know each other before we rented the house together. But we got along. All of us were... pretty chill with each other. Let everybody do their own thing. You know."

Cruz and Margie nodded. "Do you know if he has any family or friends in the city?" Margie asked.

"Yeah, his folks are here," Samantha offered. She ran her fingers through her long, blond hair and looked at the man as if expecting him to contribute something.

He just shrugged. "I guess."

"Do you know their names? Where they live?"

The two shook their heads. "Maybe... the northwest somewhere?" the woman suggested.

"Could we see Bruce's room? He might have something that will help us to find them."

"They would be on his phone," Samantha said doubtfully. "It's not like anyone these days has an actual address book." She gazed at Cruz as if he were ancient.

"His phone was in the water. I don't know if we'll be able to retrieve anything from it," Margie advised them. Of course, they would be able to get his phone logs and see who he had been in contact with, but that might take a few days. It was better if they could contact his parents the first day, not wait until they had heard it from someone else or come to the police to report him as a missing person.

"I don't know. Yeah, I guess you can. You're the cops." She still seemed hesitant. "You don't need, like, a warrant or something?"

"Not if you let us in."

Neither of them got up to show Cruz and Margie to Bruce's room. Margie exchanged a look with Cruz. He gave her a slight nod, encouraging her to take point. While Cruz generally came across as pleasant and non-threatening, a woman was less intimidating.

"Is there something you're worried we're going to find?" Margie suggested. "We understand that you're not responsible for whatever we find in his room."

"Well… I don't know what he could have. None of us are big partiers or anything, but what people do behind closed doors…" The woman gave a one-shouldered shrug. "Well, you just don't know."

"Understood. Like I said, we won't blame you for anything we find there. You're just helping us out by giving us access to the room so that we can find Bruce's parents and let them know. You wouldn't want them to be wondering what happened to him." Margie saw an opening. "Or calling you or coming here looking for him. You don't want to be the one having to break it to them."

Samantha's eyes got big. No way she wanted to do that. She pushed herself to her feet. "Yeah, I guess it's okay. He would want his parents to know."

She led them through the kitchen to the stairs. The man didn't follow them, and Margie could hear water running and the toilet flushing while they were partway down the stairs. She hoped he wasn't flushing whatever stash he had. They weren't going to search his possessions, and flushing pharmaceuticals was just bad for the water system.

Samantha led them down a hall. There were several closed doors. She stopped at one and looked at them, fist closed as if she had been planning to knock.

"Do you have a key?" Cruz suggested.

"It's… not locked. We all had keys to the house, but none of us bothered to lock the individual doors."

A pretty trusting group. Cruz nodded and angled to reach past her and open the door. She stepped back and gave him room. Cruz turned the handle and pushed the door open, he and Margie standing just to the side of the door. As far as they knew, the room was vacant, but way too many police incident reports started with, *The residence was believed to be unoccupied.*

They waited for a moment, then Cruz reached around the door frame and felt for a light switch. He found it and flipped it up. They looked around. No one there. There were places they couldn't see—under the bed, in the closet, against the wall that the door was on—but no one obviously lying in wait and no one sleeping in Bruce's bed waiting for him to get home. No pit bull or psychotic cat.

Cruz gave Margie a nod and they moved into the room. "Thank you," he told Samantha, and closed the door behind them.

The two of them quickly checked the various blind spots to clear the room and ensure that they were alone. There was no desk. There was a laptop computer on the bed. Cruz pressed a button to wake it up. Miraculously, there was no lock screen. No need to enter a password or provide a fingerprint. Cruz clicked and tapped for a few moments.

"There we go. Mom's phone numbers are in his contact list. Two of them, one will be a landline traceable to an address. Only an email address and single phone number for Dad."

"Sounded from the roommates like they still live together."

"Sounded that way. If not, I'm sure Mom will have Dad's information. Maybe she'll even want to be the one to inform him."

Not likely. Margie looked around the room. "Give it a quick once-over?"

Cruz nodded. "If you want to take a look around, I'm going to spend a minute in his email. See what's been going on in his life."

Margie shook her head as she started looking through the man's drawers. "Twenty-somethings don't use email," she told Cruz. "Try Snapchat, IM's, Discord."

She could feel Cruz rolling his eyes at her. It was the second time in ten minutes he'd basically been told that he was old. "Kids these days," he quavered in a grandpa voice.

Margie chuckled. She pulled a couple of plastic bags out of Hungry Bear's bottom drawer and tossed them on top of the dresser. There were a few pill bottles in his top drawer, but none of them were prescription. Just over-the-counter stuff. Tylenol, cold pills, caffeine.

Cruz looked at the packages of herbs. "Weed?"

"No, I don't think so." Margie continued her search, checking the backs and bottoms of drawers for any stashes. The closet, including the pockets of jackets and toes of the shoes littering the bottom of the closet. It all seemed pretty innocuous. As Samantha had said, he wasn't a partier.

Cruz closed the lid of the computer and walked over to the dresser to take a look at the packages. Margie returned to look at them with him. Cruz frowned, rubbing his thumb over the contents of one of the bags to shift the contents around. He didn't open the package to smell it. That's what a cop on TV would have done. Cops in real life didn't taste unknown white powders or smell-test baggies of dry green leaves. There were labs to do proper tests.

"What are they, then?" Cruz asked.

"Tobacco," Margie informed him, pointing to one. "Sage," pointing to the other. She'd seen and handled both of them enough to easily recognize them on sight.

"So… he uses snuff and cooks turkey?" Cruz asked, giving her a puzzled look.

"No. They're sacred herbs. For ceremonies."

"Oh. Indian—*Aboriginal* stuff. Would he smoke them?"

"More likely smudge. But he could."

Cruz looked around the room. "Nothing else? No alcohol?"

Of course, Margie might have found alcohol but not drawn his attention to it as she had the herbs. There was no reason he shouldn't have alcohol in his own room.

Margie might have taken offense at the question, accusing him of assuming, like the forensic tech, that Hungry Bear was a drunk just because of his heritage. But she didn't. She understood where the answer would lead them.

If Hungry Bear had not been drunk or high, then how had he ended up stumbling into the Valleyview pond?

CHAPTER SIX

*B*ack in Cruz's car, they didn't discuss the question, both of them content to just ponder on it for a while themselves. Margie would put the question in the back of her mind and let her subconscious chew over it for a while. See what her brain came up with.

"You want to go to the northwest to talk to the parents?" Cruz asked. "I can drop you at your car if you want to go home and spend the rest of the day with Christina."

"Uh... let me talk to her first. You can find out if there is an address tied to that landline."

They each took out their phones to make their inquiries. Margie tapped Christina's name in her favorites.

"Hi, Mom." Christina answered before the third ring. "I took Stella out for a walk, and we're back home. When are you going to be done?"

"Well, that's why I'm calling you. We need to make a death notification, and it's over in the northwest. It will be at least twenty minutes' drive each way, plus however long it takes to talk to the parents. If I go, I'll be at least another hour."

"You should go."

"I'm supposed to be off today. So I *can* bow out and just let Detective Cruz take care of it."

"No, Mom," Christina said immediately. "You need to be the one."

Margie was bemused. "Because I was the one to find the body and pull him out?"

"No." There were a few beats of silence before Christina explained. "Because... you said he is Siksiká, right?"

"Yes."

"Then... you should be the one to tell them. So they have a friendly face. Someone who looks like them, not some white dude."

"Detective Cruz is not a white dude." Margie laughed. But Christina made a good point. Hopefully, Hungry Bear's parents would feel better knowing that their son's death was being handled respectfully by someone who had at least a basic understanding of their culture. Someone who would not immediately jump to conclusions or make judgments.

"Hispanic, then," Christina said impatiently. "Whatever. But he's not Indigenous."

"Filipino," Margie informed her. "And you're absolutely right. I think I should too. You don't mind? You'll be okay for another hour or two on your own?"

"Time without you looking over my shoulder telling me I should get off the computer and get out for some fresh air?" Christina countered. "Yeah, I think I can handle it."

"Okay. Love you, sweetie."

"You too."

Margie terminated the call and slid her phone away.

"A white dude?" Cruz asked, obviously having heard part of the conversation.

Margie laughed. "Sorry. Kid's not always politically correct."

"Well, thank you for setting her straight. I wouldn't want anyone going around thinking I am a white dude." A fan of wrinkles appeared around his eyes as he smiled. "So are you going with me?"

"I am."

Cruz chuckled. "Teenagers don't mind being left home alone for a while."

"No," Margie agreed. "That didn't seem to be a problem." She adjusted to a more serious tone. "She's a good kid. We had plans for today, but she wants to make sure that I'm the one doing the notification. So that they get it from... someone like them."

"Not some white dude."

"Yeah. I don't think she has anything against white dudes or Filipinos. She just knows… well, the racism that this family faces."

He nodded his agreement. He shifted the car into drive.

"You got the address?" Margie asked. "That didn't take long."

"Got it."

"Did you put it into your phone GPS?"

He tapped the side of his head. "This one here."

"You really know the city well. How can you know all of the little crescents and cul-de-sacs? They can be so confusing."

"I've had longer to learn than you have. You're still pretty new."

"Yeah, but I'm crap at directions. By the time I've been here five years, I might be able to get to a few places from memory. But I'm not going to remember every place I've ever been."

"I don't remember every place I've ever been. Most, maybe, but not quite all of them." His voice was teasing.

Margie sat back in her seat and tried to relax and not think about the duty she was facing.

§

CRUZ WAS able to get to the parents' house pretty quickly, much faster than Margie would have liked. She took a deep breath and hoped that the lump in her stomach would go away once she did the notification. There was no way to fully prepare for these things. It was like ripping off a Band-Aid. She could completely psych herself out worrying about how bad it was going to be, or she could just pull it off and cry about it when it was done.

"Ready?"

Margie nodded. "Yes. It's not going to get any easier."

"Nope."

They got out of the car and approached the door. Cruz didn't knock as loudly as he had at Hungry Bear's house. Margie wasn't sure if it was because they were not as likely to still be asleep, or that he was showing respect and didn't want to scare them. They stood to the side slightly until the door was opened by a tiny Siksiká woman, bent over, hair almost completely white.

"*Oki*, Grandmother," Margie said, lowering her head and bending down slightly to get closer to the woman's face. "We are from the Calgary Police. May we come in?"

"Yes, come in, come in," the woman agreed, backing up a few paces to make space for them. Margie looked at Cruz. She hadn't been expecting this. She hoped that the old woman was not the only one who was home.

They followed her into the house and she motioned for them to sit down in the couch and easy chair. She sat down on another chair, maybe a dining room chair, with a straight back, but cushioned. She leaned forward to study them, her eyes quick.

"Is there someone here with you?" Margie asked. "Or are you the only one at home?"

"Alice is here. And her husband, Michael. No work today." She gazed away from them. "Canada Day," she said flatly. "A day to show pride in your country."

Margie leaned as close to the old woman as she could manage, but there was still too much distance between them for Margie to place a hand on her arm or her shoulder.

"I am proud of my family," she said. "And proud of my community. This has been a very hard time for all of us, and they have been very strong. I can tell that you are a strong woman. Like my Moushoom, you are a survivor."

"We had to be strong to survive. It was that... or die."

Margie said nothing. They both allowed some time to pass. Eventually, Cruz spoke up, uncomfortable with the silence.

"Do you think we could get Alice and Michael in here. So that we can talk to you all together at the same time? That way we don't have to repeat ourselves."

The old woman studied Cruz openly. "Where is your family from? Are you a brother?"

"I am from the Philippines." Cruz hesitated. "I hope I am a brother."

She nodded. "Your people and my people knew each other many, many moons ago."

Margie had heard of trade between the Pacific islands and the North American tribes, but didn't know whether it was true or not. Sometimes stories were just stories. Scientists believed there was a relationship between the Siberian tribes and the Alaskan Aleuts, but it seemed to be easier for them to believe that those peoples had crossed on the ice or a land bridge than to believe they could have built boats and sailed across the ocean. As if no one but Europeans could build seaworthy boats.

Cruz was willing to accept this. He nodded to the old woman and waited.

"Alice," the old woman called eventually, directing a remarkably loud and clear voice toward the back of the house. "Come out to speak to the company. And bring your husband."

There was a bit of chatter back and forth between them, too fast for Margie to follow the Siksiká words. Then a woman in her fifties or sixties, with a warm, round face joined them.

"It is so hot. We should sit outside."

No one made any move to get up. Alice sat down with the older woman, who Margie assumed was her mother or grandmother. A few seconds of silence passed, and then her husband came into the room as well. His face had sharper planes, not soft and round like Alice's, but narrow and angular as if he had been chiseled from stone. Despite his severe appearance, he gave Margie a smile, showing off several missing teeth.

With all of them assembled, it was time for Margie to make the notification. She looked at Alice and Michael.

"I assume that you are Bruce Hungry Bear's parents?"

They exchanged looks of anxiety with each other, then looked at Margie and nodded. They didn't ask what had happened. But they knew it was something bad.

"Bruce's body was discovered early this morning," she told them, as quickly and compassionately as she could. "We believe he died sometime late last night or early this morning, but will need to wait for the Medical Examiner's report before we can tell you more. I'm so sorry."

Alice let out a high-pitched keening, wailing for her son. Margie wanted to take her hands and to hold her and give her comfort. But Alice turned away from Margie, into her mother, head lowered into her chest.

"I'm so sorry," Margie repeated. She looked at the father. His face was stoic, but his shoulders collapsed inward, holding in grief and pain.

For a long time, there was no conversation, only Alice's wailing and a chanted song from her mother. They hugged and held each other, pulling Michael into their circle as well. A tiny family, lost in themselves.

The room was unbearably hot. Margie tugged at her collar and tried not to look as uncomfortable as she was. Sweat was dripping down all their faces, mixing with tears.

Eventually, the family was able to turn outward again, looking to Margie to give them more details, to make it all make sense to them.

"How? What happened?" Michael asked.

"We don't know yet. We will let you know what we find out. When was the last time you saw him?"

They looked at each other. "Yesterday. He was just here," Alice said, as if Margie must have gotten her facts wrong. He couldn't be dead if she had just seen him the day before.

"What time was that?"

"Supper… then he went home. He said he was meeting with friends later."

"Do you know who?"

"I… no. He had a lot of friends. I don't know who he was going to see."

"What were they going to do?"

"I don't know. Getting together to talk. Play games."

"Would there have been drinking?" Cruz asked.

"He was clean," Alice told him firmly. "No alcohol, no drugs. He wasn't into any of that."

"Had he been?"

"Why? Because he was an Indian?"

Cruz shook his head. "Because of your choice of words. Clean. And that he didn't use any alcohol or drugs. Most people will have a social drink. Those that don't, it is often because they have had addiction problems in the past."

Alice didn't answer right away, maybe not believing him, thinking that he was already prejudiced against her son. "Yes. He'd had a problem with alcohol." Alice looked at Margie, then glared at Cruz. "Many of our people have. How can we have strong families and communities when our children are taken away from us? Over and over again, generation after generation. Not just the residential schools. Not just the Sixties Scoop. *Now.*"

Margie nodded. Cruz looked over at her and wisely kept his mouth closed. He probably didn't see it in the city. It wasn't as bad in Calgary as it was in Manitoba. Over and over again, in trying to deal with the violence of the streets, she had seen them. Displaced children who had been unable to establish bonds. Brothers and sisters who were so *lost* by the time they reached adulthood.

"He wouldn't have been drinking," Alice repeated. "He was through that. He was back on his feet. He was clean."

CHAPTER SEVEN

*M*argie was quiet in the car, thinking about the devastated family. She knew that she should take the opportunity to talk it through with Cruz, but she needed time to ponder and think things through on her own first.

If Alice were right and Bruce Hungry Bear had not been under the influence of alcohol or drugs, then how had he ended up in the pond? Mac had remembered a previous death there, determined to have been an accidental death, no foul play involved. Someone who had been so intoxicated that he had apparently wandered into the pond at night and gotten turned around or passed out, eventually drowning. Tragic, but at least not violent.

If that was what had happened to Bruce, then at least his family would know that it had just been an accident. That might be some solace to them. But if that was not what had happened, then what?

"Did Dr. Galt point out any injuries?" she asked Cruz. "After I had gone?"

"Some bruises, but not anything that he could clearly identify. Maybe a fall. Not stabbed or shot. Not that he could see on his initial inspection."

"Face? Head? Hands?"

"Head. He'll know more once he's had a chance to examine the body fully. Can't tell if there are any bruises on the torso or knees until he's got the clothes off. He'll do x-rays, tox screen."

Margie kept her face frozen, willing herself not to grimace or make any sign at his reference to a tox screen. Of course Dr. Galt would have to check whether Hungry Bear had been intoxicated or under the influence of some drug at the time of his death. That was routine. They couldn't just take his parents' word for it that he wouldn't have had anything to drink. Parents were often the last to know. Since he was an adult and didn't even live with them, he could be drinking a lot without their knowing. Kids told parents stories to keep them happy. Margie had done it. She was sure that Christina did it. They liked their parents to think the best of them. It was uncomfortable to disappoint them.

&a.

CRUZ RETURNED Margie to the parking lot at Valleyview to pick up her car and go home. There was one other car in the parking lot, a lone dog walker, probably. Margie glanced over the park but didn't see anyone walking. They might have parked at Valleyview and then taken the Twenty-Sixth Street pathway rather than staying in Valleyview. Or they might just be around the bend where she couldn't see them. Maybe behind the trees that had initially screened Hungry Bear's body from her view.

"You okay?" Cruz asked.

"Yes. Long, hot day. That's all." Margie looked at the time on the dashboard clock. It was still only mid afternoon. Hot, but not the end of the day. "Looks like I still have some time to spend with Christina. If we can stand the heat."

"Go to the mall. Cooler there. Or a movie if the theaters are open. I heard that some of them have reopened, but I haven't checked them out."

Margie shrugged. "Not really in the mood for a movie." Though they might watch something on the computer, stretched out on Margie's bed under the air conditioner. Margie just didn't feel like going out and being around people who were celebrating the day. While she was happy about all the restrictions other than masking in public places being terminated, there weren't many other reasons for her to celebrate Canada Day. "Maybe we'll go to see my grandfather."

It had been a couple of days since they had seen him last. It would be too hot for them to take him out. He would need to stay in the cool of his apartment. But they could have a nice visit there. When the weather cooled off, they could make him some more bannock. Until then, she wasn't using anything other than the microwave to heat their meals.

"It's nice to have a grandfather in town!" Cruz's voice held a smile. "I would have to take my kids back to the Philippines to see their grandparents. Not something we can afford to do very often."

"Can they Skype?"

"When my brother goes to my parents' house, he takes his iPad so that they can talk to the kids. My wife's parents don't have anyone to help them out with technology, so we don't see them very often. Sometimes if they have to go into the city, there is a room in the library where they can connect." He shook his head. "Not the same as having someone in town that you can talk to face to face."

"He lives just a few blocks from us so we can go see him often."

"Nice. I bet he really looks forward to seeing you."

Margie's car's air conditioner was just starting to blow cold air when she got back to the house. She sat there for a moment in the parked car, just enjoying the cool air. But then she turned it off. She didn't want to overheat the engine, and she didn't want to get used to a colder temperature and then deal with being hotter again. She went into the house.

"I'm home!"

Stella, usually exuberant when one of her people returned home, let out a couple of barks but didn't get up from where she was lying in Margie's room.

"Hi, Mom. We're in here."

Margie found Christina lying on the bed just where Margie had imagined her, in shorts and a halter top. Her black hair, which she sometimes wore loose, was braided to keep it off her neck and back.

"Sorry to be away so long." Margie petted Stella and scratched her ears. "How are you guys managing?"

"It's hot."

"No kidding."

"It's *really* hot."

"I know, honey. I wondered if you wanted to go visit Moushoom."

Christina perked up. "Yes! It's way cooler there than it is here. And I want to see him. That's not second, it just came out in that order."

"Okay, why don't you go get ready, and we'll pop over there?"

"I just need to get some sandals on."

Margie looked at Christina, carefully considering her response.

"What?" Christina demanded. She sat up and looked down at herself. "I'm dressed. I'm clean. Hair done. I'm ready to go."

"Maybe something more appropriate for visiting your grandfather?"

Christina stared back at her. "What is not appropriate?"

"I'm just thinking of something that covers a little more skin."

"That will be too hot."

"It's up to you..." Margie didn't want a fight over it. She knew that Moushoom wouldn't criticize Christina for the way she was dressed, no matter what he thought of it. "It just might make everyone more comfortable."

Christina looked down at her cleavage and shrugged. "I don't see what's wrong with it." She got off the bed and used both hands to pull the hem of her shorts down an inch, but they still showed off much more of her long, brown legs than Margie was comfortable with. But what of it? They covered more than a bikini would have.

Margie just smiled and nodded at Christina, not making a big deal of it. "Okay, find your sandals, then, and we'll head out. Are you hydrated?"

The teen rolled her eyes. "Yes, Mom. I've had plenty to drink."

"Not just coffee, right? Because that's dehydrating. I don't want you getting sick."

"We're only walking like three blocks. We'll stay in the shade. And it's cool at Moushoom's."

"Okay. I'm going to grab a water bottle for myself. You want one?"

Christina patted her leg to call Stella to her and gave Margie an annoyed look. "Yeah," she agreed finally. "Grab me one too." She sighed dramatically.

Margie went to the kitchen and grabbed a couple of water bottles from the bottom of the fridge. She knew she should be using a filter and refillable bottles instead of the cases of bottles that she had picked up at the grocery store, but it had been more convenient to just grab the flat. It was bad for the environment, and she should be doing more to take care of Mother Earth.

Christina snapped the leash onto Stella's collar and slid her feet into her sandals, and they were off.

CHAPTER EIGHT

*M*oushoom's room was cool compared with the temperatures outside and at Margie's house. Warmer than she would have kept it if she had central air conditioning, but older people were often cold, so she imagined that was why it was as warm as it was. She was relieved, at any rate, that everything was working as it should. She always worried about the elderly in extreme temperatures. Without fail, whenever they had extreme hot or cold snaps, elderly people died.

But those were mostly people living by themselves or on the street. Not people in care centers like Moushoom. If they had problems with the air conditioning, they would have someone in right away to fix it. They would let Margie know if there were any concerns about her grandfather's health or their ability to provide for his needs.

At least, she hoped so.

There were other family members in town, but Margie was the closest to him, both by blood and distance-wise, and the others had been happy to put her name down as his emergency contact once she had moved in.

She'd heard horror stories about the conditions in care centers, especially at the beginning of the COVID crisis. People living in filth and without the necessities, alone and isolated, bodies piling up too fast to be dealt with. She'd been relieved when she moved to Calgary and found Moushoom in a clean, neat, well-ventilated room with diligent caregivers close at hand, an emergency alarm on his wrist, and allowed visitors if they were masked and sanitized.

"There are my girls," Moushoom said with pleasure, a big smile on his face.

Margie's heart felt as if it would burst. She loved him so much and had only been able to see him once or twice a year when she had lived in Winnipeg. Now that they were close at hand, they were making up for lost time.

"Hello, Moushoom!" Margie bent down to give him a hug around his thin shoulders. She remembered Hungry Bear's grandmother, how old and wizened she was. But still so strong. It had taken a strong will for the past generations to survive and go on to raise their families, despite the best efforts of the government to stamp out the traditional ways. She could see that strength in the survivors. "How are you feeling today?"

"I am ready to go for a walk."

"I'm sorry… it's still too hot out. It's supposed to cool down on the weekend, and then we'll go out."

"A little warm weather never hurt anyone."

"These temperatures do. We have had several deaths. I'm not risking losing you."

Moushoom scowled, but then turned it off and spoke to Christina. "And where is my hug?"

Christina was happy to give him one. Margie could see that Moushoom was not really angry or upset. He had expected her answer. As soon as the weather broke, they would take him out again.

Margie brought over chairs and she and Christina sat down close to Moushoom to talk.

❧

THERE WERE FIREWORKS AT ELEVEN. Margie stepped outside for a moment to watch them, then she went back into the house. The house was holding on to the heat of the day. The temperature outside had finally dropped to the high twenties instead of high thirties. Margie's bedroom was the only room that was reasonably comfortable, so that was where they were hanging out.

"Do you want another movie?" Christina suggested, tapping her iPad.

"No. I need to get to sleep. I have work tomorrow, and it will be busy with this new case."

"Can I watch it still if I put on headphones?"

"Sure."

Margie dropped off to sleep more quickly than she had expected to. Her brain was whirling with thoughts of Hungry Bear and his family and where the case would lead. But she'd been up early for her run, and it had been a hot, busy day, so her body took charge, and she was soon off to sleep.

A crash woke her a few hours later and, disoriented, Margie thought at first that it was more fireworks, then maybe a truck crashing into the house, and, finally, logic reasserting itself, she realized that it was thunder. The loudest, most aggressive thunder she had ever heard. And she had seen some storms in Winnipeg.

"What was that?" Christina grasped at Margie. "Are you okay?"

"It's okay. Just thunder."

"Thunder?" Christina's hand worked its way up Margie's arm and shoulder and touched her face. Christina leaned in close in order to see her. "I thought you got shot!"

"Oh, baby." Margie pulled away from Christina to turn on the bedside lamp, then returned to her previous position and cuddled Christina to her again. "I'm just fine. It was only thunder. Maybe you had a dream to go with it."

"Yeah." Christina's eyes searched Margie's face and then did a quick scan of the rest of her body. Apparently convinced that Margie was telling the truth and she had not been shot, Christina relaxed and put her head against Margie's. "Yeah, just a dream. That was really loud."

Stella whined, squeezed up against Christina's other side. She wasn't supposed to be on the bed, but neither of them tried to tell her that. They lay there watching the startlingly-bright flashes of lightening and listening to repeated peals of thunder. After a few minutes, it stopped. Margie waited for the rain, but not a drop fell.

"I guess that's it for tonight," she told Christina. "Just nature's way of showing up the fireworks."

Christina giggled. "Yeah. *I'll* show you a light show."

"Are you okay? I'll turn off the light and we can go back to sleep."

"I'm fine." The girl yawned, and Margie found herself doing the same. Back to sleep, then; she would need to be up for work in a few more hours.

CHAPTER NINE

$\mathcal{M}$argie was in the bullpen early, reading through the reports in her email and jotting down notes for the squad's stand-up meeting, where she would be expected to report on the progress in the Hungry Bear case.

There was always a certain level of stress, anxiety, and energy in the room when they had a new case. Although it could take months or even years to clear a homicide file, they all knew that the progress they made in the first couple of days was vital.

But there seemed to be something different about this case. The Hungry Bear death seemed to have affected people differently. Maybe it was just the holiday. People had taken the Thursday off to be with their families, and then had to come back in on a Friday to deal with a death that, in all likelihood, would be cleared as an accident within a few days. Maybe they just didn't feel like getting into it.

Margie nodded to Katelyn Jones as she came in, to Cruz, and to the others on the team who walked by her desk and gave her a smile, nod, or thumbs-up. Margie's initial worries over being accepted by the team when she had first moved to Calgary had mostly faded. They were all willing to work with her and treated her pretty much like any other member of the team, but Margie worried that there were still some reservations. People were still watching to see how she would act at annual review time, when salary increases or promotions came down, the first time she used her gender or her cultural heritage to get special treatment. It was ingrained. Most of them were probably not even aware of the biases they held.

"Let's go," Mac called out as he left his office and headed to the conference room for the morning meeting. Margie glanced at the system clock on her computer. He was five minutes early.

Could she safely take the last five minutes of time to prepare? Or did she need to stop what she was doing and give her report, feeling rushed and not quite fully prepped?

She decided that being seen as arriving late would be a bigger blot on how she was perceived, even though she wasn't actually late. She could go ahead with the points that she had, and answer anything additional with an "I don't yet have that information."

Five minutes more preparation wasn't going to make that much of a difference.

"Ready to go?" Mac asked, the moment Margie stepped up to the table and set down her papers.

She had never known him to be so impatient. "Yes, sir."

"Let's start with your new case."

Margie nodded. She glanced around at the attendees. There would be a few stragglers. The team wasn't used to Mac jumping the gun like that.

"I think everybody already knows the basics. The body of Bruce Hungry Bear was discovered in Valleyview Park by a runner—myself—yesterday morning. He had clearly been dead and in the water for a few hours. No attempts at resuscitation were made. Dr. Galt attended on behalf of the Medical Examiner's office. He made a cursory investigation at the scene and brought the body back for further examination. I attended at the morgue early this morning, and the preliminary report showed..." Margie took a deep breath, bracing herself for their reactions. "Hungry Bear died from a blow to the head, not drowning."

"Really?" Jones blurted. She blushed slightly, a charming shade of pink that set off her blond, wavy hair. She grimaced and shook her head, not happy being the first one to ask for more details. "So... how does that play out? He was in the water when you found him."

"Yes," Margie confirmed. "But during the autopsy they found that he did not have water in his lungs. He didn't drown."

"Was he in the water when he died? Like he was walking over slippery rocks, and he fell and hit his head and died in the water without breathing it in?"

"There are drag marks on his knees and shins."

The room was silent, as if everyone were holding his breath. Margie was holding hers for sure. She waited, looking around at all their faces. She knew what they had all thought to begin with. That Hungry Bear had just been a drunk who had happened to fall into the water and drown. But that was not what had happened. No matter what anyone had thought, that had been an incorrect assumption, and they had begun the investigation with that bias.

MacDonald's face was stern, almost angry. "This was supposed to be an accidental death."

"But it wasn't."

"The Stampede starts in one week. We have delegates coming in from out of town. We need this to go away."

Margie shook her head. "Why would anyone coming from out of town be concerned with it?"

"We missed the Stampede last year due to COVID. For the first time ever. That lost the city a lot of revenue. This year, the border is still closed, so it is only Canadian tourists. They need to at least recover costs. And if people are hearing about a homicide instead of the grandstand show…"

The rodeo, fair, exhibits, and musical performances of the Stampede were a big deal to Calgarians and, as Mac said, brought in a lot of revenue.

"I don't see what this has to do with people going to the Stampede. It isn't as though we have a serial killer attacking tourists, or someone threatening to bomb the events. One suspicious death has nothing to do with the Stampede or tourists."

"There has been a lot of… negative news lately. I've already been called by several different offices requesting that we keep this out of the news except to say that it has been cleared and there is no danger to anyone visiting or living in the city."

A lot of negative news lately. That would be the graves at the residential schools, along with calls to cancel Canada Day. Celebrations had been canceled in several municipalities, but Calgary had chosen to go ahead with theirs, paying some lip service to the tribal elders and saying that the fireworks would be in memory of the children who had died.

Margie had never attended a memorial service or vigil with fireworks.

"Did you see the news last night and this morning?" Detective Gagnon asked. "Ten Catholic churches vandalized in Calgary, statues of Queen Elizabeth and Queen Victoria and early explorers vandalized, knocked down all over Canada, even thrown into the harbor in Vancouver. And Calgary's masking bylaw still in place even though we are over 70% vaccinated." His voice was loud with frustration. He wasn't the only one who was frustrated. A lot of people who were promised that everything would be back to normal in July were not impressed that the requirement for masking had not been lifted.

Society had changed in the last year and a half. Maybe some things would never go back to the way they had been.

MacDonald nodded. "The fact that Hungry Bear was Aboriginal will play big in the news. It's going to be connected to all this other genocide stuff, even though there is no connection. And with a name like Hungry Bear, everyone will know that he was an Ind—Native person. We really need to clear it quietly. Before the Stampede parade."

Which, Margie knew, was a week away. Homicides weren't cleared that fast. It would barely be enough time for the ME to declare the manner and cause of death. If it was murder, a week's investigation was not going to put it to bed.

"With all due respect, sir… I don't think that's possible."

"I need you to be behind me on this. Whether you think it is possible or not, I need you to put all of your effort into it. Make sure that it is *old news* by parade day."

Margie swallowed. She looked down at her notes, trying to arrange her thoughts into bullet points. "Tox screen was negative for alcohol or street drugs."

"Maybe it was a wild animal," Jones suggested, playing devil's advocate. "There are animals over there, aren't there? Maybe it was a coyote attack. An animal could have dragged him."

Margie gritted her teeth and pretended to consider it. "Definitely something to look into," she agreed. "But as there were no teeth marks on Hungry Bear, and it took two of us to pull him out of the water… I can't see a coyote being able to drag him anywhere. And why would it drag him into the water?"

Jones couldn't come up with an explanation. Crocodiles pulled people into the water, but there were no crocs in Calgary. They didn't have any large predators living in the pond. Margie briefly entertained the idea of informing the press that maybe they had a lake monster like Nessie or Ogopogo in Valleyview pond. But that probably would not go over well.

"Detective Cruz and I talked to Hungry Bear's roommates and his family yesterday. None of them were aware of any of the circumstances surrounding his death. The parents believe he was going to spend the evening with friends. I will be following up on that today. If we can get his phone logs, I can start identifying who he has been in contact with in the last week. Detective Cruz got some information off of his computer." She looked at Cruz for him to fill them in.

"I got a few names from his social apps," Cruz acknowledged. "It will start us off."

"Anything suspicious in his email?" Mac asked. "Any red flags?"

"No. Everything I saw was innocuous. Spam and shopping. I'm told," he glanced over at Margie, "that young folks these days don't use email."

MacDonald cleared his throat. "Right. Anything in his social apps, then?"

"It all looked pretty vanilla. No criminal activities that I could spot. No threats or cyberbullying. From what I can tell, he lived a pretty quiet life."

"Give me an update at the end of the day," Mac instructed. "I expect to see some progress. Detective Patenaude, would you stay after this meeting, please?"

Margie nodded. "Yes, sir."

They moved on to the other cases that were being actively investigated. Margie looked through her notes, but tried to keep focused on what the others were saying so that she would know the status of each case and if there were parts of the investigation that she could assist with.

CHAPTER TEN

*I*n half an hour, they had touched on each of the active files, and Mac dismissed the group. They all headed back to their desks, leaving Mac and Margie to talk. Mac shut the door.

"I'm sorry things didn't go the way you expected," Margie said tentatively, wondering if this was a private dressing-down for not agreeing that the Hungry Bear death was an accident.

Mac nodded and waved the comment aside. "Not much we can do if the evidence points in another direction… but I'm sure this is a pretty simple case. Don't make it more complicated than it is."

And keep it out of the papers.

"No, sir. Of course not."

"I wanted to talk to you about the complaint you submitted on Oliver Symons."

"Oh." Margie nodded. She swallowed, trying to dispel the lump in her throat and butterflies in her stomach. "Yes, I was pretty shocked."

Mac looked at her and didn't say anything for a minute. "Well… I didn't find anything particularly shocking about it. I would have taken it as an off-the-cuff remark. A poor attempt at humor."

"You can't deny that it was racist."

He was silent.

"If you're concerned about people hearing that an Indigenous man was killed after hearing so much in the news focusing on Indigenous harms, then how do you think a comment like *this* from a municipal employee would play in the media?"

"I don't deny that it was inappropriate. But I think you're making too much about it. I want you to consider whether you really want to submit that report or not. Because I think… you don't want to."

"Why not? Because I should *take it?*"

"Because no harm was done. It wasn't aimed at you. It wasn't aimed at anyone who could be hurt by it. Yes, it was inappropriate. But it was gallows humor. It's just a stress relief valve."

Margie breathed in and out in long, slow breaths. "Number one, drawing attention to someone's ethnic or Indigenous name is a microaggression. An ethnic name is just as normal and valid as any white European name. Second, saying something negative about someone's ethnic name or mocking it is overt aggression and racism. Symons made fun of the name Hungry Bear. Third, by calling him Thirsty Bear, Symons implied that he was a drunk and that was why he had died. Knowing nothing about the man except for the fact that he had an Indigenous name, he made the assumption that he was a drunk. Hungry Bear didn't reek of alcohol. He wasn't carrying a flask. There was nothing to indicate that he was drunk or had died because of it."

"That's just because we had a death there previously due to someone intoxicated wandering into the pond. I understand what you're saying, but I think that filing an official complaint against the guy is taking it too far. Symons is a good forensics tech. He just needs to learn to watch his mouth."

"And maybe a reprimand will remind him to do that next time."

"I feel for the guy. You haven't been policing here very long and were never on a beat here, so you don't know what it's like. But most of a beat cop's contacts with the Native population are for drunk and disorderlies and domestics involving alcohol. That's fact, not bias. Alcoholism is rampant in that population. That's just the way it is here."

"Symons isn't a beat cop. He's just a racist. I'm fully aware of the alcoholism endemic in the Indigenous community. More so than you are. It doesn't excuse making assumptions and racist comments about victims of homicide or anyone else."

Mac held up his hands in surrender. "Fine. You're entitled to your opinion, and you're absolutely entitled to file a report on what you saw and heard. I just wanted to give you a heads-up and see if you wanted to rethink your decision. If you're determined to file it, then go ahead. I'll sign off on it."

Margie stared at him for a moment, then nodded. "Thank you, sir."

"Of course. And… if anyone on my team were to make similar remarks, I assume you will come directly to me."

Because he wanted to know about it and handle it immediately, or because he wanted the chance to bury it or talk her out of filing a report on a member of the homicide squad?

She chose to believe the best of MacDonald. If something happened, she would take it to him first. And if it wasn't dealt with, she would take it to Professional Standards.

⁊

MARGIE'S CELL PHONE RANG. Sliding it out, she saw Christina's name and picture on the screen. She swiped to answer the call.

"Hi, honey."

"People suck!"

Margie laughed. "Well, yes, sometimes they do. What's wrong? What happened?"

"You know I've been bagging up all of the empty bottles for the fundraiser for residential school survivors?"

"Uh-huh?" Taking empty drink containers to the bottle depot earned them ten cents for small containers and twenty-five cents for anything over a liter. Christina had been diligently collecting all their cans and bottles and even discarded beer cans she found on the street, to donate for a fundraiser that would benefit IRSSS, the Indian Residential School Survivors Society.

"I was going to put them in the shed, so I had them out in the back yard…"

"Yeah?"

"And somebody stole them! Somebody walked right into our yard and stole my bags of bottles!"

"Oh, honey. No! I'm sorry about that!"

"I can't believe they would do that! It isn't like I put them in the lane with the garbage bins. They were right in our yard. I was just going to take them all the way to the shed later, after I dressed."

"How many did you have?"

"Five bags. And I was going to go around the neighborhood and see if I could get some other people to donate their bottles too. Why would somebody do that?"

"Well... hopefully it was somebody who really needed the money. But I'm sorry. You've been so good about making sure nothing gets thrown out or recycled if we can get a deposit on it."

"People just suck," Christina repeated. "That's all there is to it."

CHAPTER ELEVEN

*M*argie started with the names that Cruz had pulled off of Hungry Bear's social networks and ran some initial background checks against them. They were not criminals. Any priors were for teenage hijinks, moving violations, that kind of thing. No drug dealing or violence or human trafficking. All pretty clean. A look at their social networks—not Facebook, because again, young people had moved away from Facebook when their parents had started getting accounts—showed that they were all pretty wrapped up in themselves. No hint of anything unsavory. Gaming, parties, pictures of products they were selling or closets they had dejunked, some family shots with extended family members. None of them appeared to have children of their own yet. Some mentioned their jobs, but most had no means of support that could be gleaned from the social network feeds.

Margie started making phone calls, and immediately discovered that the friends knew something was up. Maybe Hungry Bear's mother had known who her son had been going to see after all, or maybe she had just called a couple of friends that she remembered from his high school days and they had spread the word. Or maybe they had missed him, but had heard of the body discovered in the park and put it together.

"Could we all get together to meet with you?" the girl named Kennedy asked. "I mean... he was with all of us on Wednesday night, and... I'm not really comfortable talking to you alone. It would be more efficient for you to talk to us all together, wouldn't it?"

Margie grimaced. "Well, it is really better if we can talk to you separately. It is easier for us to find out what each individual knows that way."

Easier to spot discrepancies in their stories. To ask one what they thought of the other. To make sure that they weren't covering for each other.

"Well... could you anyway? I mean, none of us really know anything. And I wouldn't want to come in myself. That's just so..." Margie could practically hear her shudder. "It's like TV or something. I can't believe... I don't want to believe that anything happened to Bruce. I want to help, but I just can't. I can't do it on my own. You should come and talk to all of us at once. I'll even set it up for my house. That's how much I want to help."

"I appreciate that." Jones looked up from her work and Margie rolled her eyes at her. "I can come to you, of course, and if you'd be more comfortable with someone else there... but maybe we could limit the numbers..."

She hoped that the young woman's mother would not be there, helicoptering around her, trying to ensure that the police did not do anything to upset her child.

Jones responded with an eye roll of her own, acknowledging Margie's opinion. Margie did her best to get the meeting set up with Kennedy, who promised to call back once she had a time nailed down with her friends. Then they could all get together.

It could be a ploy, designed to put Margie off. Say that they were going to arrange it, and then never settle on a time. They would keep telling Margie, "Don't call us, we'll call you," or whatever the modern equivalent was. "I'll message you. Promise."

After hanging up with Kennedy, Margie turned her attention to the files in the workspace that had been set up for the case. She had already at least skimmed all the written reports, her own among them. Just to make sure that it was complete and that she hadn't already forgotten any of the details of the scene. It was a bit different being a witness as well as the primary investigator. Homicide detectives did not normally go around finding bodies themselves.

The photography was another story. Margie was familiar with the park and had seen everything that was there to see, so she hadn't bothered to spend much time on the pictures. But it was time to remedy that. She might have missed a clue with adrenaline pumping from her discovery, a little tired from the first half of her run, trying to preserve the evidence and keep people back from the scene before she had any way to rope off a perimeter.

There were a few establishing shots of the park, showing a pulled-back view of the pathway, pond, and the area around it. Similar to what Margie was used to seeing when she went to the park, either with Stella or on her own as part of her new morning run routine. Similar to the pictures that she took when the sky was still pink or the water was particularly glassy and clear.

The next pictures, though, were far different from any that she had taken. Hungry Bear's body where she and the bystander had pulled him up out of the water. Still stomach down because that was the way they had pulled him out. Close-ups of any mark or foreign object on his clothing. Pictures of the bruise on his head. Hungry Bear's bloated face.

Then more shots after he had been taken away. The pond, anything they found on the ground that might have had something to do with his death. Shots of the bystanders and of Margie herself, standing there talking to Cruz.

Margie wrote down a couple of pictures that she wanted to print or review over again later. The next set of photos was for the garbage excavations. The techs had emptied each of the garbage bins in the area Margie had indicated. She was sure they were just delighted with her suggestion that each needed to be checked. Especially considering the fact that they had found nothing of interest. No bloody bludgeon. No bottles of alcohol. No nasty notes about how Hungry Bear needed to be killed.

There were 7-Eleven bags and Tim's coffee cups. Chip bags and half-eaten muffins. And lots of dog poop bags. The park was well used.

"Sorry guys," Margie muttered to herself. She was not sorry that she had not been personally involved in excavating the bins one layer at a time, pulling out all those doggie doo bags. Some of the 7-Eleven bags had been used to pick up poop too, only it wasn't obvious until the techs uncrumpled the bags and spread them out. What a job.

She skimmed through the garbage pictures quickly. She wasn't expecting to find anything in the garbages related to the investigation, but one never knew. Canadians were well-known for their manners, and leaving a murder weapon or other evidence on the grass or in the water would have been very rude.

The techs had also itemized the contents of each of the bins, and each bin was marked on a map so that Margie could see where each had come from. She looked through the itemized lists for anything sinister.

Baby wipes and diapers. There were a few needles in addition to the other crap. Needles that should have been properly disposed of in a sharps box. They didn't need the techs getting stabbed while they were working.

Broken toys. Shoes. Teddy bears. Margie frowned, wondering if a neighbor's memorial to the dead residential school children had been stolen and thrown in the garbage.

THE PHONE RANG. Margie was so deep into her notes that it made her jump. She took a breath, finished the sentence she was writing so she wouldn't lose her thought, and looked at the caller display. Kennedy Johnston, the young woman who she had been talking to earlier.

Margie hadn't expected to hear from her again so quickly. She figured they would be exchanging phone messages back and forth for a few days, with both of them trying to find a time that would work for everyone.

"Detective Patenaude."

"Oh, hi… this is Kennedy? We were talking earlier about Bruce?"

"Yes, I remember, Kennedy. Have you already been able to set something up?"

"Uh, yeah, actually. Would you be able to come to my place this afternoon?"

"I'll make the time. What is your address and what time should I be there?"

Kennedy gave her the pertinent details, stammered a little about seeing Margie later, and hung up.

Detective Cruz had been good with Hungry Bear's roommates and family, but he was busy on his own cases, and Margie asked Jones whether she would be able to attend the interview with her. They had worked well together on other cases and Margie wanted Jones fully onside with the fact that it was not a case of accidental drowning. The evidence said that it could not be.

"Sure, I could do that," Jones agreed pleasantly, looking at her computer screen for her schedule. "I don't have anything I absolutely have to be here for."

"I'd really appreciate it. I know it's out of your way and it's not your case…"

"They are all everyone's cases. We're not going to get them cleared without everyone helping out."

Margie nodded. The homicide team was very good that way, but she still wanted to be careful not to impose on the others or to imply that her case was any more important than anyone else's. The Hungry Bear case was starting to get hot politically. They had all heard Mac say that he wanted it cleared within a week. It probably wasn't possible, but Margie needed to be able to show that she had used every resource within her reach to do so. Including human capital.

She gave Jones the details of where and when, and the blond nodded agreeably. "That gives me half an hour to clear my desk. I'll just tie up a couple of loose ends here and make sure that I'm ready to go."

CHAPTER TWELVE

*D*o you know exactly where this is?" Jones asked, peering out the window and studying the street signs.

"Well… not exactly. I looked at it on the map before we left, but I don't remember the exact turns. I think it's… over there?" she gestured to the right. A guess. Her phone was clearly being affected by the clouds gathering overhead and was rethinking the route.

"I think it's one of these backward lots," Jones said.

"Backward lots?"

"These ones," Jones gestured toward one of the alleys. "The fronts face onto green space and a shared multiuse trail. The backs are the only way to get to them by car; you have to go through the alleys to make deliveries or to interview someone."

Margie turned into the alley, reading the street sign as she went by it. The alley was, in fact, the street. But it was still full of garbage bins and broken-down cars and falling-down fences. It hadn't been made more presentable because it was the only way visitors could access the houses.

There were numbers on some of the fences, but not all of them. Margie shook her head in irritation. There was a bylaw that people had to have their house numbers in the back for law enforcement, first responders, and garbage collection. But a lot of people didn't know or didn't care about the requirement.

"If we're on the right street, it could be this one," Jones gestured to a house squashed away in the corner.

The GPS program on Margie's phone suddenly sprang to life, blitzing through several screens too fast to follow, showing a few different routes with the turns mapped out, and then finally settling on a picture of her car on the map and a blue dot representing her destination right on top of the corner house Jones had indicated.

Margie eased the car forward until she was as close as she wanted to get to the garbage and the decrepit fence that might blow over onto her car at any moment. She turned on her police flashers to deter thieves and busybodies, and they got out of the car and put on their masks.

"What a junkyard," Margie said, looking around.

"I know. But that's what it's like in the poorer neighborhoods. They don't have the money to have stuff hauled or to pay the disposal fees at the dump. They've got three cars in hopes of being able to get one running. And it's probably like Hungry Bear's house, with several people sharing the rent or mortgage."

Margie nodded. She'd seen it all before. It wasn't anything new. But she always felt bad when she saw neighborhoods like that. Bad that the people were so down on their luck and bad that everyone else had to look at it. The little house in Dover was only a kilometer or two from Margie's own house in Southview. Margie's area had definitely been kept up better, but that didn't mean the people in Dover were lazy. Just that they didn't make as much money.

There was a cord tied around the gate post that they had to untangle in order to open the gate and get into the yard. Margie looked for a "Beware of Dog" sign, but there wasn't anything to indicate that they might be attacked the instant they opened the gate. She could hear dogs barking nearby. Hopefully, they were caged or chained, wherever they were.

Margie had been bitten a couple of times in Winnipeg. Luckily, in both cases she had been able to find the owner and to confirm that the dog's vaccinations, including rabies shots, were up to date, which meant that she'd been able to avoid having to get shots of her own. But she wasn't eager for a repeat of the experience.

Eventually, Jones worked the cord loose and opened the gate. They walked through it and pulled it shut behind them, wrapping the string loosely around the post so it would be easier to get back out.

It felt like an invasion to walk in through someone's back yard and approach the back door. Different from when it was a friend and she just knocked on the kitchen door and went in.

Kennedy was apparently watching for them and opened the door as they approached.

"Hey. Hi. I'm Kennedy."

She held her hand out tentatively. Margie glanced over at Jones, then back at Kennedy. "I'm sorry, we're not supposed to shake. Department policy. So many police officers got sick at the beginning of COVID…"

Kennedy shrugged and withdrew her hand. "We're supposed to be back to normal now. Fully open. I know Calgary still has to cancel their mask bylaw, but this isn't a public place; it's my home. You don't have to wear them."

"It is still recommended by CPS. It's for your protection as well as ours."

"I'm vaccinated. I don't care."

Margie nodded agreeably. "So, are the others here?" she asked, prompting a subject change. She had learned not to argue hygiene measures with civilians. It never got anywhere, and people just got hot under the collar. It was hot enough without throwing irritated, opinionated people into the mix. Thinking about the temperature, Margie ran a finger around her collar. It was cooler than Canada Day had been, and it looked as though it might start storming any minute, but it was still 27 degrees.

"Yeah, come in," Kennedy agreed. She turned around and led the way into the house. Margie followed close behind her, with Jones bringing up the rear. Margie looked around alertly for anything that was out of place. There was a danger that came with walking into someone's house, into their territory, where they might feel the need to protect themselves, where they could lay a trap or just happen to have a firearm hidden somewhere close when things got emotional.

The house was somewhat untidy, but not a hovel. Cleaner than Hungry Bear's house had been. Tidier than the junk outside had suggested. Kennedy apparently did take some pride in her house.

"We're meeting in the game room downstairs," Kennedy led them to a stairway that led down from the kitchen. "It's a lot cooler down there."

It was. Margie could feel the chill as she walked down the stairs. They had left their shoes on, but she was sure if she hadn't, the floor would have been icy through her socks. Tile over concrete.

The basement was mostly the game room, which included a wet bar. There was a sliding pocket door to one side that Margie assumed was a washroom. Most of the room was empty, with some folding tables against the wall that were normally used for whatever games they played together. Role playing games, Margie guessed by the posters on the wall. She had never gotten into them, and neither had Christina, but they both knew people who were heavily into D&D and other games.

There were several other members of the group of friends waiting, sitting in chairs around the room. Margie and Jones were apparently the last to the party.

"Okay, so this is Alex, Evander, Roger, and Susan. And I'm Kennedy," she added, in case they didn't remember from the phone calls and the introduction upstairs.

"It's good to meet you," Margie said to the group.

"You want to sit down?" Kennedy pushed a couple of folding chairs in their direction.

After considering for a moment, Margie took one of them and sat down. It would be easier to talk to them on their own level. She wanted them to feel comfortable, as if it were a friendly conversation, rather than feeling threatened by a police interrogation. Jones followed her lead and sat down. Margie saw the slight movement as she readjusted her concealed holster to make herself more comfortable.

"So... I guess I'll start with whether you have any questions for me," Margie said. "I gather from talking to you on the phone that you know the sad news about your friend Bruce."

Kennedy shook her head. "I can't quite believe it. I mean... are you sure? I couldn't get him on the phone, but I never thought that something *serious* had happened. He was just here Wednesday night. How could something have happened to him in that short period of time?"

"I know. It's quite a shock, and it takes time to adjust to the idea. I'll just confirm what his family probably already told you..." Margie waited for some sort of indication that it had been Bruce's family who had told Kennedy and the other friends Bruce was dead. They looked at each other, but no one offered anything by way of explanation. "Yeah. So Bruce's body was found early yesterday morning. You know where Valleyview park is?"

They all nodded. "Of course we do," Kennedy said, rolling her eyes. "It's just over there." She made a movement to indicate one direction. Margie was too turned around to know whether she was right or not. She had to assume that Kennedy knew what she was talking about. They lived in the neighborhood; of course they knew where the park was.

"It was… in the water. Bruce was dead." Again, taking care not to use euphemisms that might confuse things and leave the friends thinking that Bruce was just hurt or traumatized rather than deceased.

"What happened to him?" the other woman asked. Susan. Kennedy was blond, Susan had dark brown hair. Poker straight.

"We are still investigating the cause of death," Margie said, giving nothing away. Hold back. Always best to hold back and see if people gave themselves away by knowing details that they had not been given.

"It just doesn't make sense," said the slight, dark-haired man who Margie thought was Evander. She hadn't had time to anchor the names to the people yet.

"It's Evander?" she checked.

They all shook their heads. "I'm Alex," the man corrected. "So what happened to him? I mean, he was playing here, it was getting late; he left to walk home. It isn't that far, just a few blocks. He should have been home in ten minutes."

"Alex. I am sorry for your loss. I understand it must all be very confusing right now. Maybe if I could ask you some questions, I would have a better idea of how things happened. It will help to set the stage."

Alex frowned, irritated by her non-answer. She had asked them if they had any questions, and then she hadn't answered his.

"Just like I said," he snapped. "We were playing games until late. Here." He raised both hands to indicate the expanse of the room. "Like we always do. No different from usual."

"Were you drinking?"

"There were drinks," Alex said a little belligerently. The others looked at each other.

"Some of us were drinking and some not. No one was drunk. We just like to do a little social drinking when we're doing our thing." This explanation came from Susan. She had a straightforward, matter-of-fact manner. Telling it like it was. Margie decided to dig a little deeper.

"Was Bruce drinking?"

Susan shook her head, eyes widening slightly. She looked around at the rest of the group. "Bruce didn't drink anymore. He was out of the closet."

Margie frowned and tried to reconcile this declaration with the rest of the conversation.

"On the wagon," one of the boys corrected. "He was never *in* the closet."

Margie smiled, understanding the mistake. Bruce hadn't come out as gay; he had stopped drinking.

"Is there a reason for that? Has he had troubles in the past?"

"No."

"He had," Alex said. "A few years back."

Susan shook her head adamantly. "No, not Bruce..."

"It was before you were around."

Susan looked at the others, who nodded. She still didn't look as though she believed this fact, but she shrugged. "Whatever. He wasn't drinking Wednesday. I've never seen him drink."

"I see. Could he have been on anything else?"

They all looked at Margie blankly.

"Drugs?" Margie said. "Maybe some weed?"

"No. Why are you asking these questions?"

"I just want to be sure that we have all the facts," Margie assured them. "A death like this... sometimes alcohol or another drug is involved."

"He hadn't been drinking or using drugs that night," Kennedy said firmly. "Not ever. Alex is right. After the trouble he had a few years back, he got into a program. Cleaned up his act. Even though we usually had booze around these meetings, he never had any. Just kept to soft drinks. We used to joke that he was the designated driver."

"Why is that a joke?" Jones asked. "He didn't drive?"

"No. He was close by; he just walked home. Everyone either stayed here overnight or walked. None of us ever drove drunk."

"Ah. That's wise. The rest of you stayed here?"

"Yeah, the rest of us did."

"Who was drinking and who wasn't?"

Walls went up. No one wanted to be judged for being a drinker. The non-drinkers didn't seem particularly interested in declaring themselves either. Margie shrugged and took over again.

"That's fine. We don't care either way. We're just trying to build a picture. Everything that happened Wednesday night. Do you usually party on a Wednesday?"

"No, we don't usually *game* on a Wednesday night," Evander corrected. "It wasn't a party. Just a game night. And usually, people have work Thursday. But because of Canada Day, we didn't. We didn't have to get up Thursday morning. We were going to play some more in the afternoon."

"You were going to? But you didn't end up doing it?"

"No." Kennedy spoke up. "Bruce was supposed to come back over, but he didn't. And we didn't feel like starting on our own and then being interrupted an hour later when he decided to show up. We called him… kept getting his voicemail."

"And I wasn't feeling well," Susan contributed. "I had a killer headache from *the heat* and couldn't play a game. So we just kind of hung out. Watched some Netflix, had a few drinks. Tried to stay cool."

Margie assumed Susan was one of those who had been drinking. She didn't want to admit that she'd woken up hung over, so it was the heat rather than the drink. The two combined could be a pretty potent combination. People got dehydrated faster, woke up sicker.

"Can you believe the heat?" Margie asked rhetorically.

Most of them nodded and made comments about just how hot it had been. Record breaking.

"It's a good thing you have this basement," Margie said. "It's really nice and cool down here."

Various nods of agreement, declarations that it was too hot to do anything but play games in the basement.

"So… how did Bruce seem Wednesday night?"

CHAPTER THIRTEEN

The friends all looked at each other. Margie wished that she had been able to convince them to do their interviews separately. So that they weren't all just giving the party line, making sure that each account fit with the others.

"He seemed fine to me," said Roger, who had been quiet until then. "He'd had dinner over at his mom's. He was chill, didn't act like he'd had a fight with them or anything."

"Did he usually have fights with them?"

"No." Roger shrugged. "But some people do. People aren't always cool meeting with their parents. Bruce liked his okay. Had disagreements sometimes, but he didn't get really worked up about them."

The others nodded.

"He wasn't upset about anything?" Margie tried.

There was a hiccup of silence. Everybody quiet for just a moment too long, looking at each other, weighing their answers.

"So, he *was* upset?" Margie suggested.

"What's to be upset about?" Kennedy asked. "It was a holiday. He had a nice dinner with his parents. Was having a nice time playing with friends. No worries about work the next day or anything. Just vibing with friends."

"That doesn't mean that he had nothing to be upset about. Sometimes something that you wouldn't think was a big deal can tip someone over the edge."

They shook their heads, sticking to Roger's and Kennedy's stories. No, he wasn't upset about anything. Just hanging out.

Margie looked at Jones for a moment, letting her mind worry over the possibilities. Had Bruce had an argument or altercation with someone in the group? Or had it happened earlier when he'd been at his parents' house? What had been on his mind?

"Who won the game?" Jones asked.

"What?" Evander said blankly, then apparently remembered that they were supposed to have been playing a game that night. Maybe they hadn't had the time to get down to these details in the story? Why would a cop care about who won the game? "Oh... we didn't finish. We were going to finish on Canada Day. Pick up where we left off. Only... Bruce wouldn't answer his phone. He didn't come back. So we couldn't finish it."

"Was he mugged?" Susan asked. "Is that what happened? Somebody wanted his money?"

"He wasn't mugged," Alex told her. "They didn't say he was mugged. Just... that he died. It must have been an accident. Maybe... he tripped and fell into the pond?"

"Maybe," Margie said neutrally.

That started them off speculating, and Margie and Jones listened carefully to the various scenarios. He was mugged. He tripped. Someone pushed him in for no reason. A gang initiation thing. A dog or a wild animal scared him. They were creative; Margie had to give them that. From what she understood, role playing games involved a lot of storytelling. They were good at spitballing, coming up with some ideas that Margie hadn't considered. But they didn't match the forensics. And no one suggested it could have been intentional or that Bruce had been confronted by someone who knew him, who was angry at him for some reason. All of their suggestions involved strangers or accidents.

"We would like to get your contact details," Margie told the group of friends as they prepared to leave. "In case I have any further questions or things that need to be cleared up." It was too late to get an untainted story.

But maybe they would still be able to separate the truth from the lies and would be able to gradually pick apart the story the friends had woven, to get down to what had really happened when Bruce had left Kennedy's house that night.

As they climbed the stairs to the kitchen, there was a crack like a gunshot. Both Margie and Jones ducked and flattened themselves against the wall, looking around quickly for the shooter, evaluating escape routes and how to protect each other.

"Thunder," Kennedy said, laughing. "Sounds like the storm has hit."

They didn't immediately accept this explanation, looking up and down the stairs and listening for anyone moving toward them. Kennedy stood on the stairs looking down at them, amused. Back in the game room, they could hear the laughter of the friends, relieved that the police were leaving and also startled by the thunder. A bit giddy. They would be breaking out the drinks soon, Margie was sure.

There was a low rumble of thunder and another crack. Enough to reassure Margie that Kennedy was telling the truth. It was just the storm. They continued up the stairs. Before they reached the door, Margie could feel the fresh, wet air blowing in through the screen door. It was starting to rain, but not yet in earnest. As they stepped out the door, Jones looked worriedly up at the darkening sky. The temperature had dropped considerably and the wind was brisk.

"It's not going to be pretty," Jones predicted.

They got back into the car just before the hail started. Margie flinched every time a big piece of ice hit her windshield or side window. "Do you think... I should drive?" she asked Jones. "See if we can get out from under it?"

"No. We're kind of sheltered by the house and tree here. Try to drive through this and you might get your windows broken."

They sat in silence for a few minutes, watching the hail pour down around them and bounce off of the car and the roof covering the porch behind Kennedy's house. Some of the hailstones were as big as a nickel.

"Do you mind if I call Christina?" Margie asked, pulling out her phone.

"Of course, go ahead."

Margie tapped on Christina's name and listened to it ring.

"Mom?"

"Hi, honey. Just wanted to make sure you're okay."

"Wow, are you in this? What a storm! Stella is scared, but other than that, we're okay."

"No broken windows? I guess this will be the test as to whether the basement leaks."

"Yeah, everything is fine. I haven't checked the basement, but everything is fine up here."

"Good. We're close by; I just don't want to drive until the hail stops."

"Okay," Christina agreed cheerfully. "I wouldn't want to be driving in this either."

Christina had her learner's license, but tended to be a nervous driver. Margie made a mental note to herself that they needed to spend some more time practicing to boost Christina's confidence. And she needed to get the girl into a driver's ed class.

"She's good?" Jones asked.

Margie nodded. "She's good. I didn't know you got storms like this in Calgary."

"A few years ago, we had a series of big storms, and that combined with the meltwater from the mountains and poor reservoir management cause flooding all over the city. Pretty much the entire downtown was under water. We couldn't get into the office. A bunch of the riverbanks in Inglewood crumbled into the Bow. Do you know the train bridge you can see from the pathway between here and the zoo? From Pearce Estate or crossing the Deerfoot pedestrian bridge from Max Bell?"

Margie nodded slowly. She had seen the latticed bridge during her Google maps exploration of the pathways to downtown.

"The deck of that bridge was actually under water. Over by the zoo, it was up over the handrails along the pathways. They had to move some of the animals because the river was up over the banks and into the zoo."

"I think I remember seeing pictures of all of that." Margie could vaguely remember the story in the news. It had been some time before she considered moving to Calgary, so it hadn't really registered. She had been concerned about her family members in the area, of course, but everyone had been okay, and she hadn't thought more about it. There had been deaths, but no one she knew.

Eventually, the hail stopped and there was just rain.

"Think it's safe to go?" Margie asked.

Jones nodded. "Yeah. Let's give it a try. But be ready to pull over under a tree if it starts up again."

Margie pulled out and made a tight three-point turn to get out of the alley. Jones was tapping on her phone.

"Are you getting directions to get out of here and back to the office?" Margie asked.

Jones shook her head. "I know the way. I'm just looking at Twitter…"

Margie rolled her eyes. "Can you tell me which way to go, then…?"

Jones didn't look up from her phone. "Hmm… might not be the best idea to go back downtown. A lot of streets have flooded. They'll drain once the rain slows down, but if you drive into a flooded street, it will stall your car and wreck your engine."

"Is there another way we can go?"

"I wouldn't count on it. You're good up here on the hill, but if you go down any of the lower-lying streets you might end up in trouble…"

Margie was just creeping along the street, uncertain which way to go. Luckily, there were not many other cars on the move, and no one honked at her to speed up.

"Why don't we go back to your house until the water goes down?" Jones suggested. "If you don't mind me hanging out for a while. Once the rain stops and the streets drain, I can just catch the Max downtown."

The Max Purple bus route ran from Seventeenth Avenue to the downtown core pretty frequently, but Margie wouldn't want Jones to get stranded if the downtown were flooded and the bus had nowhere to go.

"We can go to my place," she agreed. "I'll drive you back once we know it's safe."

"We'll talk about it. Sorry about imposing myself on you."

"No, that's fine."

Jones raised her eyes to the road, then looked at Margie. "To your house, then."

"I don't know the way. I got turned around."

The other woman laughed. "You'll get it eventually," she promised. "Some neighborhoods are easier than others. It's nice when they are on the grid system, but all the new developments are full of cul-de-sacs. This area really isn't bad once you get used to it. Just confusing because of the backward houses."

She gave Margie directions until she hit Twenty-Sixth Street and recognized where she was. "There's the park," she pointed Valleyview out to Jones. "That's where Hungry Bear's body was."

Jones craned her neck, but couldn't see the pond because of the trees and hill that were in the way. She nodded. "Don't think I want to explore it in the rain."

"Yeah, I'd rather stay dry."

In a couple of minutes, they were back home. Margie went in first, tapping on the door and calling out to Christina. "I've got company," she announced. "Hide the drugs!"

She could hear Christina's laugh at the back of the house. Stella padded out to greet them, but was not her usual exuberant self. She whined at Margie and pushed her muzzle into Margie's hand for comfort. Margie scratched her ears and jowls and crooned to her that the storm would end soon and Stella would be all right.

Christina joined them. "Isn't it so nice? It finally cooled down!"

The breeze was blowing through all of the house's open windows, cooling the house down for the first time in a week.

"It is. You remember Detective Jones?"

"Kaitlyn," Jones corrected. She had stayed with them overnight when Margie and Christina had been in danger from a killer who had targeted them. So Christina and Jones were on a first name basis.

"It's good to see you again!" Christina greeted. "Are you going to stay for dinner?" She flashed a look at Margie that said, "And what are we going to make for her?"

"Oh, it will probably just be a few minutes. There's flooding, so I wanted to wait until the rain stops and the water goes down." Jones looked out the window. "Hopefully, the weather will break before long."

Margie looked at the ominous, swirling clouds. It didn't look to her like it would break in a few minutes.

"Yeah, we'd better get something on," she told Christina. "At least it's cooled down enough that we can use the oven!"

"Yeah." Christina brightened. "We can put a pizza in!"

"Good idea. And I'll make a salad to go along with it. Just so we can feel virtuous." She laughed.

"I really don't want to be any trouble," Jones protested.

"You're not. We have to eat anyway. We've been terrible this week, just eating junk food and sandwiches, because we don't want to heat up the house by actually cooking anything. A pizza will be a nice change."

"If you're doing it anyway. Just don't go out of your way for me. I'll just stay out of your way."

"It's nice to have company," Christina assured her. "It's just me and Mom all the time."

"You can actually have friends over now," Margie realized. "Now that the restrictions have been dropped."

Moving to Calgary during the COVID lock-down had not exactly been easy on Christina. She was naturally social, but she could only see her friends at school; they weren't allowed to go to each other's houses. Margie knew that a lot of the teens went shopping or did things outside together, but she'd tried to keep Christina close to home to minimize the chances of infection.

"Yeah!" Christina looked surprised. "I guess I can."

It occurred to Margie that Hungry Bear and his friends had been breaking the gathering rules, since it had only been June 30 when they had gotten together for their gaming night, and the restrictions hadn't been dropped until July 1. And from their conversation, she thought they had been meeting together regularly even before that.

It was no wonder infection rates had gotten so high.

CHAPTER FOURTEEN

They had eaten the pizza while looking at the pictures on Twitter and Facebook showing cars up to their windows in water and people canoeing or kayaking down their streets. Margie's throat got tight looking at all that water.

But by eight o'clock the storm had petered out. Jones called the police dispatcher to find a clear route back to her house, since it was too late to bother going back to the office. She directed Margie, and then helped her to set up the Maps app on her phone to take her back home by a safe route.

"If you run into any flooded streets, then stop. Don't drive into the water. Call me, and we'll figure out a different route."

"Okay." The way there had been clear, so Margie thought she would be fine, but had to admit to herself that she was still a little nervous. She didn't like water, and the thought of driving into a flooded street and being trapped in her car with the floodwaters rising around her sent her heart into wild contortions.

"It will be fine," Jones assured her.

"Yeah. I'm sure it will."

The other woman gave her a reassuring smile and pat on the shoulder. "Thanks for supper. That was a lot of fun."

"We'll have you over again. I really enjoyed it."

"We don't have to wait until the next storm. And I'll supply the dinner next time. It will be my treat."

Margie watched her walk into her apartment building and waited a few extra minutes just to make sure that she hadn't run into any trouble. Then she steeled herself and headed back for home.

⁂

SATURDAY MORNING, Margie got up early for her run. It was only supposed to get up to 27 degrees, but she wasn't counting on it. She didn't want to wait too late and be running in the heat of the day. It had stayed cool all night, so the house was comfortable and the temperature outside was cool, just right for a nice run.

She hesitated about going back to Valleyview, even though it was her usual route. Would everyone there look at her differently, now that they knew she was a police detective? Oscar certainly hadn't been impressed when he had discovered what it was that she did. And there were also Margie's worries that she would find something else unexpected in the park or have flashbacks. Of course she wouldn't actually find another body, but that was now her strongest association with the park. And what if it were flooded from the storm the previous night? It was part of the stormwater management system. What if the entire park was now covered with water? Then she wouldn't go in, of course. She'd just stick to the Twenty-Sixth Street pathway, which was at the top of the hill and would not be flooded.

It was best to confront any thoughts of anxiety or flashbacks head on. Face her fear right away, and it would not be able to settle in and take over her life. If she avoided the area, the fear would just grow and become more entrenched. She would have a big hole in the middle of the neighborhood, an area that she could not go to. It was a great place for walks, runs, and throwing the Frisbee for Stella, and she would not let it become a place she had to avoid.

So she forced herself to cross Twenty-Sixth Street and enter the park. It was a little strange to see it empty again after having been filled with police cars and vans and all of the investigating team and spectators two days before. It was as if nothing had changed, yet everything had changed in her own mind.

Margie made one loop around the pond, watching the ducks and red-winged blackbirds and looking for the muskrat. The muskrat did not put in an appearance. Across the field, a group of gulls was congregating, mostly black-headed Franklin's gulls, which she hadn't seen much of in Calgary. She hadn't noticed any in Valleyview park before.

There was an older couple walking around the pathway together at a leisurely pace. The man had a long grabber tool that he used to reach over the short chain-link fence to the splash park—which was still padlocked early in the morning—to snag pieces of litter and put them into a shopping bag that hung on his other wrist. They strolled along, picking up trash along the way. It was no wonder the park was normally so pristine. Margie smiled and nodded as she went by them. She didn't stop and give them a chance to realize that she had been there on Canada Day and had been the one to find the body.

She looked around for the other couple, the two who had been out walking their dogs. The man who had helped her to pull Hungry Bear's body out of the water. But she didn't see them. Maybe they didn't walk there every day or were on a different schedule on the weekend. She was sure she would see them again at some point.

Margie stopped for a quick swig of water, then pushed herself to run faster around the long pathway, then back across Twenty-Sixth Street to head home.

%

SHE WASN'T SCHEDULED to work on Saturday, but she headed downtown anyway. She wanted to transcribe all of her notes from the interview with Hungry Bear's gaming friends while it was still fresh in her mind. She was also determined to go through all the reports and photos one more time. And maybe she could start making individual calls to the friends to see if she could shake anything loose.

As much as she tried to make Hungry Bear's death fit the scenario for a mugging or gang activity, it just didn't fit the pattern. He'd had a wallet on him but no cash, it was true, but fewer and fewer people carried cash anymore, especially since the pandemic had hit and people had been encouraged to tap rather than handling cash or using the touch pad, reducing the number of times a point-of-sale machine had to be wiped down. If he'd been mugged, the thief would have just snatched Hungry

Bear's wallet and phone, he wouldn't have asked for his cash and let him keep the rest.

And gang violence? A single blow to the head didn't look like gang violence. There was nothing on Hungry Bear's record to indicate that he'd had anything to do with gangs in the past. Dire Facebook warnings notwithstanding, attacking or killing strangers was not a typical way to initiate new gang members. Not in Calgary, anyway. Even with blood-in gangs, initiates tended to target people that they knew or who were members of a rival gang, not complete strangers.

Margie called Jones, hoping she wasn't too busy, and asked her for her impressions of the interview with the friends. They had briefly discussed it in the car and while Christina was out of the room making pizza, but not in any depth. Just agreeing that the friends had intentionally gotten together to make sure they all told the same story. Whether that was because they were trying to hide something or protect one of their number, or just because they were nervous about being questioned by the police and wanted the moral support, was not yet clear. Margie would dig down and try to get to the truth when she followed up with them individually.

"Made it home safe?" Jones asked cheerfully.

"Yes. And downtown without any problem this morning. There are a lot of disabled vehicles still on the road, though. You can tell that something happened."

"I don't envy Traffic Division."

"No... I guess they'll be out there ticketing and towing. I hope they give people time to retrieve their own vehicles, though..."

"I imagine they will. They won't be looking for more work. Easier if people pick up their own vehicles."

"So... just wondering if you have a few minutes to talk through the interview last night. I'll get your notes on Monday, but if you had any feelings, any red flags..."

"Well, just the fact that they circled the wagons and wouldn't talk to us separately says something to me."

"You don't think it was just because Kennedy was anxious and wanted someone else there?"

"No... she didn't strike me as the nervous kind. If it had been Susan, okay, I could see that. If it had been a group of all girls, I could see how they would want to band together. But Kennedy seemed pretty strong and put together, and the boys were confident enough. Susan is the weak link."

"You think I should talk to her first?"

"Definitely. If anyone is going to talk, it will be her."

Margie nodded thoughtfully. She clicked through photographs of the scene while she talked to Jones, looking for anything out of place or unusual. Sometimes there just weren't enough clues at a crime scene to come to any conclusion. It wasn't like on TV when there was always enough evidence to catch and convict a killer.

"Do you think one of them knows what happened? Or all of them?"

"It just seems 'off' to me. They all stayed overnight except for Hungry Bear? They just sent him off on his own late at night? Why didn't he stay?"

"His house was close by."

"They are all close by. Relatively, anyway. I looked at their home addresses. They're not all in Dover, but most of them could walk home if they wanted to. So why didn't they? And why *did* Hungry Bear?"

Margie thought about the dynamics of the group. What had they learned?

"Maybe there was an argument or a fight? The others were drinking, tempers might have been high. Or they might have been pressuring him to drink and he knew he needed to get out of the environment."

"Could be," Jones agreed. "If he was trying to stay clean, and they weren't supportive of his sobriety, that would be good reason to leave, even if it was late. Maybe especially if it was late, since inhibitions are reduced as you get more tired and he would have known that he was more likely to take a drink the later he stayed."

"They said they didn't have much to drink."

"So they said."

"Yeah. That's not necessarily true," Margie admitted. "It was a party. Get together and play games, get a head start on celebrating the holiday."

"Uh-huh. I suspect they had more to drink than they told us. They wanted to show themselves in a good light. Portray themselves as some friends who got together to play a game and have a glass of wine or bottle of beer."

Margie pictured the wet bar. It had appeared to be well-stocked but, of course, she had not gotten behind the counter to have a good look at it. Any empties had been cleared away, there were no bags of bottles to be returned for deposit. Margie frowned, clicking through the photos on the screen.

"If they hadn't already cleaned up, we could check fingerprints on the glasses or bottles, see how much they had each been drinking in reality."

"I suppose. But what would the point be in that? Hungry Bear wasn't drinking, or it would have shown up in his bloodwork. No alcohol, no drugs."

"Just to show if they were lying, I guess," Margie admitted.

"You're not going to get a warrant from a judge based on 'we think they're lying about something, but don't know what.'"

"Uh, no."

"I don't think there is anything we can go after them for until we get confirmation from one of them that someone is lying. Preferably someone with a motive to kill Hungry Bear."

"*Did* someone have motive to kill him? We haven't really talked much about motive." Motive is always the crux on TV. In real life... not so much.

"Maybe he was too friendly with one of the girls?" Jones suggested.

"Or one of the guys?" Margie countered wryly, grinning. "Jealousy? Or protecting someone's virtue? It's always possible. There's nothing that gets people upset as fast as a love triangle."

Margie looked down at her notes for a moment, considering each of the members of the group of friends. She hadn't noticed any romantic attachments between any of them. There had been no long looks or flirting. When they talked about staying over for the night, there hadn't been giggles or significant looks. No discussion of bedroom assignments or other sleeping arrangements. They had just acted like friends.

But that wasn't conclusive. Some people wore their emotions and attractions on their sleeves and others did not.

Christina, for example. Margie had been watching for signs that she was attracted to anyone at school or pairing off when school let out. But so far... nothing. She told herself that Christina was just still trying to fit in and make friends. She had put in a full year at a new school, but with all the back and forth between online schooling and in-person schooling, and time off for quarantines half a dozen times during the year, it seemed as if she had never been at school for more than a couple of weeks at a time. And when they weren't allowed to have other people in their house, it was pretty hard to tell who Christina was friends with, other than through overheard conversations.

Margie reached the itemized lists of what was in the garbages, skimming over them quickly for anything that shouldn't be there. It was a long shot, but sometimes people did throw things into public garbages just out of habit. Or someone else picked up something that had been dropped to put it into the garbage himself.

CHAPTER FIFTEEN

O h!"

Jones had been speaking, but stopped at what she heard in Margie's tone. "Oh, what?"

"It isn't something that is there. It's something that is missing."

There was silence on the other end of the phone. Margie pulled up each of the garbage inventories, looking through them carefully.

"I missed it," Margie murmured. "We all missed it."

"Missed what? Do I dare ask? Have you broken the case?"

"I don't know. It's probably nothing. But we also might be missing evidence from our crime scene."

❧

MARGIE LOOKED through the pictures taken of the people hanging around after the body was discovered, rubberneckers trying to catch a glimpse of the body or something equally horrifying.

She recognized a lot of the faces she had seen there on her morning runs or evening dog walks. It was a well-trafficked park, a place to go and watch the children play in the water or the playground, watch a volleyball tournament, run, bike, walk your dog, sit on a bench and visit while watching the ducks… Despite how small it was, many people made use of it.

Frustratingly, she couldn't find the couple she was looking for. It would have been so much easier if someone had taken their statements. She would have names, addresses, and phone numbers to go with the faces. But apparently, they had not stayed around to find out what was going on. Or maybe they hadn't even been there that day and she was on a wild goose chase.

&.

MARGIE AND CHRISTINA took Stella to the park to play ball and Frisbee Saturday afternoon, and Margie returned on her own on Sunday morning to watch the walkers and look for familiar faces. The old man with the cane went walking every morning on his slow circuit around the pond. Lots of dog walkers, including the one who had helped Margie to pull Hungry Bear out of the water. She got out of her car, admired the dogs, and thanked him for his help.

"I'm just glad *you* were here," he said. "I wouldn't have known what to do by myself."

"You would have called 9-1-1 and they would have sent help, just like they did. I didn't really need to be there for that."

"Maybe… but it was nice to have a cop there who knew what she was talking about."

The man's girlfriend gave Margie a friendly nod but didn't have much to say. Margie let them continue on their walk and sat on one of the benches by the pond, overtly looking at the ducks, but also watching the people in her peripheral vision. They didn't have any reason to avoid her, but people didn't like knowing they were under surveillance.

And then she saw them. The tall, slim man with a garbage grabber and his wife or friend, taking a leisurely stroll around the park, eyes open for any litter to be picked up. Making the world around them a better place. Margie waited until they were closer to her before standing up. She let them approach her, trying to look non-threatening. Just another person enjoying the beauty of the park.

"Hi. Nice day."

"Cooler," the woman agreed. "Nice to have a break in the weather. Between the heat and the storm…"

Margie nodded. It was an overcast day, and would probably rain later on, but there at least weren't any thunderstorm warnings. Yet.

"I'm actually with the police department. I wonder if you could help me out."

They exchanged looks.

"We're not doing anything wrong," the man protested.

"No, no, this is not about anything you have done wrong. It's about the body that was found here on Canada Day. You heard about that?"

They nodded in unison. "Horrible thing," the woman observed. "I guess he was drunk and fell in?"

"It doesn't look like it, no. But I can't discuss the specifics with you. But you may be aware of evidence that could help us."

"We don't know anything."

"I've seen you here before, picking up garbage."

The man nodded. "I want it to look nice here. People litter, or stuff blows in from somewhere else... I don't want kids picking it up, or dogs eating it, or just having it cluttering up the park. So I pick up a little each day." He looked around, admiring his handiwork. "And it helps to keep things looking nice."

"That's so admirable. I'm really impressed that you do that."

That seemed to relax him a little. Margie smiled, trying again to reassure them that she wasn't there to accuse them of anything.

"You may not know, but we took all the garbages from this area and looked through everything for any evidence."

"Evidence of what?" the wife asked, her brows wrinkling.

"Anything. Anything at all related to the victim's death."

The man spoke up. "And what does that have to do with us?"

"I realized yesterday when I was looking through all of the garbage that had been inventoried... there were no bottles."

"Well, no. You don't throw out bottles. They're worth money if you take them back to the depot."

"Yes. My daughter is doing a fundraiser by collecting cans and bottles for refunds."

"It adds up. Might just be ten cents here and twenty-five there, but it adds up once you've collected a few bags."

"I wondered... whether you collected any bottles from the park."

They looked at her, not answering. Still thinking they were going to be accused of something.

"I clean up the park. There's nothing wrong about that."

"No, there's not. You're doing the community a service. There's nothing wrong with you picking up cans or bottles if you find them here."

He nodded slowly.

"I imagine that sometimes people throw them in the garbage can. And if you open it up to put the litter you have picked up in there and you see bottles or cans, you would probably retrieve them. They shouldn't just be going to the dump."

"No, that's right."

"So if there were any bottles on the ground or in the garbage, you would pick them up."

"Sure."

"Again, there's nothing wrong with that and I'm glad that you're taking care of the park and keeping it so nice for everyone. But I would like to see any beverage containers that you have picked up here since Wednesday."

He stared at her. "Why?"

"Because it might be evidence. There's no guarantee that it is, or that it will have any significance at all… but if I can get those bottles, they could be very important."

"I don't see how," he grumbled.

His wife gave him a little tap on the arm. "Myron. There's no reason to act that way. This officer has been very polite. She's trying to solve a homicide!"

"If you're going to take my bottles, I'm going to expect to be paid for them."

Margie blew out her breath in relief. "I would be happy to."

She wasn't in the habit of paying for tips, but giving Myron a twenty for what might be important evidence? She could do that.

"Well, then…" Myron brightened. "What are we waiting for?"

CHAPTER SIXTEEN

*M*argie had each of the friends back in over the weekend to review their testimonies and get their fingerprints, which she told them would be used to eliminate any of their fingerprints found on Hungry Bear's possessions. Margie did her best to find out more details of what had happened that night while the techs analyzed the evidence, hoping that she could make some progress on the case independent of the physical evidence. But the friends all stuck to the same story, with little variation. A sure sign that they had discussed the details among themselves to make sure that they all told the same story.

It wasn't until Monday that she was ready to move forward.

She welcomed Alex into the interview room and offered him a seat. They were both wearing masks, so it wasn't easy to see his expression, but in the past year she had grown more skilled at watching the eyes and the other muscles of the face to discern a person's expression behind the mask. People seemed to be freer to let their faces shift while they were wearing a mask, assuming she couldn't see a smile or scowl behind it.

Alex looked around the room, uncomfortable. He had trouble choosing a chair to sit in for their interview. He dithered between two or three chairs before finally choosing one. It wasn't like any of them were farther away from the bottle that sat in the middle of the table.

"Thanks for coming in," Margie repeated, smiling at him and being sure to make her voice pleasant and soothing. "I know that you must have a lot to do, probably back at work today, so I appreciate you taking the time."

"I don't understand why you needed me to come in today." He looked around, as if waiting for her to bring the other friends in. Had he already talked to them? Did he realize that he was the only one who had been called in?

"Well, I just had a few more things that I was hoping to cover with you, like I said on the phone."

"We've already told you everything that happened that night. None of us know what happened to Bruce." He gave an exaggerated shrug. "We weren't there."

"Hmm." Margie looked at the bottle in the middle of the table. "I think that one of you was."

He kept his eyes away from the bottle, as if it were invisible and he didn't know what she was talking about. Margie continued to gaze at it, until he felt compelled to follow her eyes and acknowledge the presence of the bottle.

"What's this?"

"It's your bottle."

"My bottle?" He rolled his eyes. "I don't even drink that brand."

"Interesting… then why would your fingerprints be on the bottle?"

"I don't know where you got it. I don't know that it *does* have my prints on it."

"This is the bottle you were drinking at the party Wednesday night. The bottle that you took with you went you left the party with Bruce."

"We were just gaming together. That's all. You make it sound… like it was more than it was. Just some friends getting together for some whole-some games. We weren't out on the streets making trouble. We don't run with a gang or deface property or anything like that. And we don't go around…" He twirled a finger, at a loss for words.

"Killing each other?" Margie suggested.

"No. We don't. Look, I've never been in any kind of trouble, and I've answered all your questions. Can we just wrap this up? If you're going to make ridiculous suggestions, then we're done here."

"Did you and Bruce leave together? Why? Were you walking him home?"

"No. I didn't go anywhere with him. I told you that."

"How did this bottle with your fingerprints on it come to be in the park, then?"

"If it has my prints on it, I probably just moved it to the side that night. You know, pick it up and move it over so I could grab a beer."

"The positioning of the fingerprints suggests that you drank from the bottle, among other things."

He shifted in his chair. "But you can't tell whether I did drink from it or not, can you?" He looked triumphant. "I can hold a bottle like I'm going to take a drink of it, and then not. Right? You can't tell the difference."

"Maybe by DNA swabs of the mouth of the bottle," Margie suggested. She shrugged. "It doesn't really matter whether you drank from the bottle or not, though, I just wanted to establish that you had it with you went you went to the park. With Bruce."

He shook his head. "No. I don't know what you're talking about. I don't know how it got to the park. Maybe one of the others went over there looking for him after I fell asleep."

Margie stared at him steadily. "That doesn't sound very likely, does it?"

"But you can't prove that's not what happened."

Margie leaned back in her chair and raised her eyes toward the ceiling. "I would just like to know what really happened. I can't figure out why you would want to hurt Bruce. Did the two of you have a fight? Did you think he had done something to you? Maybe both of you were interested in the same girl and you thought he was weaseling his way in on you?" She didn't see any response to this scenario in his eyes. "Or maybe you were interested in Bruce, or he was interested in you?"

"No!" She could see his grimace of disgust behind the mask. That wasn't it then, but that still left many other avenues open.

"No? What was it then? What was it that made you so angry?"

"I wasn't there."

"The bottle was there. Your fingerprints are on the bottle. And not just in the position they would be for you to take a drink. There were also prints in the right position for you to swing the bottle and bring it down on someone's head. To bludgeon them."

Alex's eyes were icy. He was doing everything he could to look casual and not at all concerned about the accusation. He had friends, after all. Friends who would back his alibi and say that he had never gone out of the house. He had been there all night, sleeping over like everyone else.

"You hit him from behind," Margie said. "Why? What reason did you have to sneak up behind him and—"

"Sneak?" Alex objected "What are you talking about, sneaking?"

"Why else would he have his back to you? You don't turn your back on your enemy. In the middle of the night, in the dark. Why would he do that?"

"We weren't enemies, we were friends. We all told you that."

Margie waited, letting the silence draw out, compelling him to fill it. The silences in an interview were just as important as the words.

Alex looked at the bottle again. His expression under the mask shifted, but it was too subtle for Margie to tell exactly what had changed. He sniffled.

"He was my friend," Alex insisted. "We were friends long before anyone else in the group. I knew him from the time we were in junior high. When it was just him and me, learning how to play D&D, the geeks that no one else was interested in. He was *my friend.*"

"Tell me what happened that night."

"I've already told you."

"No, you haven't. And if he was your friend, then don't you think it's time to clear this up? His family needs to know what happened. Why this happened. Don't you owe it to Bruce?"

"You think his parents would want to know—" Alex cut himself off, shaking his head.

Would they want to know that he had been killed by his best friend? Was that really what would make them feel better about their son's death and help them to find peace? Margie doubted it. But she was a seeker of the truth. She had to follow this line of questioning to its conclusion. Just like when breaking the news of a death to a family member, she had to hear the true story, unvarnished. No hiding behind euphemisms, just the cold, stark truth of it.

"Yes. The truth needs to come out. It will be better for you. It will be important to his parents. All of us need to be able to close this chapter. We can't begin to heal until the truth is known."

Alex's eyes flared. He shook his head angrily. "You sound *just like* him!" he blurted. "Talking about truth and healing. I was so sick and tired of it!"

Margie's own anger flared, but she kept it hidden. He wasn't attacking her. He was reliving what had happened between him and Bruce. And if something she did or said prompted him to do that and to tell her about it, then that was what needed to happen.

"What was Bruce talking about?"

"It never stopped. I grew up with the guy. I knew the kind of home he came from and the way he grew up. He didn't live on the reservation and he went to the same schools as I did. Not some residential school where he was abused."

Margie nodded encouragingly, a picture starting to form in her mind.

"All night while we were gaming, he was on about this 'hashtag Cancel Canada Day' and 'No Pride in Genocide' stuff. He just wouldn't shut up about it. We would change the subject, and he would be right back to it two minutes later. No one wanted to hear it. We were there to have a good time together, not to rally against the government. Everyone was sick and tired of it."

"He didn't go to a residential school, so it had nothing to do with him?" Margie asked.

"He had to go all the way back to his grandma to find someone who had gone to residential school. So how does that affect him? She wasn't one of those little kids who died. He didn't go to residential school, and neither did his parents. Why did we have to keep hearing about all of the abuses? That stuff is all in the past and there's nothing we can do about it." He met Margie's eyes. "Can you explain that to me? What exactly are we supposed to do? We aren't the ones who abused anyone. We had nothing to do with it."

Margie could have given him a list. Pressure his elected officials to follow through on their promises and the recommendations of the Truth and Reconciliation Commission. Support Indigenous outreach and counseling programs. Help with memorials for those whose deaths had been ignored or hidden. Or just be a supportive ear to a friend who was dealing with inter-generational trauma.

"And you were fed up with it," she suggested instead. "You didn't want to hear any more."

"Exactly. Just shut up already. It was getting late, so... I said I'd walk home with him. I'm a good friend. I didn't just tell him to get lost. I could tell it was getting on everyone else's nerves too, so I said I'd walk home with him. He probably just needed a good sleep, and then he'd feel better about it. He wouldn't be so wound up. It was just because he'd been with his parents, you know. He wasn't usually like that with us."

"He just acted like a normal white guy with you."

"Normally," Alex agreed. "We're not racist. We don't look at him and say that he's brown so he can't play with us. I don't see color. He's just my friend."

"So…" Margie gazed at the empty bottle on the table. "What happened then?"

"We went through the park. He was getting on my case. Saying why didn't I stand up for him, if we were friends? Why did I just sit there like I didn't care? I told him he was the one being rude, tiring everyone out with his complaining about something that didn't even affect him." Alex rolled his eyes up toward the ceiling. "I told him if he wanted to play with us on Canada Day, to leave his agenda at home."

Margie nodded.

Alex shook his head, eyes glistening. "I just don't know why he had to be so up in our faces about it. He said it wasn't an agenda, it was who he was, and that I could go… *you know*. And he turned around and started to walk away from me."

"And…" Margie said gently, trying to encourage him to complete his statement. "It was just too much for you…?"

He put his hand to his face, rubbing the bridge of his nose with the back of his thumb. "I'd had a bit to drink. It all happened so fast. I was mad, he was mad, we were yelling back and forth. He told me to… just walked away from me, like nothing that happened in the last ten years meant anything to him, that we weren't anything."

"And you hit him."

Alex shook his head, staring at the bottle. But it wasn't a denial. Maybe disbelief. "I'd never hurt Bruce. He was my best friend. He used to be."

Margie nodded.

"I hit him," Alex admitted, staring down and talking to the table. "I never meant to do anything to hurt him. And when he went down, I laughed, and I expected him to get back up. He'd be boiling mad, but I wouldn't care. As long as he got up again."

But he hadn't gotten up again, and Alex had been left with the body of his best friend on his hands, the murder weapon in his hand. Drunk, he had made the wrong decisions.

"Why did you drag him into the water?"

"I just thought… that would be more natural. Someone could see that he'd just fallen in. An accident. There was a body discovered there a couple of years ago, you know, and the police said right away, not foul play. And I figured they would again. Just a… tragic accident."

Margie breathed out slowly. And there it was. The explanation of what had happened to Bruce Hungry Bear and how he had ended up dead, floating in the pond Canada Day morning where Margie had found him.

Alex raised his eyes to Margie. "What's going to happen to me now?"

"You are under arrest. Charges will be brought. You'll make a court appearance. You'll want to get a lawyer, talk with him about what you will plead to."

"I'm not going to have to go to prison, am I?" He stared at her beseechingly, clearly not understanding the full impact of everything he had said. "It was just an accident."

"Tripping and falling is an accident," Margie told him softly. "Whacking someone over the head with a bottle when his back is turned… that's something else."

CHAPTER SEVENTEEN

*M*ac had been pleased that Margie had put the case to bed so quickly. He was happy to write it off as a drunken argument between friends, something that he could explain away to any higher-ups in the city's organizational structure, to any Stampede officials, sponsors, or celebrities. It could all be explained away and there was no need for anyone to be concerned that Calgary was a dangerous city.

Margie reported back to Hungry Bear's heartbroken family that it had been a fight between friends, not a premeditated murder or a hate crime. She pictured the face of the white-haired grandmother, someone who had already been through so much in her life, seen so many of her friends and loved ones die. And now Bruce.

She didn't tell them what the fight had been about.

Wednesday morning, she reached the crosswalk across Twenty-Sixth Street to Valleyview park, and didn't hesitate to cross for a loop or two around the pond. From the top of the hill, she could see West Dover school. Low fog clung to the grassy fields. She could see the orange ribbons still tied along the fence.

Margie watched the ducks and the blackbirds as she circled the pond. She no longer felt anxious and afraid that the park would always represent something ominous. It was still the same place it had been before she had discovered Bruce Hungry Bear's body immersed in the pond.

As she ran by the fence of the splash park, which Myron had diligently cleared of all litter, she saw that there was something tied to that fence too, between the signs warning pathway users to stay two meters apart from each other. Orange paper hearts with pictures glued to them tied together in a chain. Printed on each heart: *An act of reconciliation.*

She read the explanatory card at one end of the chain and thought about the two school pals whose friendship had ended on almost that very spot. The school children who had made the paper hearts had no way of knowing that. Hopefully, their offering would help to heal other wounds, so that other friends could be reconciled.

VALLEYVIEW PARK

While Valleyview Park is the tinniest of the parks so far, it packs a punch, with a pond, a playground, a children's splash park, beach volleyball courts, baseball diamond, and soccer field, along with a few park benches and picnic tables. There was also a fire pit there for a few months earlier in the year, though it has disappeared again.

Just across 26th Street from the multi-use pathway, leash-free area, and a lookout platform, Valleyview Park is well-used by neighbourhood walkers, runners, and dog-walkers. The red-winged blackbirds, ducks, and a muskrat enjoy the use of the pond, and you can occasionally spot coyotes, foxes, and rabbits in the fields.

The multi-use pathway runs under 17th Avenue to the Max Bell Arena pathways, then over Deerfoot Trail to the east side of the river, past the zoo, and downtown. There is also a connection over Deerfoot Trail beside the Max Purple bus route, then under 17th Avenue/Blackfoot Trail to the Bow River Pathway (west side of the river), through Pearce Estate Park and Inglewood downtown.

SKIMMING OVER THE LAKE

A PARKS PAT MYSTERY #5

For those who feel differently

CHAPTER ONE

*M*argie was settled in front of the TV with her teenage daughter Christina as the Calgary Stampede parade began. The Stampede had been canceled the previous year due to COVID so everyone was eager to see its return. The much-shorter parade could only be watched on TV and not attended in person. At least it was still going ahead.

It had been a long time since Margie had seen the rodeo/fair, dubbed "The Greatest Outdoor Show on Earth," while visiting cousins in Calgary over the summer.

"Do you think we can go to the Stampede?" Christina asked. "There will be lots of stuff to see. Including the Bow River Camp."

"The Bow River Camp?"

"What used to be the Indian Village. Tipis and dances and other Indigenous culture. You want me to go to stuff like that, don't you? To be educated about my background?"

Margie pushed her own long, black hair back over her ears, smiling at Christina. "You really don't need to pull the 'culture' card to go to the Stampede."

Christina had a sip of her coffee. "I didn't think it could hurt."

Margie chuckled at this. "Well, we'll see. I don't really have anything against it, other than crowds and noise and possible contaminants. And people drinking and getting out of control. The heat and the dust, or the rainstorms…"

Christina shook her head. "Maybe we could take Moushoom down if they have a seniors' day. He remembers what it used to be like; he can tell us how it compares."

"I don't know that I want to be taking an old man down there." Margie thought about the hazards that she had already mentioned. Her grandfather's immune system wasn't as strong as a young man's. He could be a target for drunks—someone small and frail who couldn't fight back. He would look strange to them in his brightly colored clothes and buckskins. And the heat was more likely to affect a senior. "Maybe we could take him to one of the pancake breakfasts around here. Or find something that is closer to home. Taking him in his wheelchair on the bus and train…"

"Why can't we drive?"

"Because there isn't much parking, and it is expensive. The Stampede gate tickets are expensive enough without having to spend a hundred dollars on parking. Or on hiring a taxi or Uber."

"Can't you park for free with your police tag?"

She had a point. But Margie would only use her police tag if she were actually on the job. She wouldn't use it just to get more affordable or convenient parking. She was scrupulously careful in not taking advantage of anything because she was a police detective. Or playing the race or gender cards, for that matter. She was determined to only get what she had worked hard to earn.

"No, I can't," she told Christina flatly. "That's not the way it works."

Christina huffed and rolled her eyes. Stella, lying at her feet, opened one eye to examine her to see why she was making such a noise, then decided it was not anything to be concerned about and closed it again. She made a little groan and rolled over so she was right on top of Christina's foot. Christina wiggled her toes. "Hey! It's too hot to have a fur rug on my feet. Get off."

Stella didn't, and Christina didn't immediately pull her feet out, but instead reached down to scratch Stella's ears and then her belly. Stella's tail thumped loudly on the floor.

"There are the Calgary Police!" Christina exclaimed, as a series of police cars and motorcycles led the parade. "Do they have a float too, or is that it?"

"I think the mounted unit is in it later."

"It's a good thing that you're a homicide detective, so you don't have to be downtown blocking off streets and keeping drunks away from the parade."

"You're right." Margie was very happy to be right where she was, watching the parade from the comfort of her own home. The convenience more than made up for any pang of regret that they could not see it in person.

They were watching the Native Princess who had been appointed parade marshal when Margie's phone rang. She looked down at it, hoping that it would not be work. She'd even take a telemarketer. Which was easy, because she didn't have to answer the phone for a telemarketer. She'd even take a call from Christina's school saying that she hadn't handed in some final assignment or they had lost her final exams.

It was work. The name and picture on the display were Detective Siever's.

She didn't know Siever well. He was pretty quiet. Good with technical stuff. If she had a computer problem or was trying to figure out how to process a large amount of data, he was the one she would go to. They hadn't worked very closely on previous files. He seemed to prefer staying in the office over getting out and doing field work. More comfortable with a computer than real people.

Maybe it was just a call to let her know that she had a new login or hadn't responded to an email he had sent previously.

Margie looked at Christina, who was watching her closely.

"That had better not be work," Christina warned.

Margie raised her brows in an expression of surrender and swiped the screen to answer the call.

"Detective Patenaude."

"It's Siever. I'm heading in your direction. Looks like we might have another case for 'Parks Pat.'"

Margie thought immediately of Valleyview Park, her last case, just barely put to bed. It couldn't be another death in Valleyview.

"What's going on? Where?"

The other possibility that presented itself was Ralph Klein Provincial Park. It had almost been a year since that one, but Siever would still consider it to be "in her direction." It was only a fifteen-minute drive away. Margie hoped it wasn't Ralph Klein. She did not like the murky black water in the reservoir beside the education center. The canals and other waterways caused her anxiety enough; that black pool was so ominous and foreboding.

"Elliston Park. You know it?" Siever asked.

"Uh… no, I don't. I've heard of it. I think it is east down Seventeenth Avenue?"

"That's right. Surprised you haven't taken your dog there. It's a nice area."

Margie had plenty of multi-use pathways close to the house and hadn't ventured much farther than Valleyview Park. Or north to the winding pathways around Max Bell Center.

"It's on my list."

"Well, today you get to see it in person."

Margie looked over at Christina, sighing. "Do you really need me there?"

"I'd appreciate it. I know everyone is supposed to be off today, but homicides don't wait for anyone. You're the closest one, it would disrupt your schedule the least."

"I'm watching the parade with my daughter."

"She's a teenager, isn't she? She can look after herself until you get back. It will be an hour. Maybe two. You can DVR it and watch it with her later. Fast forward through the boring bits and watch the good stuff over again. Much more entertaining."

"How long until you'll be there?"

"I'm about ten minutes out. Probably going by your house about now. I'll meet you in the east parking lot. You know how to get there?"

"No." Margie's stomach tightened. "There is more than one parking lot?"

"Sure."

And probably only the main one would show up on GPS. By the way Siever said she should meet him in the east parking lot, she assumed that it was not the main entrance.

"Maybe I should use the main parking lot. You can secure things on the east, and I can see if there is anything of note going on in the…"

"The west access." Siever was silent for a minute. "I don't think there is going to be anything on that side. The vic's car will be in the east lot. That's where we will be collecting evidence."

"We won't know if there is anything of note in the west end unless we check. I may as well do that."

"Do you think you can find your way from the west end to where the body is?"

Margie had an uncomfortable feeling that he knew or guessed more about her lack of sense of direction than she had ever told anyone. Why else would he have asked that?

"How big is this park? Are there are lot of pathways?"

"Not really. They're just in a loop around the lake. Sort of an outer loop and an inner loop."

"Okay. And which should I be on?"

He considered for a few seconds. "Fine. Shortest to go around the north side of the lake. If you're facing the lake from the west parking lot, that's the left. Doesn't matter which path you take. The outer loop will be longer, obviously."

"I can do that." Margie grabbed a pen and a flyer from the coffee table and scribbled down his instructions. "I'll be on my way in five minutes."

He grunted and hung up the phone.

Christina looked at Margie, one eyebrow raised. "First, no Canada Day, and now no parade day?"

"I'm sorry, honey. Like Detective Siever says, you can DVR it and we can watch it together later."

"I don't want to watch it later; I want to watch it now. With you. Not a taped version later. We can just watch the news or YouTube for that."

"I'll be back as soon as I can be." Margie knew there was no point in arguing. It wouldn't get them any closer to overcoming the disappointment that once again, Margie was being taken away from Christina on a day that was supposed to be set apart for the two of them. Christina wasn't the only one who was upset about her being called in.

"I can't control when the bodies are found." Margie divided her hair into sections behind her head and began to braid it. She would have to change out of her casual shorts and t-shirt and into something more appropriate for a homicide detective. And then jump in the car and get to the park as quickly as she could. She didn't want to keep Siever waiting for too long and it was going to take time to walk to his location.

She hadn't even asked him how far a walk it would be.

CHAPTER TWO

She was right about the GPS on her phone only giving her one option for a route to Elliston Park. She didn't even see the second parking lot marked.

Happily, there wasn't much traffic on Seventeenth Avenue and she was able to get to the park in good time. There were more cars than she expected in the parking lot. Apparently, a lot of people did not care about watching the Stampede parade. It might be sort of a holiday to Calgarians, especially those who normally worked downtown, but there were obviously plenty of people who didn't watch the coverage.

It was a sunny day, the sky a clear, pale blue. Margie could see people walking dogs, carrying little children on their shoulders, and strolling around the park at a leisurely pace. No one seemed to be aware that there was a dead body somewhere at the other end of the park. It was just a normal day for them.

Getting out of the car, Margie put on a mask and consulted the corner of the flyer that she had torn off and put in her pocket. *Facing the lake, take the left-hand pathway.*

There were several pathways to the left, and not all of them appeared to loop around the lake. But they might meander other directions first and then turn around. Margie walked slowly, trying to fix the other end of the lake in her mind. She would keep going left, or clockwise, and she would eventually meet up with Siever on the other side.

Margie walked past flower beds vibrant with colors. Keeping left, she discovered some kind of monument and walked closer to take a look. Various cylindrical concrete blocks stood in a half circle, numbers on top of them. There was a grid of months and horseshoes embedded in the pavement in front of them and a starburst shape like a sun or a compass at the top. Margie looked at it, bemused. Public art? A puzzle?

"It's a sundial," said a voice behind her.

Margie turned and looked at the woman behind her. Shoulder length brown hair under a baseball cap, somewhat overweight, in a t-shirt and shorts, pushing a stroller with fat wheels seating two toddlers. The children were lolling over, eyes glazed, obviously tired out from walking or playing.

"A sundial?" It didn't look like any sundial that Margie had ever seen. There was no pointer to cast a shadow on the numbers. The pillars themselves cast shadows, but Margie couldn't figure out how that would tell her the time.

"You stand on the month," the mother instructed, pointing to July.

Margie positioned herself on the rectangle.

"Then put your arms over your head like this." She demonstrated, pressing her palms together, arms extended over her head.

Margie did so.

"Now look at your shadow."

Margie followed her shadow out to the numbers and found it falling between the eight and the nine. She looked at her phone, thumbing on the screen. Eight-thirty. "It worked!"

The woman laughed. "It does," she agreed. "Every time."

"Except if it's too cloudy or dark to see your shadow," Margie pointed out.

"Right. Of course." She gave Margie a broad smile. "Reliable enough for me to know that it was only six o'clock when they were racing those stupid boats."

Margie looked toward the lake. She couldn't see any boats from where she stood and didn't remember seeing any from the parking lot. There were no cars with boats in trailers. Maybe in the other parking lot, where Siever had gone.

"They were racing boats in here?"

Margie would not have thought it large enough for a boat race. It wasn't just a pond like the one in Valleyview, but it was nothing like Chestermere Lake or the reservoir.

"RC boats."

"RC?"

"Remote control." The woman mimed working a controller in her palm. "Little remote control boats. They play with them out on the lake."

"Oh, I see." Margie nodded. "Six o'clock does seem a little early to be playing with remote control boats. I suppose whoever it was had the morning off for parade day. But maybe he has to go into the office in the afternoon."

"Maybe. I still don't like having the serenity of the morning broken by those whining, whizzing boats. They go so fast. Did you know they can go, like, two-hundred-fifty kilometers per hour?"

Margie tried to picture it. She shook her head. She had been thinking of the remote control cars some of her cousins had had when she was a kid. They didn't go any faster than a brisk walk. Slower if their batteries were getting low. She had pictured something similar putting along the surface of the lake. But that wouldn't have irritated the woman so much. It would have been quiet. Little boats going over two-fifty, though... that was a different story. Margie could just imagine them screaming over the water.

"That's incredible. I had no idea."

"It's cool to see people playing with them here. The kids like it. But you would think people could be more considerate and not do it while people are trying to enjoy the peace and quiet of a morning walk."

"Mommy..." one of the toddlers whined, not sitting up, but still lying back, looking exhausted. "I'm firsty..."

The woman shook her head at Margie. "When we get into the car, I'll give you a juice box," she promised.

"I'm firsty too!" the other insisted more loudly.

"I'm sure you are. We'll be in the car in a minute."

The woman waved at Margie. "Well, I guess I'd better get on my way." She looked Margie over, taking in her slacks and blazer. "You... know where you're going?"

"Just around the lake," Margie said lightly.

"There's something going on down the other end. I don't know what. Saw a bunch of flashing lights and uniforms. Maybe some vandalism or a homeless person causing trouble. They camp out here in the trees sometimes."

"I'll watch out," Margie promised.

"Okay. Have a nice day."

"You too."

The woman pushed her stroller back toward the parking lot. Margie reoriented herself to the lake and followed the path that ran along the edge of it.

Ducks and other waterfowl floated serenely on the glassy surface of the lake. The skies were blue with big fluffy white clouds. She could see a few Canada geese floating at the end of the lake as well, one of them clambering up onto the shore to poke through the grass for something tasty. Margie didn't know as much about wildlife as she should, but she knew enough about Canada geese to give them a wide berth. Being attacked by one of those big birds and their hard beaks was something she would prefer to avoid. They might look like stately, graceful creatures, but cross one, and you'd better be ready to run. It was probably too late in the year for there to be goslings to protect, but Margie was not going to find out.

The single pathway split into two, and Margie hesitated over which to follow. Siever had said that there was an inner loop and an outer loop. She could stay on the inner loop, where she could keep the lake in sight. It would be a shorter distance for her to walk. But if the woman was right and there were sometimes homeless people camped in the trees, then maybe she should take the path that led into the grove of trees. There might be witnesses to interview. Evidence that someone had discarded in the trees in the hopes that the police would never see it.

It would take longer, which would probably irritate Siever. But it would be more efficient and save time in the overall investigation.

Margie unlocked the screen on her phone and tapped Siever's recent call record. She walked into the trees as she waited for him to answer.

"Did you get lost?" Siever asked dryly.

"No, your directions were good. I'm on my way around to you. I just thought I'd let you know that I'm taking the longer route, through the trees. I could see a good deal of the shore, and I don't see anything suspicious by the lake. But something could easily be hidden in the trees, and a woman I just passed said that sometimes the homeless camp out here. So I'm going to take a quick walk through to see if there is anything that we need to take a closer look at."

Siever was silent for a moment, considering this. She waited for him to tease her that he thought she had gotten lost and was just looking for an excuse for her lateness. Cruz or Jones would have. But Siever was quieter, a bit shy or awkward. He didn't press it.

"I suppose if you think that's the best course," he allowed. "You're the one with experience in parks."

She didn't have *that* much experience. She certainly wasn't a tracker of any kind. She hadn't inherited that gene through her Cree or European explorer ancestors. But Siever had agreed to her chosen course.

"Thanks. I'll see you in a few minutes, then."

CHAPTER THREE

*W*alking into the trees, it was almost as if the rest of the world ceased to exist. There were still occasional traffic sounds, but all the busy-ness of the walkers and other park users disappeared and she was alone, her view limited by the trees that pushed close in on the trail. Birds chirped and twittered. She had expected to hear a lot of red-winged blackbirds, like she did at Valleyview park, but she couldn't pick out their songs. She heard many sparrows and smaller birds like she often heard from her yard. Always fighting and bickering with each other, declaring their territory, calling back and forth.

It wasn't a paved trail like at the other parks she had been to. A worn footpath rather than a multi-use pathway. It was kind of nice that way, making her believe that she really could be in a forest, removed from the constant hum of civilization, rather than walking beside busy Seventeenth Avenue.

"Coming through!" a voice called out.

Margie looked up, startled, to see a bicycle hurtling toward her. She stepped to the side, off the worn path.

"Thank you!" the cyclist called out as he whipped past her. And in a few seconds, he was gone again.

So much for being isolated. Margie laughed to herself.

She was there for a reason, and it wasn't just to take in the trees and nature around her. She was supposed to be looking for anything that was out of place. Any homeless encampments or possible evidence. She scanned back and forth, looking for anything that might have been dropped or thrown to the side.

Like the other Calgary parks she had been to, it was pretty clean and tidy. Not much for her to find.

A few minutes later she could see a large rock that was obviously out of place. The forest ground cover was mostly grass and pine needles. It was a river rock, round and smooth. And it had been painted. Margie left the trail to look at it.

It was robin's egg blue and painted on it in a cursive script were the words "Pray Always."

Margie studied it for a moment. Was it evidence? There was nothing to indicate it had been placed there recently. There was no blood spatter or other obvious contaminant. Did it indicate that someone frequented the park who was evangelical? Maybe even a religious zealot who would rail at and try to convert park goers? Religious mania could sometimes lead to violence.

The two painted smiley faces on the rock dissuaded her from this line of thought. A violent zealot might have painted fire and brimstone, but not smiley faces. Still, the rock was out of place and she should make note of it. Margie took a couple of pictures with her phone. Using the toe of her shoe, she lifted the edge of the rock, and could see by the dampness of the ground underneath that it had been there for some time. Not just dropped there the night before.

She returned to the trail and continued through the trees. The next people who came through from the opposite direction were a man walking a big, black dog, and two more cyclists. Margie would not have expected so many bikes through there on a trail that wasn't made for them. She wouldn't have wanted to be bumping over all of the rocks and roots on a bike.

As she emerged from the grove of trees, an older woman, thin and deeply wrinkled, was walking toward her. She nodded a brisk greeting at Margie.

"You might not want to go this way," she told Margie. "They're blocking the pathway. You can't get around."

"Oh, okay. Thanks." Margie smiled and nodded. "Any idea what's going on?"

Sometimes there was more to be learned from gossip than through official channels. Margie was curious as to what people were saying about the police activity.

"Police roping off the area. I guess they think it's unsafe. The lake is a stormwater catchment, maybe they're worried about it getting too deep with the last couple of storms."

"Oh, okay." Margie nodded. "There has been some spectacular lightning lately, hasn't there?"

"Yes, and there was a lot of flooding last week with that sudden storm. Lots of people got stranded in their cars. Dangerous to be near a basin like this if there is a sudden downpour."

"That makes sense. Thanks."

Margie continued to walk in the direction she had been.

"You can't get by them," the woman warned again. "You can't get all the way around."

"That's okay. I don't need to get around."

The woman frowned. Then she shrugged. She had done her neighborly duty by informing Margie of the problem. If Margie still wanted to follow the ill-advised route, then that was her own business. She would just find herself blocked at the other end of the lake anyway.

They went their own ways. A leg of the lake jutted out to the left and, as Margie started to follow the perimeter, she realized that the lake was bigger than she had thought. She hadn't been able to see all of it from the parking lot.

Which meant it would take that much longer to get to Siever and the body.

Margie picked up her pace.

CHAPTER FOUR

*I*t felt like it took a lot longer than it should to get around the lake. Margie had thought that it would take her only a few minutes, but it took nearly half an hour, and she was drenched in sweat once she got there. She should not have worn her blazer when she knew she was going to the park. Homicide detectives were supposed to look professional, but she probably would have looked more professional in khakis and a white t-shirt than dressed for the office and drenched in sweat.

She approached Siever, trying to look as calm and cool as possible. He glanced over her. He was heavyset, his face slightly rounded with extra weight. Hair buzzed short. His expression, what she could see of it around his mask, was neutral. "Glad you could make it. Ready to go?"

Margie nodded. "Yes, what have we got?"

Siever pointed at something in the lake. Margie could see a brightly colored inflatable raft and some other indiscernible shapes. She squinted, trying to force her eyes to adjust to the bright reflection of the sun on the surface of the water.

"And we think that's a body?"

He handed her a pair of binoculars. Margie put them up to her eyes and adjusted the focus. She could make out an arm and hand protruding from under the raft. There was also a smaller boat; Margie assumed it was the RC boat that the woman at the sundial had been complaining about.

"So… is someone coming to tow it all to shore?" *She* certainly wasn't going to be swimming out there to get them.

"Fire department has some boats. They're going to send someone over."

So Margie had not held anyone up in taking so long to get to the scene. They still couldn't even access the body. She took a few pictures of the raft with her phone, though she knew that the chances she would actually be able to see anything significant in the pictures were extremely low.

"I would think that they would be faster getting someone here. We can't even confirm that the guy is dead. What if he's just injured?"

"Hasn't moved for an hour and he's under the water. I don't think there's any chance of a successful rescue."

"Who found him?"

Siever motioned to one of the spectators standing close by. "Dog walker. His dog kept going into the water and banging into the boat. Eventually he figured out that something was wrong. A birdwatcher had binoculars," he made a gesture toward a tall, gangly woman who was also waiting and watching the water through binoculars. "She was able to see the arm once the dog had moved the raft enough."

"Do we know who he is?"

"Hopefully, he'll have some ID on him. Otherwise, we might have to wait until the parking lot clears out and see which car is left."

"He could have walked in."

"Not with a raft and other equipment," he pointed out.

"Oh." Margie nodded. "No, not very likely. How big is the parking lot at this end?"

"Smaller than the one you saw and less well-known."

"So now we're just waiting."

Siever shrugged. "Forensics is on their way. Mostly, it's rock by the edge of the water, but I could see some footprints, so we want to keep everyone back until they have documented everything."

Margie looked around. He had taped off a nice wide perimeter, and no one seemed inclined to cross the barrier. People stood back watching the activity or looking into the lake and pointing at the raft, but so far no one of the type who thought they had the right to march into an area, caution tape notwithstanding.

"Looks good."

She was regretting that she had hurried to get there. Margie took off her jacket and folded it over her arm. She was probably showing huge sweat rings under her arms, but there was no point in getting overheated or dehydrated because she was dressed too warmly.

"So… what do you think happened? He had a problem with his remote control boat and went out to get it?"

Siever nodded. "Probably. And then he overturned or fell out reaching for it. Wasn't as strong a swimmer as he thought or hit his head on an underwater rock. Freak accidents happen."

They listened to the whoop of a siren making its way down Seventeenth Avenue and looked toward it, though their view of the traffic was blocked by the trees. It pulled into the parking lot behind them and turned off the siren, still out of Margie's view. It sounded big and heavy, so she assumed it was the fire department, not another police car.

In a few minutes, a group of firefighters came out of the trees carrying a boat. It wasn't an inflatable like the raft on the lake and required several firemen to carry it.

"Just over here," Siever directed, pointing to the raft. "There's a body under it."

"What a pity," one of the men said, heavily accented. Bahamian, maybe? West Indies? He certainly wasn't a Calgary native.

Siever directed them around the tape perimeter, so that they wouldn't go walking across the area he believed the evidence was in. They set the boat into the water, talked back and forth for a bit, getting everything ready, and then started the motor and buzzed slowly over to the bright yellow raft. Margie tried to see what they were doing, but their boat blocked most of the view as they turned the raft right side up and examined what they found underneath for a few minutes, talking to one another, before they worked together to heave the body out of the water into the rescue boat. Margie found herself tensing, her own body remembering pulling a man out of the Valleyview pond. She hadn't been able to do it herself, but had needed help to lift his weight and break the surface tension to get him out of the water.

She tried to relax her muscles and breathe evenly. She wasn't the one doing the physical work this time. The firefighters would bring him to shore, the death investigator would examine him and take him away in his van, and Siever or one of the others would attend at the autopsy. Eventually, Margie would get the medical examiner's report in her inbox, neat and tidy.

It was a few more minutes before the rescuers tied the raft to their boat and putted back to the shore, again staying well away from Siever's evidence. Margie walked along the tape perimeter down to the water's edge. She could get close to the water without getting anxious, as long as she didn't have to step into it or take a bridge over it. Then things got complicated. But she was fine standing on the shore to get a good look at the victim and any of the evidence that came with him.

He was a large man. A good thing that they'd had several firefighters to pull him out of the water. One or two wouldn't have been able to manage. His t-shirt had pulled up, exposing a wide expanse of white belly and rolls of fat. He was sandy blond, with short, thinning hair. His face had not yet begun to swell, which indicated to Margie that he hadn't been in the water for very long. But she already knew that. The mom with the stroller had said that she'd heard him running the RC boat, alive and well, at six o-clock.

The firefighters left the body in the boat as they pulled the boat up onto the rocky shore, not stretching him out on the grass to be on display to all the spectators. Pulling the tow rope attached to the inflatable raft hand over hand, the Caribbean firefighter smiled at Margie, flashing bright white teeth at her before pausing to pull up his mask as she approached.

"You are a detective?" he asked. "I don't think I have met you before."

"Yes, I've been in Calgary less than a year, so... that's not surprising. Detective Margie Patenaude." Margie didn't bother offering her hand. Besides the fact that many people no longer felt comfortable shaking hands, he was obviously occupied with his job. He pulled the raft up onto the shore and started to look it over carefully.

"Anton Carter," he introduced himself. "Parks Pat!" he said after a minute. "I have heard of you, ma'am."

"Well, yes, that's what they've been calling me." Margie was a little embarrassed by the name. But it was so much better than the other names that she imagined her fellow law enforcement officers giving her, she didn't fight it. Parks Pat was a little ostentatious, but that was all.

"You are the lead?"

"No." Margie pointed to Siever. "Detective Siever is in charge. I'm happy to help, of course, in any way I can, but I'm only assisting on the case."

"I do not see anything wrong with the raft." Carter poked and prodded at the seams. "And it should be sturdy enough to hold his weight, even though he is a big man."

"What do you think happened, then? He fell out?"

A nod. "That's usually what happens in these cases. Like falls off of ladders while people are painting. They think they can reach farther than they can, and overbalance."

"I guess you probably see a few of those too."

"Ladders? Yes ma'am. If we're the closest first responders, we will take the call until paramedics can get there."

Another of the firefighters showed Margie the remote control boat. She leaned in closer and studied it with interest.

It wasn't like she would have imagined a remote control boat. She had pictured a child's toy, like a normal boat, only reduced in scale and made of plastic. Like she had played with in the tub as a child. But it was wider and flatter, not looking much like a pleasure craft or any speedboat she had seen in real life. She wasn't sure what it was constructed of, but it didn't appear to be plastic or metal.

"Where is the engine?"

He turned it around and opened up an access panel to show it to her. "This one takes nitro. There are others that are solely battery powered."

"Which is better?"

"You could research that all week long and not be able to decide. Everybody has a different opinion. It really just comes down to your personal preferences."

"Do you have one of these?" She assumed by his familiar handling and lingo that he knew something about it.

"My brother does. I gave it up years ago because he always beat me or wrecked my boats. It can be an expensive hobby. We've had a better relationship since we aren't competing against each other. I can just go to a race day and cheer him on."

"That's too bad. It sounds like it could be fun."

"Yes, if you don't get too obsessed about it and are just in it for the fun. But many people... take it too seriously. Takes the fun out of it, in my mind."

He had the experience, so she assumed he knew what he was talking about.

"Do you know the victim? If you've gone to your brother's races, maybe you've run into him at some point."

The firefighter shook his head. "No, I wouldn't recognize anyone. Don't go often enough to remember anyone else from one meet to another."

He looked the boat over one more time and then handed it to her. "I guess you're going to want that."

Margie pulled on a pair of gloves before taking it. "Yes, I guess we'll need it as evidence until the ME confirms that it was an accidental death."

CHAPTER FIVE

The van from the medical examiner's office and techs arrived at around the same time, and neither of them paid any attention to the fact that there was no road from the parking lot and simply drove out onto the grass. Margie could understand their not wanting to carry a heavy stretcher all the way across the grassy expanse or to have to carry their various bits of equipment from the van to the scene to collect the forensic evidence.

Margie stood back and let Siever give directions to the team. Not that he needed to tell them where to go or what to do; everyone knew his job without being told. Margie nodded at them as they went by. They went to the body first so that the techs could gather any necessary evidence before the investigator touched the body. They took pictures, tweezed a few bits that Margie couldn't see from where she was standing, and eventually nodded to the death investigator that he could go ahead. Margie watched him check for a pulse and put on a stethoscope to check for respiration or a heartbeat before starting. Despite the fact that they all knew the body had been face down in the water for over an hour already. Margie didn't see how he could have survived that, but supposed that it was part of the prescribed routine.

The death investigator took some pictures of his own, examined the body in situ, and looked out to the point that the firefighters pointed to on the lake. Carter showed him the raft that they had brought back in and described the positioning of the raft and the body.

During his examination, the man retrieved a wallet and held it out to Margie. She opened it up to reveal that the victim was one Simon Hustler. She did a quick flip through the wallet but didn't find anything of note. No pictures of family, but who kept those in their wallets anymore? It was all on phones.

"Did he have a phone?" Margie asked, looking back at the body. The pathologist patted all the likely places. "Not that I see yet. Maybe it went in the drink." He looked over his shoulder to the lake. "Or maybe it's with his things by the water."

Margie looked at the backpack and luggage that Hustler had obviously used to carry his boat and equipment in, which he had left on the shore when he went into the raft to go after his RC boat. She hadn't touched anything yet. Let the tech guys go through the cases and contents and collect any evidence they needed. If there were a phone in there, it would turn up. But if it were in the water…

"Maybe he dropped it in the water and that's how he ended up tipping out of the raft. Trying to dive after it."

A shrug from the investigator. "Possible."

People kept their lives on their phones and, even if their information were stored in the cloud, it would be natural for Hustler to reach or jump after it in a split-second of panic, only realizing afterward that he had made the wrong choice.

Eventually, the remains were bundled up in a double layer of body bags and prepared for transport.

"Do you have a preliminary cause of death?" Margie asked, unable to hold her tongue.

The pathologist raised his brows at her. "Nothing to indicate that it was not drowning. Pretty good guess, to begin with. We'll know better after the autopsy."

Margie nodded.

Her last drowning case had turned out not to be drowning.

But this one seemed to be pretty clear. Guy had been out there alone on a raft, retrieving a boat that had stopped working. Somehow, he tipped himself into the water and wasn't able to recover.

It would be an open and shut case, easy to clear.

❧

EVENTUALLY, all the evidence had been collected and taken back to the lab. Siever talked to the dogwalking man and the birdwatching woman, getting the same statement that he had gotten from them the first time. Margie couldn't detect any discrepancies or any sign that either one of them was not telling the full truth.

Neither of them professed to know Hustler from other visits to the park. They had just happened to be the lucky ones to stumble across the body.

Margie knew what that was like!

Her stomach was growling loudly and she felt like it was going to eat itself from the inside out. She should have grabbed a couple of granola bars on her way out the door. Just drinking a cup of coffee was not nearly enough to last her all morning. Had she even finished her first mug of coffee? Margie suspected that she had not. Siever looked around the scene for anything that they might have missed.

"You didn't find anything significant in the trees on the way over here?"

"No," Margie admitted. "Oh—but I did run into a woman who was complaining about the noise of the RC boat this morning. She said that six o'clock was too early to be racing it out here, that it disturbed everyone's peace and quiet."

"She was sure of the time?"

"She used the sundial in the corner. It's pretty accurate; I tried it out myself."

"Well," Siever nodded. "Assuming she did it right, that gives us a window for time of death."

"She showed me how to use it. So she definitely knows how."

"Did you take her name and contact details?"

"Uh... no. It was just a casual conversation while I was coming to see you. I should have. I'll come back here a few times to see whether she comes back. Sorry about that. She seemed to know the place pretty well, so maybe she walks here every day... or at least a few times a week."

"Yeah... if you could find her, that would be good. We can find out if there are cameras recording people as they walk into the park. Or taking pictures of their license plates. I assume there's some kind of security other than just saying it is closed at night."

"If we're done here... I should be getting home to my daughter."

"Do you want a ride back to your car?"

Margie looked across the lake to the parking lot on the far side. It was a beautiful day, the clear blue sky reflected in the water. But she had been on her feet for hours and didn't really feel like walking all the way back, either the way she had come or via the other side of the lake, which she had not yet walked.

"Actually, that would be really nice."

He started to take down the yellow tape to allow people to walk through the area. "You should have just come down this end to start with."

Margie shrugged. "Then I wouldn't have run into the woman at the sundial. So it's probably a good thing that I did."

Siever tilted his head, then nodded. "Maybe you're right."

Margie started at the other end of the tape and they worked together to take it down, meeting in the middle.

❧

SIEVER DROPPED Margie at her car. She got settled and touched Christina's name on her phone before pulling out.

"Hi, Mom."

"Hi! How was the rest of the parade?"

"There were different floats, marching bands, and stuff. There were a couple of Indigenous groups. The Stoney Nakoda and Niitsitapiiks. The parade was kind of cool. Seemed more... small town-y than I expected."

"It had become pretty big and commercial the past few years," Margie said. "Probably good for them to scale back a bit. Are you hungry? I thought I would stop for something on the way home."

"Yeah, lunch would be good."

"Burger King?"

"Get me an Impossible burger?"

"Sure. You want a shake? They have those mini ones right now."

"Yeah. Strawberry."

"Okay, I'll be home soon!"

❧

THE AFTERNOON WAS MORE RELAXING. Margie watched a few highlights of the parade and discussions of the special rules the Stampede was working under and gave Stella a thorough brushing, which hadn't been done for a while. Margie figured she had enough extra fur for a whole new dog.

"I'm going out with Tracy for a while," Christina told her, marching into the living room and tucking her phone into her pocket.

"Whoa, wait! I thought we were going to go see Moushoom."

"Tonight, you said. I can go out for a few hours."

"With Tracy?" Margie remembered that Tracy was a boy, not a girl, from Christina's school. Were they dating now? Was this a thing? "Why didn't you mention anything before?"

"We just decided. We were both kind of bored and didn't want to stay inside all day. You said you wanted me to have friends and that I'd be able to do things once the restrictions were lifted." Christina stood there, looking expectant, one eyebrow raised.

"Sure. I didn't say you couldn't," Margie reassured her. Though she wished that she had a good reason to ask Christina to stay home. "I'm just surprised. You kind of ambushed me."

"I'm just hanging out with a friend for a while. It doesn't have anything to do with you."

"I was planning on us having the afternoon together, that's all. Since it was my day off."

Christina rolled her eyes. "Yeah, and I thought we were going to have the morning together, *since it was your day off.*"

Touché.

"Okay, well… say hi to Tracy for me. What are you guys planning to do?"

Christina's stance relaxed slightly, reassured that Margie wasn't going to go all hardcore and insist that she had to stay home. "Like I said, we're just going to hang out. Go to the mall maybe, since we don't have to wear masks and social distance and all the capacities are back to normal. We can just… be normal again."

They had been under health restrictions ever since moving to Calgary, so Christina hadn't yet had the chance of a normal life and normal relationships there. It had been nice to cocoon at home and not to worry about her getting into trouble as much, but Christina had to spread her wings and have some independence. Hopefully, she would make good choices. Margie couldn't help worrying about what else they might decide to do now that they were allowed social gatherings.

"Have a good time. And you'll be back in time to see Moushoom?"

"Yeah. Of course. We're just going out for a few hours."

Christina was out the door, jogging down the sidewalk to get into the car that pulled in at the curb. Margie hadn't even had a chance to ask whether Tracy had his full driver's license yet.

CHAPTER SIX

*A*fter a long weekend, Margie felt refreshed going back to the office. She had not spent as much time as she had hoped with Christina, but it had been nice to have a little downtime, and she had been able to catch up on some of the cleaning and home maintenance stuff that had fallen behind lately. She'd actually unpacked the last of the moving boxes. Only seven months after their move; that wasn't so bad.

Except for the boxes that she had decided didn't need to be unpacked, that would just stay in storage in the basement. She wasn't sure how they had accumulated so much stuff or why she had decided to move everything she had. They could have had a garage sale or given some items to relatives. But they had just packed everything up.

Margie took a few minutes to look through her in basket before going to her email. Despite the promise of the paperless office and having had to work from home as much as possible during the pandemic, there was still a significant amount of paper floating around the department. And too much of it was just printouts of what she had already received in mail or seen posted on the case file virtual workspaces. They just went straight into the garbage, because Margie didn't want to keep track of physical paper as well as everything else. Filing everything twice was not efficient.

She moved on to email and reviewed everything that had happened over the weekend. Most of it she had already skimmed over anyway, unable to just disconnect from work, even when she was supposed to be off. She saw that the medical examiner had posted his report to the workspace for the Hustler file and clicked through to have a look at it.

Hustler's death had been determined to have been caused by drowning, Margie was happy to see. She hadn't expected to have two cases in a row where an apparent drowning had turned out not to be a drowning. That would have been too coincidental. But as she read on, she frowned.

"What are you looking so glum about?" Kaitlyn Jones asked as she walked past Margie's desk to get to her own. "Didn't you have a good weekend? Or maybe you had too good of a weekend and didn't want it to end." Jones gave her a wide grin. Though she had her hair pulled back in a bun, a few tendrils of wavy blond hair had escaped and framed her face, making her look younger and less like the seasoned homicide cop she was.

"It was good," Margie said. "This isn't anything about my weekend."

"What's up, then?"

"You heard about the new case on Friday? A body found in Elliston Lake?"

Jones nodded. "Sure, I saw that. And of course Siever pulled you into it. You are Parks Pat, after all."

"I think it was more the fact that I'm just ten minutes from there. So... yeah. Body floating in the water, face down, under a raft that had tipped over. It looked pretty obvious that he just fell in while trying to reach for his RC boat."

"Uh-huh."

"But the ME hasn't made a finding of accidental death."

Kaitlyn's brows went up. "Really?"

Siever apparently heard the conversation and wandered over to join them. "You talking about the Hustler case? He said it needs further investigation. I really don't understand why. It's open and shut."

Margie read over the words on her screen, trying to take them in. She felt like the screen was too far away from her, the words difficult to concentrate on while the other two looked at her, waiting for her response.

"He says that there was a lot of perimortem bruising. Which I guess would be unusual if this guy just happened to fall into the lake...?"

She looked at Jones and Siever for their thoughts.

"I guess," Jones said, shrugging. "But he could have gotten bruised from a lot of different things. Not necessarily anything to do with the accident."

"And I guess that's what he wants to establish. Where the bruises came from."

"Click the pictures," Siever instructed, looking over Margie's shoulder.

She was sure that he would already have looked at all the pictures on his own computer. But she did as he suggested and brought a couple of them up on the screen. Blue-purple bruises on white skin. At seemingly random places on Hustler's shoulders, arms, chest, and face. In a couple of places, it wasn't just bruising, but tearing of the skin as well.

"What the heck caused that?" Jones wondered, leaning in closer for a better look.

"I have no idea. And I guess the ME didn't either, or he would have made a finding based on that. What do you think?" She turned her head to face Siever. "Can you think of anything at the scene that would have caused that?"

Siever shook his head slowly. "I initially thought maybe he hit his head on the bottom of the lake, diving after his phone or something. And he could have been bumped by the boat. Even though it was an inflatable, those things still have some hardware and can do damage."

"I can't imagine this being done by a collision with the bottom of the lake or the raft. It would have to be multiple collisions."

"Ready to go?" Sergeant MacDonald asked as he walked by the bullpen. Siever looked uncomfortable. He waited until MacDonald was in his office, then looked at Jones and Margie.

"What am I going to say? Mac is going to be expecting us to put this one to bed, but I can't do that with the ME saying that it needs to be investigated further."

"Just tell him that, then. You can't control what the ME finds," Jones told him. "You're not responsible for that. You just summarize it and figure out what we're going to do next."

Siever looked a little green. "You're so much better at this than I am."

"What's Mac going to do? He's not going to fire you. He can't even criticize you for continuing the investigation, considering that is what the medical examiner says to do. Now if you tried to close it, that would definitely be a problem." Jones laughed. She went over to her own desk, putting down her purse and straightening things on her desk. "We'd better get ready, then; looks like he's raring to go."

According to the system clock on Margie's computer, they still had another twenty minutes before the scheduled stand-up meeting in the conference room. She looked at Siever. "We still have time to prep. No one can tell you that you're late just because Mac is eager to start the meeting. Why don't we take one of the small meeting rooms, and we'll go over your notes and what you want to say? You can write down bullet points or rehearse or whatever helps you."

Siever's eyebrows went up. "You would do that?"

"Sure. Grab your stuff and we'll do a quick run-through. Mac doesn't need to hear everything; it's only supposed to be a brief."

Siever returned to his desk to grab a folder of loose papers and his tablet. They closeted themselves in one of the small interrogation rooms and bent their heads over the papers.

It wasn't a particularly comfortable setting. The plastic chairs and wobbly table were not meant to make suspects feel good. While on the surface, a suspect was kept comfortable and given everything he needed, there was subtler effort to keep him off his game. To make him want to get out of there as soon as he could.

But Margie knew she and Siever were only going to be there for fifteen minutes. How comfortable the furniture was didn't come into it. Siever briskly paged through the reports and statements in his folder. He opened a note on his tablet and began to type bullet points. Margie didn't really do anything other than to act as a sounding board and encourage him to get down what he needed to in order to be comfortable.

"It's okay if everyone's questions are *not* answered," Margie reminded him. "People will ask questions and the answer will be 'we don't know' or 'I will look into that.' That's perfectly reasonable. Today may officially be day four, but it is really only day one. We didn't know this could be classed as anything other than an accident until today. Now we will start making inquiries of a more personal nature."

"What about the scene? Should we have done anything else at the scene to preserve evidence? Was there anyone else that I should have talked to, or any other follow-up?"

"You followed all the correct protocols. Even though it looked like an accident, you taped off the perimeter, identified forensic evidence beside the lake, and stayed out of the way to let the techies' and ME's office handle the evidence collection. There wasn't anything else to find."

"And you helped to establish time of death," Siever pointed out.

"Yes." Margie flipped through the ME's report and saw that his time of death window had been much larger. Because Margie knew that he had still been alive and playing with his boat at six o'clock, the TOD had to be between then and when the first witness had spotted the body under the raft, sometime around eight. It was good to have a narrow window. It made it much easier to identify or eliminate suspects.

Were they looking for a suspect? Of what? Murder? It seemed bizarre that they would be thinking about suspects instead of just an accident. How could it have been anything but an accident?

"The death occurred between six and eight," Margie said. "That is something that we know. Concrete."

"Yeah. That's good. When we look at the video coverage, we can eliminate anyone who left before or came after that." He caught Margie's eye. "As a witness, I mean. It will help us to identify witnesses."

"Yes. Someone might have seen something without even knowing that it was important."

Siever made a couple of additional bullet points and was looking far more relaxed. He nodded slowly. "This is better. Thank you. I just needed to get my mind around it all. You really helped."

Margie checked the time on her phone, though she had been watching it pretty closely throughout their meeting. Having a prep meeting was great. Showing up late for Mac's stand-up meeting would not be.

CHAPTER SEVEN

*a*s usual, the stand-up meeting moved briskly. It was a chance for everyone on the team to hear of the latest developments on each active case. They gave reports, asked questions, and spitballed solutions at a rapid pace.

She listened to Siever's efficient outline of the Hustler case and what they knew so far. He gave no sign of his earlier anxiety, sounding confident and self-assured.

"Any idea what it was that caused these bruises?" Mac drilled.

"We don't know yet. We will need to investigate further."

"There wasn't anything on the scene that you could identify as a weapon?"

"There were plenty of rocks, some sticks or branches. But whatever it was didn't break the skin most of the time. Only once or twice. There were no signs of blood on the shore, but it's rocky; they could have been missed. But he died of drowning, not the blows or any blood loss. My guess would be that whatever hit him was in the water." Siever shook his head. "We just don't know what that was yet."

"What about this dog that found him, that kept swimming out to the boat. Could he have shifted the boat and caused the bruising?"

"Not with the number of bruises that he had. It wasn't just the boat landing on top of him. It was multiple blows or collisions."

Margie tried to envision what might have happened and still couldn't fathom it.

"Is it something that happened before he went out on the water, then?" Cruz asked. "Maybe he had a fight with someone. Then he went off to get the boat, overturned, and presto, we're back to accident again."

"Could be," Siever agreed. "We'll need to find out if there were any bad feelings with anyone. If he was the kind of guy who normally got into physical fights. Questions for family and friends."

"Was anyone there with him?"

"Not that we're aware of. We have some video footage of traffic going into or close to the park. I'll be watching to see whether anyone arrived at the same time as Hustler, or sometime during the time of death window."

The discussion went on to other cases. Siever's shoulders relaxed slightly. He stayed engaged, commenting and asking questions on the other cases that were presented. The meeting dismissed and they all headed toward the door. Margie hung back a little so that she could exit behind Siever. She slapped him on the shoulder. "Good job."

"Thanks again for the prep."

Margie nodded. "So, what do we tackle first? You have the names of his family?"

"His mother. Father is either dead or not in the picture. Hustler wasn't married, no children."

"Well, that's something, at least. Those little guys... they just tear your heart out."

Siever nodded his agreement. "I did the death notification Friday and explained that I would be doing the investigation into her son's death and would be in contact if I had any further questions. So now... I guess we go ask her further questions."

"Was he an only child? Is she on her own now?"

"Yes. All alone."

Margie sighed. "Poor woman."

"Hopefully she has friends, maybe extended family. She couldn't have just relied on her son for all of her social interaction."

છે.

Mrs. Hustler, the decedent's mother, lived in a small home by herself in Inglewood. It was an older part of town, and Margie suspected that she had probably lived there all of her life. Or at least since she had gotten married and/or had her son. Everything about the house spoke to it having been there for a long time, with Mrs. Hustler making only the very necessary technological advancements as time marched by her or upgrades when something fell to pieces. It was like walking into a church, only less cheery.

Mrs. Hustler herself was not that old. Certainly not as old as the house. If Hustler had been forty, she was probably sixty. She looked older than that, but she wasn't a wizened, tottering old woman. She had wrinkles, extra weight, and what Margie suspected was a wig. She moved decisively, showing Siever and Margie into her living room and showing them to their seats. She offered them tea, which both turned down, and she sat down in a chair a few feet away from them. Margie looked over to Siever to see whether he would start the questioning. He looked back at her, widening his eyes slightly in an expression that Margie thought was intended as *go ahead*.

"Mrs. Hustler. We are terribly sorry for your loss. And sorry about having to come back here to bother you with more questions."

"Yes, I know," she agreed. "Nothing one can do but go on."

"You remember Detective Siever. And I'm Detective Patenaude. Some people prefer to just call me Detective Pat."

"Okay."

"Had you seen Simon recently? How long was it since you had seen him?"

"We Skype every week. I have not seen him face-to-face in months. With the pandemic, you know."

Indoor gatherings had been prohibited for some time prior to July 1. Although a woman living on her own, as Mrs. Hustler was, was allowed two regular visitors. It was odd that her son hadn't been one of hers.

"So what day did you usually talk to him?"

"Sunday."

"And did you talk to him last Sunday?"

Mrs. Hustler hesitated. "Sunday a week ago, yes."

"Had you talked to him any time since? Emailed or messaged?"

"We might have emailed during the week. I would have to check."

"But nothing that jumps to mind."

"No. If we did… it was just to share a joke or a news article, that kind of thing. Nothing important."

"How was he when you talked to him on Sunday?"

She thought back, leaning her head back on the headrest and closing her eyes. "I don't remember very much about it, I'm sorry. They all run together after a while."

"Was there anything that he might have been upset about? A complaint about someone else?"

"Oh… he *always* had grievances, that boy." She shook her head. "I don't know why he chose to be so miserable. He had a good life. You know, before you have children, you have all these wonderful ideas of what kind of a parent you will be. How your children will be so well-behaved because you know how to do it all. Other people's children act up because they weren't raised right."

"Uh-huh…?" Margie could see where this was going and smiled slightly.

"And then you have your own child. Welcome to reality. You find out that they come with their own personalities and sensitivities, their own ideas about how the world should work. We do our best to lead and guide them, but they aren't just miniature versions of ourselves. We can't just train them to be the way we think they should be."

Margie nodded. "I have a teenager."

"Well then, you know. During the teen years… you can do nothing right. You don't know anything about anything. And they do."

Margie chuckled. "When you're right, you're right."

"Simon was miserable as a teenager… and he never really grew out of it. It's like he got stuck on that one track, complaining about everything and being unhappy about the rest of the world and how they treated him. And he could never appreciate the good things about his life."

Margie jotted a couple of notes in her notepad. Not because there was really anything to write about Simon Hustler having a bad attitude about life in general, but because she wanted Mrs. Hustler to get used to seeing the pen and notepad in Margie's hands, so that when she did have something important to write, it wouldn't distract the woman from what she had to say.

"What was his life like? I understand that he wasn't married, didn't have any children?"

"No. And he had a lot of sour grapes about that. No woman ever saw what a great catch he was. He was so smart and would be a good provider. She could stay at home with the kids and be the kind of mother that he always wanted. But the women that he was interested in were never interested in him. Sometimes he would go on a date or two, but it never lasted."

"That must have been disappointing for him. And for you."

"You want to die knowing that your children are cared for and are in good hands. I always wanted him to find the woman that could be... a soul mate for him. Someone who understood his quirks and could put up with his nonsense when he got worked up. He was never violent. He just... had a lot to say."

Margie nodded. "And no relationships that produced children?"

"Certainly none that I was ever aware of. And I think that he would have told me if he'd had any. He would have been so proud. But as it was... No. I won't ever have any grandchildren. He even tried doing the big brother thing for a while. I don't know which organization it was, but one of these programs where they mentor children. Uncles or brothers or whatever."

"But that didn't work out the way he hoped?"

"No. He went through two or three different children, but it was the same as the dating game. He would see them a few times, and then he would be assigned someone else. They never told him what he was doing wrong or if the children were complaining about him. He just bounced from one to another for a while... and then they stopped assigning him. They told him they would call when they had a match for him. And then they never called."

If he had been as negative as his mother perceived, then Margie could understand that. That wasn't a good influence around children. They would either be irritated by his attitude, or they would copy it and drive their parents and everybody else crazy. Mentoring programs had very high standards and, if he had failed a few times, they might have decided to just let him down easy. Ghost him until he got the message and gave up.

"That's too bad. It would have been rewarding for him if it had worked out."

"Maybe it would have," Mrs. Hustler agreed. "Or maybe it wouldn't. He didn't seem to... feel the happy stuff. The negative stuff, yes; he would talk about it for hours. But the good stuff never seemed to lift his spirits. I suppose they have a name for that now."

"Depression?" Margie suggested.

"Alexithymia," Siever said.

Margie looked at him, surprised. Mrs. Hustler frowned and leaned forward.

"I've never heard of that. What is it?"

"Well... it's sort of a broad term for not being able to feel emotions or to identify the emotions you are feeling. Sometimes it can be like you said, never being happy about things." Siever shrugged. "I don't know if he had that... but it's a possibility."

Mrs. Hustler nodded slowly. "Could you write that down for me so I could look it up later?"

Siever's brows drew down, studying her. Then he took out his notebook, wrote the word down carefully, and tore the page out of the notebook for her. Mrs. Hustler put it on the side table under the lamp and put a pen on top of it to keep it from fluttering away in the breeze from the fan oscillating back and forth.

"Did Simon get cross-threaded with people?" Siever asked. "Was there anyone in particular who had a problem with his personality or negativity? Maybe someone at work?"

"I don't remember him talking about any one person more than another. Simon... complained about everyone at some point or another. I hate to think about what he might have told people about me. I'm sure he wasn't any happier with our relationship than he was with any other. He didn't shy away from saying hurtful things to my face. I can only imagine what he might have said behind my back."

"So at work... there isn't anything that jumped out at you lately that he was unhappy with?"

"No. No more than usual."

"And what about his social life? I know you said he didn't get along well with women... but did he have any friends that he spent time with? Somebody who might have gone with him to the park for a stroll..."

"The only people I know of that he ever met at the park were those boat people."

"Those boat people?" Margie echoed.

"His club. The group that he ran. Racing the toy boats. They were always getting together. Not a lot during COVID, maybe, but whenever they could. They met a couple of times a week, normally."

Margie captured this point in her notepad, leaving Siever free to continue with his questions.

"He didn't just use the RC boats by himself."

"Oh, no. There was a big group of them. He was very well-regarded by them. They made him the president of their club. If that's what you would call it. He could talk for *hours* about his boats and racing on the lake."

"So there was something that he enjoyed in life," Margie suggested.

"I suppose so... though he wasn't ever telling me about how wonderful things were going. If he didn't win a race, there was always a reason, the other boaters cheated or didn't follow all the rules like he did. If he did win, then he would complain about how the others hadn't congratulated him or had complained about something he had done that was totally within the rules. They were very competitive, from what he said."

Margie remembered the first responder at the park saying the same thing about his brother. How it had become too competitive for him and he had had to bow out to keep their relationship intact.

"I never even knew about RC boat racing before this case," Margie said. "But you must know a lot about it."

"More than I ever wanted to, my dear. I wish I had never bought him that first boat!"

"He got into it when he was a boy?"

"I'm not sure how old he was... a teenager, probably. Yes, I remember the principal at his school saying that he needed to find a hobby. Something to keep him busy. I think he was rather disruptive in his classes. He was very bright and not shy about letting everyone know it. They didn't want to put him ahead, so he was bored. We went to the hobby craft store... the same one as is still there on Thirty-Second Avenue. I let him browse around to see what caught his fancy, and it was those boats. I thought they were just model boats to start with, and I thought that gluing together all those little parts would be a nice, quiet hobby for him to occupy himself with." She shook her head, laughing at herself. "Well, I have gotten my education since then!"

The boat that Margie had seen hadn't looked like a model boat. No tiny pieces to glue together and then show the completed piece on your mantle or float it in the bathtub. The boats had been much sturdier and utilitarian rather than showy. She nodded her understanding.

"Well, it must have brought him a lot of joy over the years. So even if it was an irritation to you... at least you know that it was something he loved."

Mrs. Hustler considered this. "I don't know if it brought him joy... but he did love his boats."

CHAPTER EIGHT

*M*argie looked out the window again, wondering where Christina was. It had been easier during the lockdown, when her daughter had either been home or at school. There hadn't been much opportunity for her to go anywhere else. But now that the health restrictions had been repealed and school had let out for the summer, it was a double whammy. Christina was free to go wherever she liked and when Margie was at work, there was nothing she could do about it. She wasn't sure there was anything she could do about it if she had been home either. Christina was at the age where she should be more independent, but Margie had hoped that she would still let her know where she was going to be and when she would be home. And maybe that they could talk about the appropriateness or inappropriateness of her activities.

But Christina was being like any other teenager. Close-mouthed about what she was up to, irritated and oppositional if Margie asked too many questions about it or hinted that she would like Christina to be home or thought that she might be getting herself into a situation that was not ideal.

And what could Margie say? She really didn't know anything. Tracy seemed like a nice enough boy, though all Margie had been able to do so far was to wave at him from the front step as Christina climbed into the car. But Christina never came home with bruises or mentioned any trouble from the police or anyone else. Margie had talked discreetly with the school resource officer, and he said that Tracy was a nice boy, not the kind to cause any trouble, not into drugs or drink or gangs, as far as he knew. Christina said that they just hung out, which was not very enlightening. She didn't like the thought of Christina hanging around malls where kids could get into trouble. There had been trouble at the malls with assaults and robberies by or aimed at teenagers in the past. She had checked.

Maybe she shouldn't have checked. Maybe she should have just been another oblivious parent, thinking that kids were perfectly safe if they were meeting somewhere in public.

She sighed. She had made supper and Christina had said that she would be home for it, but there was no sign of her. Margie eventually sat down to the vegetable stir fry with rice by herself. Christina was mostly vegetarian, so Margie had fried up just a bit of chicken for herself and kept it in a separate dish. A little bottled sauce from the cupboard, and it made a nice meal. But not one she had intended to eat alone.

She texted Christina as she sat down to eat. She tried not to constantly phone and text Christina, figuring that if she did, the girl would just tune her out like so much background noise. If she only made occasional contacts when she really needed something, Christina would be more likely to pay attention.

I'm going ahead and eating. Will you be home in time to visit Moushoom?

She switched her phone over to one of her social networks immediately after sending the text, so that she wouldn't be staring at the texting screen wondering whether Christina was going to text her back and how long it would take if she were. The time would pass much more quickly if she weren't waiting for those little dots to appear on her screen, indicating that Christina might be typing a reply.

The vibration and banner across the top of her phone came just a minute or two later, and Margie tapped the banner to switch back to the text messages.

Sorry got held up will be home soon see moushoom

Margie read the message a couple of times and let out her breath in a slow, controlled stream. Christina was fine. Nothing untoward had happened. And she would be home soon. That was all that Margie could hope for.

She tried not to gobble the meal down, but to go slowly and savor it.

Eating alone didn't mean that she couldn't enjoy herself and what she had prepared. Maybe Christina would be home quickly enough to have a bite or two to eat before they went over to Moushoom's. Or maybe she would eat some after they got back, when she was looking for an evening snack. She might have already eaten somewhere with Tracy.

Margie was just putting the leftovers away when she saw Tracy's car drive up to the curb. Christina did not get out immediately, apparently taking a minute or two to wind up their conversation and say goodbye. Then Christina popped out the door and jogged up the sidewalk. The front door banged open.

"Hi, Mom! Sorry to be so late. I didn't mean to be."

Christina bounced into the kitchen and gave Margie a quick kiss on the cheek.

"Really, I'm sorry."

"No problem. Maybe you could just pop me a text next time. Let me know you're running late and what your plans are."

Christina nodded. "Yeah, I should have. That smells good, how was it?"

"It was good. Plenty left if you want some later."

"I might."

"So how is Tracy? What did you guys do?" Margie was careful not to put too much emphasis on the words. Just a casual conversation. Two people who lived together asking each other about their days.

"He's good. We had a nice time. Went over to his sister's house to help her pack for a move. I didn't know that it would take so long."

"Oh," Margie was a little surprised at this news. She added the tidbits of information to what she knew about Tracy. He had a sister who also lived in Calgary. She would be older than he was if she had a place of her own. Margie knew that Tracy's family had immigrated from China, so she assumed that there was probably only one sibling. "Well, that sounds like a lot of work. Maybe you'd better have something to eat before we go out." She paused in putting the leftovers into the fridge.

"No, it's okay. We had pizza earlier and I'm still full."

"Okay." Margie put the last plastic container into the fridge and closed the door. "All taken care of, then. Are you ready to turn around and go right back out, or did you need to freshen up first?"

"We can go. I'll relax while we're visiting."

Margie nodded. "Do you want to walk over or drive? Are you tired?"

"Umm… maybe drive over in case Moushoom wants to go for a walk when we get there. I don't think I can walk over *and* go for a walk with him *and* walk back."

If Christina had spent a good part of the day packing for a move. Margie was inclined to agree. She grabbed her purse. "Let's go, then. Stella! Go for drive?"

Stella jumped down from the couch where she had been sleeping and ran over to the door. Margie had to laugh at how eager she always was to go out.

Christina got to the door first and gave Stella ear scratches, cuddled her face, and kissed her on the snout. "How is my Stella? How is my doggie? Did you miss me today?"

"I'm sure she did," Margie obliged. "She isn't used to you being gone so long."

"Oh, poor Stella." Christina loved her some more. "She's used to me going to school, though, and that's all day."

"You're usually back before supper. That's different for her."

"I guess." Christina grabbed Stella's leash from the peg beside the door and clipped it onto the D-ring on her collar. "Come on, then, girl. Go for drive!" She opened the door and took Stella out to the car. Margie locked up and followed them.

"Can I drive on the way back?" Christina asked. "I need to get more practice time in."

It was only a two-minute drive. Margie shrugged. "Sure, of course."

They took Stella into Moushoom's building with them. Margie had been hesitant to do that at first, thinking that people would be averse to having a strange dog in the building. There were bound to be rules about dogs, especially larger dogs. But she had found that the opposite was true. Whenever they took Stella in with them, it took three times as long to get to Moushoom's room, because everyone wanted to say hello to Stella and to give her a pet and a kind word. Margie didn't hurry people, thinking of it as sort of a service to them. Not a formal visiting-dog program, but something that brought them joy and should not be rushed. So she just provided them with a wipe or squirt of sanitizer so that Stella did not become a vector to transfer diseases from one resident to another.

Eventually, they reached Moushoom's door. They knocked and went in.

Moushoom was asleep in his wheelchair in front of the TV, and it took a few minutes of gentle prodding before they were able to wake him up.

Moushoom looked at them for a moment, eyes blank, not taking them in. Then all of a sudden, a smile bloomed across his face and he reached for them. "There are my girls!" He gave them both hugs, and Margie brushed his wrinkled cheek with a kiss.

"*Boon swayr*, Moushoom. How are you?"

"I am good. *Maarsii.*"

"Are you tired? We can help you to get into bed?"

"Oh, no." He shook his head briskly at this. "I'm not ready for bed. And I am not so old that I cannot get myself into bed anymore."

"Okay. I just wanted to make sure. We wouldn't want to wear you out."

"I was just napping so that I would be ready when you came. Now I'm bright-eyed and bushy-tailed."

Christina laughed. Moushoom scratched Stella's ears, smiling at her. "She reminds me of a dog I used to have," he reminisced.

Margie and Christina had heard this story many times from him, but neither gave him any sign that it was one they already knew.

"Tell me about your dog," Margie encouraged.

"She was just a stray when I got her. I guess we didn't have the humane society back then, or maybe people just didn't use it. There were a lot more stray animals around. She kept hanging around my back door, and I started feeding her some scraps. She was very skittish, did not like people approaching her. But she got more used to me, always coming back for more scraps, until she would come right up to me and eat out of my hand. And then I started being able to pet her. And eventually… to give her a wash with the garden hose and brush her…"

"What was her name?"

"Queenie." Moushoom's eye were far away. "She was a good dog. She would never come into the house, but we were used to keeping dogs outdoors. It wasn't a big deal back then. Now, I suppose if you had a dog that you kept outside all the time, the bylaw people would come and take her away. But whatever had happened to her before she started showing up at my back door… she would never let herself be tricked or tempted into going inside."

"She was probably abused," Christina said.

Moushoom nodded. "Probably. I don't know who had her before she showed up at my door. But we got on very well, once we were friends."

"Did you want to go for a walk today?"

"Yes. It looks like a beautiful day out there." Moushoom looked toward his window and the bright blue sky.

"There are some clouds coming in. We'll have to come back if it starts to rain."

Moushoom leaned back in his wheelchair, looking serene. "I will not melt in the rain."

Margie chuckled. "No, but you might catch pneumonia. I'm not willing to risk it."

"You don't want to go to hospital during COVID," Christina said wisely. "Especially not with pneumonia."

Margie nodded her agreement. "We want to keep you as far away from infections as possible."

Moushoom threw up his hands in surrender. "You are like two mother hens. How is a man supposed to fight both of you?"

"You're not supposed to fight us," Margie told him, bending down to give him another kiss on the cheek. "You're supposed to do what we say when it is for your own good."

He looked again at the window. "We'd better get outside before it starts raining."

CHAPTER NINE

*M*argie was at her desk looking through some of the surveillance video footage of Elliston Park when Siever texted her. She looked at the message and then looked across the room to where he was sitting at his own desk.

You want to go back to the park?

Margie could have texted back to him for more details, but it seemed a little silly to be texting across the room when she could just go over and talk to him. It wouldn't disrupt anyone else's work. She got up and went over to his desk.

"What's up?"

"Apparently, the RC boat club that Hustler led sometimes meets at Elliston Park on Tuesday mornings. Around ten o'clock."

Margie looked at the time on her phone. It felt like she had just gotten into the office, but she had been there an hour already.

"Sure. I'm up for checking that out. Do you want to drive together?"

"If you want to come back here afterward to pick up your car. If you're going to go somewhere else or go home after, it would make more sense for us to take separate cars."

Margie considered. While it would be nice to just spend a couple of hours at the park and then go home and work from there, she wasn't sure how productive she would be. It was easy to get distracted at home and to start on something else not work-related, when she really needed to focus.

"I think I'd better come back here after and keep looking through those videos."

Siever nodded. "Sure. I'll drive, then. Unless… you want to drive." He looked at her, cheeks getting a bit pink. "I don't mean to dictate that I should drive. If you wanted to."

Maybe it had occurred to him that when a male and female law enforcement officer went out together, it was almost always the man who drove. But there was no reason it should be that way. But she imagined Siever fidgeting in the passenger seat beside her with nothing to do and decided she would prefer his driving.

"No, that's fine. I don't mind."

"Okay." He looked relieved. "If you really don't mind."

"I don't. I won't tell you one thing when I really mean another."

Siever didn't move, very still as he considered her statement. In the end, he shrugged it away. Margie suspected he didn't believe it. He had dealt with too many other people who said one thing when they really felt a different way. He'd learned to accept it as a human behavior and wasn't willing to believe that Margie would be any different.

Siever put the papers on his desk neatly into one file and put the file into the file drawer in his desk.

"Just give me a sec," Margie told him. She went back to her desk to lock her screen and get out her purse and water bottle. She checked that her notepad was in her purse where it was supposed to be, then nodded to Siever. "Okay. Let's go."

It didn't take as long as Margie expected to get from downtown to the park. Really, no longer than it would have taken Margie to get home, and it was much faster late in the morning than it was during rush hour. It made a difference when they didn't have to deal with bumper-to-bumper traffic.

Siever went directly to the parking lot he had used the week before. Margie looked around, assessing everything. Had Hustler been there alone or with someone else? Had someone else gone separately? Or had he gone with someone? Had they met there intentionally or by accident? Or were they wrong in assuming that someone else had been there? Maybe the bruises were from something that happened before he got to Elliston Park. Maybe not even that day. Sure, the medical examiner could guesstimate when the bruising had occurred, but doctors could be wrong. It was still a guess.

Siever stood waiting for her. Margie shrugged. "Just getting a feel for the place. Seeing if I can picture what might have happened."

He nodded.

"Lead the way," Margie invited. It was true that she had gone out that way the previous week, but she wasn't sure how many ways there were in from the parking lot and how easy it would be for her to get lost.

Siever didn't have any trouble finding his way through the trees to the end of the lake where they had watched the firefighters retrieve the body and the boats. Before they even got there, Margie could hear the high, whining buzz of the little boats.

"Looks like you were correctly informed."

Siever nodded. "You must be able to hear them all over the park. So your witness was probably telling the truth. Both about being able to hear Hustler's boat and about it being annoying to those who come out here to walk in peace and quiet early in the morning."

"Yeah, it would be."

They walked in silence the rest of the way to the east end of the lake, where there were now a number of portable tables set up where various club members had their boats displayed or awaiting launch. The club members were not concerned by their approach. They were probably used to all kinds of people asking them questions about what they were doing. It was something new and interesting to many people and would attract attention.

"This looks like fun," Margie offered, raising her voice so that they would all hear her over the noise of the boats that were skimming over the surface of the lake. Despite the fact that they didn't look a lot like regular manned boats, they were very fast and maneuverable, making hairpin turns and avoiding each other when there were more than one out on the water.

A couple of the men who were waiting for their turn to put their boats in the water turned toward them. Margie suspected that they must only allow a certain number of boats on the water at the same time to avoid collisions.

"It is fun," a man in a red ball cap answered, giving Margie a tolerant smile. "Nothing like getting your boat out on the water."

"Are you here often? Is this some kind of club?"

He nodded. "Once or twice a week if I can. We are a loosely formed group. Not a club, exactly. But it's more fun to enjoy the boats together than separately, so we get together when we can."

"Do you have a lot of members?"

"There's a core that is generally the same." The man gestured to himself and the others who were there, some of them listening to the conversation and others ignoring it as they worked their boats out on the water. "And then there are others who come and go. People who are just starting out, experimenting, or new in the city."

"And does Simon Hustler play with your group?"

The members looked around at each other. "Well… yes, he's here sometimes."

"Pretty often," offered a woman with long gray hair. A couple of dogs stood near her, watching everything she did. They were obviously well-trained not to go into the water after the boats. Margie wasn't sure how hard it would have been to train Stella not to go after little boats. It would be doggie heaven for her to have something to chase in the water. "He was an enthusiast."

"I heard that he was the president of this club."

There was a snort from a dark-haired, heavyset man. He looked at Margie and rolled his eyes. "He told you he was the president of the club? I'll just bet he did. No, we don't have a president. We meet together as friends and enthusiasts when it is convenient. There isn't anyone in charge. Not Simon. Not anyone."

"You don't have anyone who… makes the decisions? Recommendations?"

"No. Everyone does their own thing. And if you can meet when everyone else can meet, then you get together and do it. If you can't… then you try to rearrange your schedule for the next time. There's no… special privileges for anyone."

"Aren't there rules?" Siever spoke up.

"Well…" the gray-haired woman conceded this point. "There have to be rules. For races or meets. But they were just established over time. There wasn't any one person who created them and who enforced them for everyone else."

There was a pause as several of them looked at each other. Of course, they were going to have some thoughts that they didn't think were appropriate to share. Were they thinking about Simon and how he'd tried to enforce rules? Or was he a rule breaker? Margie couldn't be sure from all that had been said so far.

"And Simon doesn't try to enforce the rules?" Siever asked. "Or to make any changes to them? To report people when they aren't following them?"

"He might," the heavyset man conceded. "But what I'm saying is… he doesn't have any special privileges or duties over anyone else. We all just take care of ourselves and our own equipment. If you're going to fight and argue with people, no one is going to want to run their boats with you."

"What was Simon like?" Margie asked.

At their sudden looks of surprise and alarm, Margie realized that she'd done it. Siever glared at her. She'd blown any effort that he was making of being quiet and round-about in his questioning. One wrong question, and everyone knew something was up.

Margie opened her mouth to correct herself, then decided there was no point. They weren't going to believe it and, sooner or later, they would find out the truth, so there was no point in trying to lie now.

"I'm sorry. I mean…"

"What *was* he like?" asked a man with a controller, watching the boat that he was guiding out on the lake. "Did something happen to him?"

"I'm afraid so," Margie said. "I'm sorry, I hadn't planned to put my foot in my mouth like that. I don't mean to be insensitive."

"What is it, then? What happened?" the gray-haired woman asked.

"He was killed last Friday."

"Killed? What does that mean? In an accident?"

"We are investigating his death," Siever said. "We don't know yet."

The members of the group were all turning around to look at the two of them. Those who had boats on the water cut their engines and left them floating out on the lake while they turned their attention to the detectives.

"What are you talking about?" the woman asked.

"I'm sorry, we can't give you any details at this time. It is under active investigation."

Margie studied the faces of each of the members of the group. Were they upset or just shocked? Was there anyone who was closer to Hustler than the others? Who had spent the most time with him? Known him for the longest? Were there any reactions that seemed wrong or out of proportion with the rest?

"You're cops?"

"Maybe we could get everyone's names," Siever said. "It will be easier if we know who we are talking to, and then we can contact you when we do know something."

People were not eager to hand out their names and contact details, but they came forward gradually. The more people who introduced themselves, the more the remaining members of the group were under pressure to comply as well. No one walked away or refused to give their names.

The gray-haired woman was Monica Ellis, the dark-haired stocky man was Michael Richards, and the one in the red ball cap was Larry Brown. One of the men with his boat on the water was Terry Hall, and the other was Vernon Nash. Siever diligently wrote down everyone's names, phone numbers, and email addresses. He didn't get addresses, but he would be able to pull up their driver's licenses to figure those out, and they could do background checks on each of them.

"So you can't tell us what happened?" Monica demanded. "It seems like you should be able to tell us something. Obviously, if you are investigating it, Simon didn't just die in his sleep."

"Unless someone poisoned him," Larry pointed out.

"I'm sure no one poisoned him," Monica snapped.

"The police are investigating it; he could have been."

Monica turned to Margie, maybe picking her as the softer target. "Simon *wasn't* poisoned, was he?"

"The medical examiner's findings have not been released yet," Margie fudged. If she told them that he'd died of drowning, then they would know why she and Siever were there at the lake. It wouldn't be too hard to figure that out. "He said that more investigation was necessary."

Margie and Siever both watched everyone's faces for any tells. Terry Hall and Michael Richards were both wearing masks, though Michael pulled his down occasionally to have a drink of water and grab a few breaths of fresh air. The others, maskless, were easier to read. But none of them were giving anything away.

CHAPTER TEN

"When was the last time each of you saw Simon?" Siever asked.
They looked at each other.

"He wasn't here Sunday," Larry answered. The others were giving him dirty looks for being the first to speak up, but he ignored them. "Was he here last Tuesday? He's usually here every time I am… he likes to get his boats out whenever he gets the opportunity."

"He was here Tuesday, a week ago," Vernon agreed. "Same as he is every week."

"Were you surprised not to see him on Sunday, then?" Siever pressed.

"Well, yes. A couple of us said something about it. Wonder what happened to Simon. Maybe he's sick. Just the usual stuff in passing."

"Anyone call him to find out if everything was okay?"

Heads shook. They weren't close enough to be comfortable calling him up, even if they thought that he might be sick. But of course they hadn't had any reason to believe that anything bad had happened to him. Just because a guy didn't make it to one regular boating day, that didn't mean that there was anything wrong. He could have been working, visiting his mother, getting a vaccination. A hundred other things.

"So the last time any of you saw him was last Tuesday?" Margie asked.

They all nodded, some more emphatically than others.

"How did he seem then?"

Looks were exchanged. People thought back, tried to remember clearly.

"No different than usual," Larry said. "Simon was Simon."

"Yeah. Just the same," Monica agreed.

"He wasn't upset about anything?"

"Well… Simon was usually upset about something. He liked to complain and make a big drama over little things," Larry contributed, picking his words carefully.

"Larry!" Monica reprimanded.

"Well, it's true. Are you going to deny that it's the truth?"

"No… I just don't think… you need to make it sound like he's a bad person. He complained, but a lot of people do. Something bothers you, you go rant to your friends about it for a while, and then you feel better. That's the way society is these days. Did he argue any more than the average person…?" Monica opened her mouth to answer her own question "No," then stopped, looking stricken.

"Yes," several of the others answered together.

They all looked at each other. Monica was still trying to bring herself to say no, he was just like anyone else, but she couldn't seem to manage it, knowing that it was a lie.

"Well… maybe," she admitted. "A little."

"A lot," Larry corrected. "He always had something stuck in his craw. You know it's true."

"But that doesn't mean that he was dramatizing. Some people just have… a more negative outlook at life. Maybe he had a difficult childhood."

"I'm sure his mother thought he had a difficult childhood," Terry said dryly.

"You guys! I don't know how you can joke about this, or not think about the fact that Simon is dead! He's dead, and you're joking about him or saying things about him that are… exaggerations."

"Was there something in particular that he was upset about on Tuesday?" Margie interposed.

"That's a long time ago now," Larry said, shaking his head. "I'm lucky if I can remember what I did before breakfast. Last Tuesday…?" He looked at the others, hoping one of them would remember.

"This and that," Monica said, shaking her head. "I can't think of anything in particular. He was looking for a part that the hobby craft store didn't have and wouldn't order in. He said something about his mother. I forget what, that he had to go see her to help her with the garden, or something. I think. Anything else?"

"Work?"

"Maybe."

Simon had been an accountant, according to the background they had gathered on him. Margie was sure that an accountant would always have something to complain about at work. Clients who didn't know what they were talking about. The other accountants in the firm. A messed up financial statement. A missed delivery. A CRA audit. There was plenty that could go wrong in accounting.

"Was he here most of the days that your club meets?" Margie asked.

"Sure. He was almost always here. If he missed, it usually meant that he was sick. He didn't skip out because he had something else going on."

Margie nodded. "And what about days that you guys aren't here? Did he come on his own too?"

Monica and the others looked at each other. "I guess so," Larry said. "Most of us only get here on either Tuesday or Sunday, not both, but I know Simon sometimes mentioned being here other days too, in case anyone wanted to join him."

"And did anyone ever take him up on it?"

There was a definite hesitation, the group not wanting to answer the question.

"Not anyone who knew him well," Michael said finally. "A newbie might, someone who wants to get some more time in or thinks it would be a good time to pick a pro's brain about some of the ins and outs of the craft…"

"But those of you who knew him well, you wouldn't come here to boat with him?"

They shrugged or shook their heads. "Simon was quirky," Monica tried.

"Simon was a pain," Michael countered. "I know he probably couldn't help it, but the guy drove me up the wall. His voice, his negativity, his… social skills, I guess? Always wanted to talk about himself, made inappropriate comments, would change the subject and try to take over the conversation if he wasn't interested in what someone else was talking about. He was just awkward, I guess. Not someone I enjoyed being around. I put up with him in order to meet with the others and have a chance to try out my boats or have a race, but come here with him on another day? No, not me."

Margie looked around and the others in the group. "Was that the general consensus?"

They looked up or down or out at the lake at the boats bobbing on the surface.

"He was awkward," Larry agreed.

Margie made some notes in her notebook, but she didn't see how any of it could relate back to Hustler's death.

CHAPTER ELEVEN

argie was frustrated by the lack of progress on the case. Some cases took months or years to close, of course, but the Hustler case had seemed so open and shut that she was irritated that they hadn't yet been able to establish the manner of death and to move it forward.

She and the others spread out a representative sample of the photos of the body on the conference room table and printed off the medical examiner's preliminary report and emails regarding what they knew about the bruises so far. They ordered sandwiches for lunch and all walked around the table looking at the pictures and rereading the description of the object or objects that had caused the bruises.

Margie worried that it was a wild goose chase. What if Hustler had sustained the bruises earlier in the day from something that was totally unrelated to his death? None of them could identify anything that had been out in the water that might have cause the bruises. Would they have to drain the lake or send in divers to see if there was something under the surface that was dangerous? People sometimes disposed of old cars or other junk in lakes like that. Margie couldn't understand why they would since there were plenty of auto junkyards and the dump right beside the park.

But there could be something under the surface that he had run into while trying to save his dropped phone. It was really the only logical assumption.

"They're all on his upper body," Cruz observed, "nothing below the shoulder blades or chest."

"Do you think that he could have dived down and gotten caught in something?" Margie suggested. "He had to fight his way out…?"

No one seemed to think this was a possibility.

"Blunt object, sharp edges," Jones mused. She examined a couple of pictures, holding them close to her eyes and turning them around to see them from all angles. Margie wasn't sure how that was going to help. The bruises were not giving much away.

On TV, there were always distinctive chain patterns, an emblem, or some other shape that could be matched directly with one unique item. But in real life, bruises were usually indistinct, and a person had to be able to connect the dots and be creative in trying to think of what object or activity had caused the injuries.

"And a lot of force," Siever pointed out. "This wasn't something that he just bumped into. He was hit with a fair amount of force."

"But we don't know exactly how long it was before his death," Margie said. "I don't think there's an exact science to how well the bruises would be developed by the time he died."

"They were new bruises. Not purple or yellow. Still fresh," Cruz said. He looked at the array of pictures. Shades of red. Blood collecting under the skin. Nothing, as he said, that could be days old.

"But minutes or hours?" Margie asked. "What if he'd had a fight with someone earlier in the day?"

"Earlier than six o'clock?" Jones asked. "Who would he have fought with before six o'clock in the morning? He didn't live with anyone, right?"

"No. No family or roommates."

"Then it wasn't likely a fight with anyone. And those aren't from a car accident. Whatever happened to him must have happened in the park," Jones asserted.

"Well, the only things in the water were the raft and his RC boat."

"You got pictures of the RC boat?"

Margie went to the laptop on the boardroom table and browsed through the pictures in the workspace for the Hustler file, eventually bringing a couple of pictures of Hustler's RC boat up on the screen.

"Here it is."

Everyone grouped around the laptop to look at the pictures.

"Well," Cruz ventured, "It could be from the boat, don't you think? That would explain why everything is shoulders and above. He's in the water, the boat is floating on top of the water; it would hit his head and shoulders."

Margie looked at the picture and shook her head. "It makes sense, but it doesn't. Why did he go out on the lake? Because something was wrong with his boat, and he had to retrieve it. So it was disabled, it wasn't going anywhere."

"How fast did you say those things could go?" Siever asked.

"The woman I talked to said two hundred and fifty kilometers per hour. We could talk to one of the other guys in the boat club to verify that or look it up online."

"It's good enough for an estimate. Something that can move like that over the water, it could cause some pretty good bruising."

"Bruising?" Jones asked. "It could take your face off. It obviously wasn't going that fast."

"But his boat wasn't operational. He wouldn't go after it in the raft if it was working."

"Maybe something else was wrong with it," Cruz suggested. "Maybe the controller wasn't working properly. Or the brakes. Maybe he couldn't get it to stop, and he didn't want to run it aground."

The shoreline had been very rocky. Trying to run the boat aground at a high speed would have destroyed it.

"But even then, he wouldn't have been in the water with it. He would be in the boat."

"He reached out to grab it and overbalanced, just like we thought in the first place," Siever suggested.

It could fit. Almost. But Margie still couldn't play it out in her head. Hustler ended up in the water, and the boat kept hitting him? Multiple times from different sides? How could that have happened? He was using the controller to drive it toward himself, but couldn't catch it and just kept smashing it into himself? He wanted to drown? The RC boat developed sentience and decided to kill its creator?

"What?" Cruz asked, studying Margie's face.

"There's only one solution that fits," she said finally.

"Which is?"

"Someone else was there with another boat."

CHAPTER TWELVE

They all looked at her and thought it through.

Margie played it through in her head. It was the only scenario that made sense. He wasn't there by himself. He wasn't controlling the RC boat and it wasn't trying to kill him by itself. Someone else was there with another boat, and *that* was the boat that had hit him multiple times.

Hit him over and over again until he could no longer fight back or escape it, out there on the water, far from the shore.

"And… it was intentional," Margie said. "It wasn't an accident."

"It would fit," Siever admitted.

"Yeah."

"The people in his club seemed pretty nice. I didn't get the sense that any of them had anything against him. Not anything serious. Just that he was annoying."

"Then I guess we'd better dig deeper and see if we can figure out who *wasn't* so nice."

❧

SIEVER TALKED to the medical examiner on the phone and described the RC boats and their theory in as much detail as possible. The pathologist agreed that it was a possibility. The bruises could very well have been

157

sustained from an RC boat while Hustler was in the water. It wouldn't have needed to get up to top speeds to have caused the bruising they had seen. And it would have been very painful. It would easily be enough to make someone panic and drown, even if they were an experienced swimmer.

While Siever was talking to the medical examiner's office, Margie started running the names of the members of Hustler's RC boat group through the computer to see what she could find on them. She saved each report to a folder with the person's name. Driver's licenses to start with, which established their addresses. Any criminal charges against them. Credit checks. Complaints made by them against someone else. General background, including their social media accounts.

Everybody seemed pretty clean. Larry had a couple of drunk and disorderlies, but Margie figured that probably spoke *against* his being in the park at six o'clock in the morning.

There were others who were part of the group too, though. People who might have attended other meetups and just hadn't happened to be there when Siever and Margie showed up to talk to them. They could get the names of some of the other members of the club. Maybe there was someone with a grudge against Hustler who had judged it better not to show up at the club's next few gatherings. Or someone who happened to have work on a Tuesday morning and couldn't adjust his schedule to give him the time to attend.

Some of the participants had been carrying quite a bit of equipment. It had to take time to get everything together and set up, play for a while, and then take everything back down and pack it away. And maybe then to take it home and put it in the garage until the next time. It would take a half day. Hustler could apparently take off a morning each week, but not everyone could. There would probably be more people there for the Sunday meets.

And it was customary to give employees in Calgary parade day morning off.

🐚

"Anything promising?" Siever asked, hovering over Margie's shoulder.

"Well... nothing that really points one direction or the other. I've started to get a clearer picture of the group, but I wouldn't put my money on anyone at this point. There might be other members of the group that we don't know about yet. We can start by re-interviewing some of the people we talked to this morning and ask each of them for the names of other people who are regular members of the group."

"It's too bad there's no members roster. At least an email list that they give out for people who want to be notified of the next meet-up."

"That would be helpful," Margie agreed. She sighed, leaning back from the computer screen into her chair. "Do you have anyone in mind who you would like to interview first?"

Siever shook his head slowly. "I'm not great with people. I would just pick someone at random."

"Then I'm going to say Monica first. I think she might have said more if she had been alone."

CHAPTER THIRTEEN

"Thanks for having us here to talk to you," Margie told Monica. She looked around at the inside of the house. It was neat and tidy. Not quite a "little old lady" house. Way too many RC and model boats around for that. Margie could see that the dining room table was not set with dishes for company, but held a case, with tiny individual drawers containing different parts for building or repairing the boats, and a roll-up tool case.

The nautical theme extended to paintings on the walls and the white-on-white wainscoting around the living room. Monica appeared to be just a *little* obsessed with boats. Margie hoped that she had grandchildren to share her passion with. What little boy wouldn't love a grandma who built and played with boats?

"I don't think there's anything that I can tell you that we didn't already cover this morning," Monica said. "So I'm hoping that this won't take too long."

"Our investigation has been proceeding, and new facts have come to light. With each new fact, there are new directions for us to investigate, new questions for us to ask," Margie explained.

"You can take those masks off. I find it really hard to understand what people are saying with them on. They aren't required anymore, and I, for one, never saw the need for them."

They were far enough away from Monica that there really wasn't much of a chance of infection unless she started singing or screaming, and she didn't look likely to do either. The CPS rules were flexible enough that they could use their own judgment and take off their masks despite strong recommendations to continue using them.

Margie looked over at Siever, saw that he agreed that it would be appropriate since she had trouble understanding them otherwise. They both removed their black masks. Margie smiled at Monica. "How's that?"

"So much better. I never realized how bad my hearing is until people started wearing the darn things. Between people's words being muffled and me not being able to see their lips, it makes it really difficult to communicate sometimes."

Margie gave a nod. "Anyway, as I was saying, new facts have come to light…"

"What new facts?"

"I can't give you that information. But if you could answer my questions, we would really appreciate it."

Monica leaned back in her seat, giving a shrug that indicated *ask away*.

"I gathered from our discussion this morning that there wasn't anyone who was particularly close to Simon?"

"No… not that close. I mean, we all talked to each other and boated together, but… we weren't particular friends with each other. Sometimes someone brought a little Christmas cheer or we marked an important holiday, but it was just… a meetup. A couple of times a week, we got together and played with our boats."

"Was there anyone who was antagonistic toward him?"

"No."

"The men that we talked with this morning didn't seem to have much of a connection with him. Were there any… ongoing feuds or arguments? Even just a feeling of not being able to click together?"

With her finger, Monica traced the piping in the arm of the couch she was sitting in, frowning slightly.

"I don't think so. Not really. You know how men are, they enjoy being competitive. Badmouthing your friend isn't really badmouthing them. It's just something you do to show that you like them."

"So you think they were just teasing each other? Being macho?"

Monica nodded. Her eyes slid to Siever, analyzing what he thought of this suggestion. Siever didn't look like the macho type, but you couldn't always tell by looking at a person. Someone might have to wear a suit to work but still be a redneck with his buddies.

"What kind of things did they say about him? What things did they compete in?" Margie asked.

"I don't know. Just being sarcastic, saying silly insults to 'burn' each other. And as far as competing… we were all competing with each other all the time. Not just Simon. We try to build our boats to be lighter, faster, and more maneuverable. We tweak them with different ignition systems, replacing this valve with that, trying a new fiberglass shell. Getting a new boat with all of the latest advancements… electrics, computer controls, AI. You wouldn't believe the number of options. It's what keeps us going back year after year, tweaking, and buying new stuff and testing it out. Just like a kid with a new toy. There's always something shiny to grab our attention and then we aren't happy until we have that too. I have a garage full of old boats. And some of them were barely even used before I jumped onto the next thing. I've got old wooden boats with gasoline engines. Fiberglass with nitro. Electrics of all sorts." She shrugged. "It's more than just a hobby for me. Some of the guys have families, work, school, wives, and all kinds of other commitments and the only time they can take for themselves is Sunday morning. I don't have a lot of other things to occupy my time."

"You sound like you've got a really good collection," Siever said. "I don't suppose we could see them…?"

Margie hadn't heard him say anything about enjoying boats during the investigation, so she glanced over at him, trying to analyze his angle. She decided that he just wanted to have a chance to see if any of her boats could have inflicted the damage that they had seen on Simon Hustler's body. Chances were, most of the boats would have been capable of such damage. And if she'd gotten Simon's blood on the boat, chances were that she would have washed it well afterward. Probably with bleach.

"Yes, maybe," Monica agreed. She looked a jeweled watch on her wrist. "We'll see how the time goes."

"You're sure that there wasn't anyone who had a particular grudge against Simon?" Siever asked. "No one who you thought… was going overboard on the insults. Or who seemed to mean them more. Or just that you thought… things were off between them, more than normal."

"Simon wasn't an easy guy to get along with."

Margie nodded understandingly. "Maybe there were a few people who would rather not be around him or to have to hold a conversation with him."

"I really couldn't say. I always thought that... he tried to get along. He had goals that would require him to get along with people. But he just... didn't have the right personality to make friends"

"But there was no animosity?"

Monica stared off into space. She wasn't denying it, and Margie thought it best to wait and see what came out if Monica were left in silence for a while.

"I thought..." She was still hesitant. Margie and Siever gave her time, both sitting still and waiting for her to get it out. As much as Margie wanted to jump in and offer suggestions, she knew that it wasn't the right time. Monica had to come up with it on her own. They didn't want to be accused of implanting memories or suggesting what testimony they wanted her to give. "I thought that Terry Hall was kind of... He really didn't want Simon around. Avoided him rather obviously... said things sometimes that were... more than teasing. Kind of cruel."

"Oh? Like what?"

"I don't know if I can think of anything specific right now... I tried to ignore that kind of thing and just go on with my own stuff. There's no point in worrying about anyone else's issues. We have enough to do dealing with our own."

"There wasn't anything particular that you thought Terry had against him?" Siever asked.

"No. I don't know. I thought maybe that they'd had an argument, something outside of the meetup. But no one ever said what it was."

"Did the others notice this tension as well?"

"I don't know what anyone else noticed. We didn't talk about it. 'Oh, what's going on between Terry and Simon?' No, nothing like that."

Margie thought that Monica was done, but as she prepared herself to ask another question, Monica said as sort of an afterthought, "Terry *did* damage one of Simon's boats once."

"He did?" Siever asked. "I don't imagine that was looked on too kindly by the others."

"No. Like I said, we were competitive, but damaging someone else's boats, that's going beyond. We don't do that. We're always very careful, we have rules about how many boats can be in the water at a time, and about taking turns and such. And of course no one ever touches anyone else's boat without permission. You wouldn't just walk up to someone's table and pick up their boat or take it out of the water. Nothing like that."

"What did Terry do to damage Simon's boat?"

"They were both in the water at the same time. I'm not sure what Simon did to get Terry's goat, but it seemed like Terry was really upset about something. He had his kids there that day, and maybe Simon had said something that he shouldn't have in front of them. I don't know. He was the kind of guy that would do that, and then look at you and ask what your problem was, because he really was clueless."

Margie and Siever nodded, encouraging Monica to go on and explain what had happened. "They both had crafts out on the water, and Terry was in a bad mood. He knocked Simon's boat off course and made it run into one of the rocks on the shore. Damaged one ski pretty badly. Simon freaked out, said that it had been on purpose... we all told him that it was just an accident, but I think we all knew that it wasn't."

"Did Terry apologize? Give an explanation?"

"No. Didn't say sorry or that it was an accident. Just said that Simon had better keep his boats to himself and watch where they were going?" Monica's voice rose at the end of the statement, turning it into a question. "That's paraphrasing, I can't remember his exact words. It was sort of strange, anyway."

"And you weren't aware of any incident leading up to this? Simon having bumped one of Terry's boats or cut it off? Nothing that you think would have explained Terry's words?"

"No. Nothing that I knew about. But something could have happened the week before that I didn't remember. Or something might have even happened there that morning, and I just hadn't noticed it. I do tend to get pretty wrapped up in my own boats."

"Sure," Siever nodded. "We all do that sometimes."

He waited for a few seconds, letting the silence grow. Monica looked uncomfortable but didn't seem to have anything else to offer. She looked at her watch. "I really should be getting back to things now. I've done my best to answer your questions, but I'm still not sure where they're supposed to be going. Whatever happened to Simon, I'm sure it couldn't have had anything to do with our boat club. It wasn't even one of our days."

"Maybe we could see your boats before we leave?" Siever asked, voice slightly wheedling. Margie was surprised. She'd never heard that tone from him before. Was he really interested in the boats? As someone who was into technology, he too might be attracted by shiny objects and want to try his own hand at the RC boats game.

"I don't think so," Monica said stiffly. "This has really taken enough of my time. I didn't expect to be taken away from my work for so long."

She had told them that she didn't have much else to do, so Margie couldn't feel too bad about the amount of time they had taken. Monica was just trying to express her displeasure at having to talk to them again when she didn't know what it was all about.

Siever and Margie stood to go. Siever gave Monica a grave nod. "Thank you for your time, ma'am. We do appreciate it."

Her cheeks turned slightly pink, and she escorted them to the door.

CHAPTER FOURTEEN

They were not able to schedule an interview with Terry until Wednesday. Margie felt like they were right on the edge of figuring out what had happened to Hustler but tried not to let it affect her. If they could discover the truth from Terry Hall, that was great. But he might not know anything. He might have some petty reason for holding a grudge against Hustler and yet never have mentioned it to anyone else.

There was no guarantee that their discussion with Terry Hall would lead them any closer to Hustler's killer.

While they usually like to invite people in to the homicide department meeting rooms for interviews, that wasn't always possible. Sometimes people didn't want to come in. It was inconvenient. Parking was terrible. They didn't want to deal with traffic. Or maybe they didn't even have a running vehicle and it was a pain to get there on the bus or on foot. Terry said that he could not spare enough time to make it all the way downtown, and if they wanted to talk to him, they could come to his house. So they did.

Terry lived in Applewood, a neighborhood adjacent to Elliston Park. Nice and handy if he ever wanted to pop over there and play with his boats for a while. Margie and Siever were greeted at the door by Mrs. Hall, a short Filipino woman who smiled and nodded a lot and probably missed half of what they were saying. Margie was sorry they hadn't known ahead of time that she was Filipino. They could have brought Cruz with them. Or Cruz could have gone in Margie's place, as the three of them ganging up on the family would probably be too much.

Instead, they smiled and nodded and tried to speak slowly so that she would be able to understand them.

Margie wondered how she liked her husband's boat hobby. Did she think it was silly? A good thing to relax and de-stress? Something that took too much of his time and attention? Margie saw a couple of giggling children run across a hallway behind her. They were perhaps four or five and cute as buttons. A boy and a girl.

Mrs. Hall had them sit down and bustled into the kitchen to fix a beverage or snack; Margie wasn't sure which. In a few minutes, Terry Hall joined them in the living room.

"I hope this doesn't take too long," he said. "It's my daughter's birthday today, we have a special evening planned."

"Oh, is it? Well, happy birthday to her. How old is she?"

"Four. We're going to go out for supper, and then go to the park for a while, let them burn off some steam. Have some cake. A few of our friends are going to join us there."

Margie had a feeling that "a few of" their friends probably had the same meaning in the Filipino community as it did in Margie's family. Somewhere under three hundred people. She smiled.

"How nice. I'm sure she'll love that. We'll try to wrap things up here pretty quickly."

"I don't know what happened to Simon. I thought I made that clear. I don't know anything that happened and I can't think that anything I could tell you would be helpful." He shrugged. "You're wasting your time."

"If we could just go over things again. Sometimes being in a quiet setting, where you are not distracted by the boats and everything else that's going on, makes a difference. I'm sure it won't take long."

Terry shrugged and folded his arms, a closed-off gesture that told her he wasn't going to be trying too hard to help her out.

Mrs. Hall returned carrying a tea tray. She said something aside to her husband, then encouraged everyone to take some tea and the other treats that she had prepared for them. Or had pulled out of the freezer so that it would look like she was prepared for company when she was not. She spoke to them mostly in Filipino, pointing to the tea and cookies and asking her husband in English if there was anything else that he wanted her to do.

"It's fine, honey," Terry assured her. "They're just here to talk to me. Not to have dinner."

She nodded a few times and eventually retreated, leaving them alone to discuss the case once more.

"When was the last time that you saw Simon?" Siever asked.

"Tuesday before last. I think. The days run together sometimes. It's hard to remember what happened at one meeting and what happened at another."

"No problem." Margie smiled. "Just do your best to answer the questions, and we'll try not to take up any more of your time."

He nodded.

"Had you ever gone to the park with Simon? Just with the two of you, I mean?"

"No. Why would I? The guy bothered me when we were together with a group. I wouldn't want to spend *extra* time with him."

"What was it that bothered you about him?"

"Just a personality conflict. He rubbed me the wrong way." Terry's face was a mask; expressionless. "That kind of thing happens. Just because we were both interested in RC boats... that doesn't mean we were best buds."

"I heard that there was some kind of problem with the boats. You hit Simon's boat with yours?"

"I think they just got too close together and he panicked. I don't think that they actually collided."

"How did that happen?"

"He didn't stay to his side of the course. If he had, I wouldn't have spooked him."

"So it was his own fault. And his boat was damaged?"

"The boats are made of lightweight materials. They don't fare well when they collide with rocks."

"I don't imagine so," Siever agreed dryly.

Terry smiled at the irony in his voice. He appreciated having someone there to share his wry sense of humor.

"But Simon blamed you for the damage done to his boat?"

"Yes. He did."

"Did you apologize? Agree to help him out with the cost?"

"No. Like I say, it was his own fault."

The two children came thundering down the stairs, then stopped where they were and hid behind the banister post, peering around at the two police detectives.

"They can still see you over there," Terry told the children. "You guys need to leave me alone for a few minutes, and then I'll get ready to go."

"Cute kids," Margie said, smiling at the children. This made them giggle and duck down to hide again.

Terry gave her a wary look. "Thank you."

"Do they like racing boats?"

"Yeah, what kid wouldn't? They don't usually come with me, but sometimes as a treat or to give my wife a break, I bring them along."

Margie smiled at the children again. But Terry didn't invite them to come closer and she didn't want to disrupt the interview or irritate him, so she turned her attention back to him, resolved to ignore the children's giggles. They would get bored and go play until Terry was finished and ready to take them out to eat.

As she turned back to Terry, she noticed his eyes on Siever, watching him with a frown. Siever had been looking at the children but, like Margie, apparently decided that the best course of action was not to engage with them, and his attention turned back to Terry.

Sometimes it was helpful to admire or talk to the interviewee's children. With mothers especially. They became more engaged and liked to show off their offspring. But Terry was clearly not one of those people. He had already told the children to go and did not talk to Margie and Siever about them without encouragement. When Siever turned his attention away from the children and back to Terry, Terry's shoulders dipped down and the tightness in his face softened.

"How long ago was this accident with Simon's boat?" Siever asked. "It sounds like it was recent, but I might be making a wrong assumption."

"It was a few weeks ago. Not long."

"And was Simon still upset about it?"

"We weren't speaking to each other. Which was fine with me. I assume that means that he was still upset about it."

"How did Simon feel about the children?" Margie asked. "Did he enjoy having them around? Was he irritated or distracted by having them around when they came?"

Terry's face immediately contorted into a scowl. It was something that he felt so strongly about that he was not able to control his expression for a

169

second or two. The change in expression was not subtle. Terry ground his teeth and didn't answer at first.

"Simon seemed quite comfortable around children," he said through gritted teeth.

Margie tried to reconcile the words to Terry's reaction. Most people would be happy that other people didn't mind kids around. It would be a problem if the opposite were true and Simon Hustler hadn't liked having kids there when they were playing with the boats. Margie could understand a bachelor being irritated by kids getting underfoot, asking a lot of questions, and squealing at the boats racing around the lake.

"Why does that upset you?" she asked finally, unable to find a more tactful way to approach it.

"I didn't like him around my kids."

"Oh. Why is that? Was he mean toward them? Too loud?"

Terry shook his head. "No. He was… too close to them."

CHAPTER FIFTEEN

*M*argie studied Terry's expression and then looked at Siever. *Too close.*

"Did he behave inappropriately toward them?"

"Depends what you call inappropriate, I guess. I kept a close eye on him, made sure he couldn't do something behind my back. But he... he'd get down on their level, close to them, hug them close to show them something. Patting their heads or shoulders. Sometimes he would bring them treats or toys. Something from the hobby craft store."

That all sounded pretty innocent to Margie. Things that anyone engaging with a child might do. But what sounded innocent and what looked innocent to Terry could be two totally different things.

"And that made you uncomfortable."

"You know what they say about grooming children. About the molester making friends with the parents and the kids, giving the kids presents, building a special relationship with them. Seeing how close they can get to desensitize the parents."

Margie nodded slowly. "Yes... you're right about that."

"That's what he was like. Showing them more attention than anyone else. Doing things to get them to like him. Touching them too much. Buying them things. I didn't like it, and I told him to stay away from them."

Margie met Siever's eyes. This was a new direction. One that they hadn't foreseen.

"You need to go with your gut," she acknowledged. "A parent can't afford to take chances."

"Did he listen to you when you warned him off?" Siever asked.

"No. He didn't."

"The man with the boats?" the little boy piped up, still watching them from behind the banister. "We like the man with the boats like Daddy's."

However much Margie wanted to start asking the boy questions directly, she had to school herself not to. Terry had already demonstrated that he was protective of them and, if she showed them what he thought was too much attention or he thought that she was scaring them or putting words into their mouths, he would not like it. Their interview with him would be over.

She could already see him shutting down at the little boy's words. Closing everything off.

Siever followed Margie's lead and did not ask the boy anything directly.

"How did that make you feel?" Margie asked. At Terry's look, she clarified. "When you told him to stay away from your kids and he didn't?"

"How do you think it made me feel? The guy should know better than to mess with someone else's kids. If I tell someone to stay away from them, I expect them to do it. I could call the police, tell them that he was causing trouble. I could get a restraining order."

Margie wasn't so sure that he could get anything on the basis of not feeling comfortable with Simon being friendly with his kids. There wasn't much the police would be able to do other than to advise Simon that he needed to listen to the children's parent and stay away from the kids. And to advise Terry to stop bringing the kids to the park for the meetups.

Take the kids to the lake on days when the rest of the group wasn't there.

Margie made a few notes in her notebook, more to avoid looking at Siever or Terry than because she was afraid she might forget anything. She documented the meeting with Terry and wrote down her thoughts about Simon and the children.

"Was there anything else?" Margie asked eventually. "Any other disagreements with Simon? Problems with his behavior?"

Terry shook his head, his mouth an angry straight line.

"How about the others? Are you aware of any disagreements between any of the others in the group and Simon?"

"You would have to ask them. I don't know anything about any of them."

"You don't think that anyone had a grudge against him?"

It gave Terry the opportunity to point the finger away from himself and focus the police department's attention on someone other than him. But he didn't take her up on the opportunity. He just shook his head.

"Nothing I know about. You would have to ask them."

⁊❧

MARGIE WAS sure when they got back to the car that she and Siever were both thinking the same thing. She pulled her seatbelt across her body to buckle herself in and looked at him.

"He thought Hustler was a pedophile," Siever said.

"Yeah. That certainly puts Terry at the top of my suspect list. If I thought that a predator was hanging around my daughter…" Margie's heart started to race and she felt a warm flush over her skin just at the thought of it. "I wouldn't wait until he hurt her."

"He told Hustler to stay away from his kids, and he didn't. He kept behaving inappropriately…" Siever hesitated. "If what Hustler did was inappropriate…?"

"Even if he didn't mean any harm, he should have backed way off when Terry told him that there was a problem."

"Yes," Siever agreed. "Once he knew there was a problem, he should have backed off. Stopped talking with the kids or bringing them presents. Just ignored them when they were at one of the meetups."

Margie flipped through her notepad, thinking. "His mother told us about him trying to become a mentor. An uncle or big brother through one of those programs."

Siever nodded, remembering. "But they kept switching kids on him. And then they ghosted him."

"I think we should find out what they knew."

⁊❧

IN ORDER TO join the mentorship program, Hustler had been required to go through a police check. That police check was clean; he didn't have any accusations or charges against him. The results had been sent directly to the organization, so they knew which one Hustler had applied to.

Siever managed to get an appointment with Amanda Sorken, the director of the program, within a few hours.

Sorken was a tall, dark-haired woman. She offered to shake hands with each of them, and Siever and Margie both shook, though they preferred not to have physical contact with more people than they had to. They were all seated in Sorken's small office. There were stacks of paper everywhere, on the desk, the shelves, and even a few piles on the floor.

"We are required to keep things confidential," Sorken started delicately. "For the sakes of both our children and our mentors. We need to be very careful of anything we say."

"Simon Hustler, the man that we are inquiring about, is dead. So you don't have any requirement to keep anything regarding him confidential. You can keep the names of the children involved confidential for now. I can't promise that records won't be subpoenaed later but, for now, we don't need any names."

She didn't look quite comfortable with this declaration. She sat stiffly, waiting for their questions.

"From what we understand," Siever said, "Hustler was assigned several different children to mentor, but each one lasted only a few meetings. They would meet together once or twice, and then he would get changed to another child."

Sorken nodded. "Yes, that's a fair summary."

"Were there accusations against him of inappropriate behavior?"

She shook her head. "There were not."

Margie let out a breath. That, at least, was a relief.

"Were there any red flags in his behavior that led you to believe that he might not be an appropriate person to mentor these children?"

Sorken had to think about that one. She waffled, shaking her head and making several false starts before she was able to get going. "Not in the way you are thinking, no."

"What am I thinking?"

"There wasn't anything that made me or anyone else think that he might be abusive in any way. But as far as being the appropriate person to be a mentor... that's a different question. A mentor should be someone that the children look up to. A good example of what they can achieve. Something that they can reach for."

Margie nodded. She thought about what she knew about Hustler. A bachelor with a very negative world view and an obsession with RC boats. He had things going for him—he was an accountant, so he had succeeded in his schooling and post-secondary training and was at least competent at what he did. His mother had said that he was very bright, that she had fought to have him moved ahead in school because he was bored. He was diligent, getting to all of the RC boat get-togethers. And he had shown interest both in mentoring children and in the children of his fellow enthusiasts. All positive traits.

"He just wasn't a very good fit for this kind of work," Sorken said. "He had... a certain social awkwardness. Saying the wrong thing or saying it in the wrong way. Blunt. Critical."

"The children didn't like him," Siever suggested.

"No. They didn't. He was 'creepy.' He leaned too close. He breathed on them. He 'told it like it is' when they needed tact and understanding. We tried to find a child that he could get along with. Someone with similar interests or a compatible personality. But we did not have good success. We were still trying to find someone... told him to wait and we would see what we could find... but eventually, we knew there wasn't going to be anyone. He just didn't have a way with children."

"Did you give him any advice about it?" Margie asked. "Give him some tips on improving his relationship with the children? How to get along without creeping them out?"

"We really don't have time for any kind of intensive training. We expect people to have a basic understanding of how to get along with others."

"So you didn't give him any information at all about what the problem was or how to deal with it?"

Sorken looked at her for a moment, then shook her head. "No. We did the best we could with what we had, but we were not prepared to train him or impose him on any more children."

Siever was making a few notes in his notepad. "Did anyone else ever inquire about him? Make a complaint about him?"

"No." Sorken shook her head. Then she stopped and thought for a moment. She shook her head. "There... might have been one. Someone who wanted to know if he was still registered with us... I'm afraid I don't remember the details. We don't give out any information on individuals, so the answer was no, we don't give out that information."

"And that inquiry didn't come from another organization that was vetting him. It was from an individual?"

"Yes, I think so. I'm sorry to be so vague. We get a lot of calls through here, and if I don't write them down, I don't remember."

"And you wouldn't have written that one down?"

"No. I would write down a call that someone needed to follow up on. No one needed to follow up on this one, because we couldn't give him the information he wanted."

"Male?"

"Um... maybe. That's what sticks in my mind, but I don't know. I might have everything backward."

"How long ago was this?" At Sorken's bewildered look, Siever clarified. "Days, weeks, months...?"

"Days. I don't think it was much more than a week. Maybe. Maybe two weeks at the outside. But not long."

Siever looked at Margie. Two weeks. Just a short time before Hustler had been killed.

They finished up with the interview, then sat in the car in silence for a few minutes.

"So is this what we're thinking?" Margie asked. "Terry Hall thinks that Simon Hustler is a pedophile, trying to groom his kids and mentoring teens in his spare time. He knew that Simon was going to be at the park with his boats. He either said that he would join him, or just 'accidentally' met him there. Then what? How do we get from A to B? Or D, or however many steps it takes. They're both at the park..."

Siever closed his eyes, thinking about it. "Terry Hall rams Hustler's boat. Disables it."

"The only way for Hustler to get his boat back, even just to see what damage there is, is to take the raft out on the lake to go retrieve it."

Siever nodded. "Right. So he does. Maybe he thinks that Terry has left, or maybe he just isn't worried about Terry still being there. What's he going to do? He doesn't know that Terry has it in for him."

Margie nodded. "So he goes out on the raft. Which Terry knew he was going to do, so others must have seen him use the raft before."

A fact that they could verify. Others in the group would know that Simon had a raft he would use if his boat couldn't make it back to shore on its own.

"And then... what? He reaches for it and falls in?" Siever suggested.

"No, Terry uses his boat again at that point. Bumps the raft or knocks the boat farther away. Something that makes Simon overbalance and end up in the water."

"Could he bump the raft hard enough?"

"If those things can go two hundred and fifty kilometers an hour? I should think so. Maybe he could even puncture the raft. Maybe he thought that it would. Deflate the raft, Simon goes down with it, end of story."

Siever grunted his agreement with this.

"So then Simon Hustler is in the water." Margie said.

"If it was just a prank or a warning, then he could have left it there," Siever pointed out. "He could give Simon a scare, tell him to straighten up and fly right—or whatever the appropriate nautical metaphor would be—or something worse would happen to him."

"But he didn't leave it at that." Margie rubbed the palms of her hands on her jeans, frowning. "Is it as hard for you to believe that he would intentionally kill someone over something like this as it is for me?"

Siever's brows drew down. "I guess not. It seems pretty straightforward to me. This wasn't just one RC boater getting angry at another for crossing him off or damaging his boat in a collision. He was afraid that Hustler was going to molest his kids. That maybe he already *was* molesting others with his mentoring gig. You said yourself that you would do whatever you had to if someone was a danger to your daughter."

Margie swallowed. "Yeah. When your children are threatened, or even being hurt already... So... Hustler is in the water," Margie returned to describing the scenario, making sure that all of the other pieces fit. "Terry is still around and has his boat in the water. Maybe he pretended to leave or maybe Simon just didn't think there was anything to fear from him. And Terry rams him with his boat."

"Multiple times."

Margie tried to remember if the medical examiner's preliminary report had said how many bruises Hustler had sustained. She couldn't remember. But she did remember looking at photo after photo of bruises.

"And kept hitting him until he let go of the raft. Until he went under the water and didn't come back up."

Siever nodded his agreement.

"However much this guy thought he was in the right, we need to prove that he did it," Margie said quietly.

Siever nodded again.

CHAPTER SIXTEEN

*M*argie looked in on Christina before she went to bed.

Now that it was summer holidays, there would probably be a lot of days that Christina stayed up to watch TV or chat with her friends after Margie had gone to bed. She still had work and Christina hadn't landed a job for the summer. She hadn't even tried, really. Margie couldn't blame her. Things had been so strange in the past year; Christina probably just wanted some downtime to assimilate and try to get back to normal again. With the restrictions having been lifted, it was the first time that Christina could actually go out places with her face uncovered and be places with her friends without being accused of breaking the rules for gatherings.

But she had been out with friends all day and had come home exhausted. She had spent a lot of time outside in the heat and Margie made her drink plenty of water, even though Christina protested that she didn't want to be up twenty times during the night to pee. She had almost been nodding off during dinner like a toddler, and soon after everything was cleared away, she had collapsed into her bed and not moved.

Now that she had her own air conditioning unit in the window, she could be comfortable in her own room and not have to go to bed with Margie in the only cool room in the house.

She was still sleeping soundly. Margie could hear the rhythm of her slow, steady inhales and exhales. Not quite snoring, but a little loud.

It was good to know that her daughter was home safe and well.

Margie didn't have to lay awake wondering what she was up to or what time she might make it home. Or if she even would make it home. Margie had seen too many parents of teenagers in Winnipeg come in to file missing person reports on their daughters. And there had been nothing that Margie could do. She would take the report and see that all of the appropriate actions were taken, but she knew that in many of those cases, they would never know what had happened to the girl.

In some of them, they would know what had happened, but it would be too late to save them.

Too many missing and murdered.

But Margie knew where her daughter was and that she was safe.

AT THEIR REQUEST, Terry Hall came downtown for a second interview. Or a third, if you counted the first meeting with the whole group. Margie could picture Terry that day—just two days ago—a stranger to her, concentrating as he ran his boat out on the water, looking as though he knew nothing about what had happened to Simon Hustler.

They had said that it might be better for him to come downtown this time. Rather than worrying his wife and kids with another visit to the house. But of course, it was far less convenient for Terry. He was impatient when he got in, having had to make the trip downtown and to find and pay for parking. And then he would get to do the reverse after the interview, dealing with downtown traffic and the drive back to his house. All for the convenience of the police department, a couple of bumbling detectives who couldn't seem to get their story straight and get all of the information they needed the first time.

"Thank you for coming in, Mr. Hall," Margie told him pleasantly, setting him up in the interview room with coffee that was fairly fresh, but not hot enough to do anyone damage. "Hopefully today we'll be able to get this all wrapped up."

"I don't see why I'm here. We already went over everything."

"We didn't, actually." Margie shook her head. "And I wouldn't have wanted to do all of this in front of your wife and kids."

She left him to think about this, while Siever came in, set the folder of evidence on the table in front of his chair, and sat down. Even sitting and with his jacket off, he looked very stiff and official. More than he usually was when Margie watched him unobserved. He really didn't like dealing with people face to face. And this interview in particular was going to be an uncomfortable one for everyone involved. But it needed to be done.

Terry looked at Siever, waiting for him to begin. The silence drew out, making everyone uncomfortable. Even knowing that Siever was using it as a tactic to make Terry want to talk to fill the silence, Margie still had a hard time with it. She looked down at her nails and picked at the tip of one nail to clean it.

"You haven't told us everything," Siever said in a flat, serious tone. "Don't you think it's time that you told the whole story?"

"I've answered all of your questions," Terry snapped. "I don't know what else you're looking for."

"No?"

Terry shook his head. "No. I've answered everything you've asked me, and I've come down here, and if you have anything else you want to know, then you should ask me now. Because after that, I'm done. I don't want to keep running around. I don't want this to be a part of my life and to be disrupting my time with my family."

"Family is very important to you, isn't it?"

"Yes, of course it is."

"You are lucky, having a wife and children. A happy family. A lot of people would like to have that who don't."

"It isn't something that you just fall into by accident. I've worked hard for what I've got."

"Yes, you have, haven't you?"

Terry looked at Siever, not liking the tone. But he didn't argue it or challenge him to explain why he was sounding so sarcastic. Maybe Siever had gotten up on the wrong side of the bed that morning. Maybe he hadn't had enough coffee. Maybe he was just naturally a grumpy, sarcastic kind of person.

"Some people would like very much to have what you do," Siever repeated. "Simon Hustler would have liked that kind of life."

181

"What was stopping him? He could have made the same kind of decisions that I had, and then he would have a happy family."

"What is stopping him is that he's dead," Margie said. "He can't really correct any of those decisions anymore, can he?"

"That's not my fault."

"It's the fault of whoever killed him."

"Exactly," Terry agreed.

"You were up pretty early last Friday morning, weren't you?"

"I don't really remember… no earlier than usual, I don't think."

"Maybe your wife would remember what time you got up." Siever suggested.

Terry looked wary, like they might already have captured his woman and be talking her into testifying against him. "I doubt if she would either. She's usually still asleep when I get up. She gets up when the kids get up, a couple of hours later."

"Didn't the kids want to go to the park that day?"

"They were still sleeping. I like to get up early and get some work done."

"Or to go for a walk?"

"I guess. Sometimes."

He didn't sound like it was something he would ever do. A workaholic, one who tackled things early to leave time for his family later.

"Maybe a walk in Elliston Park," Margie suggested.

Terry shrugged and didn't answer.

"Did you ever go to the park early in the morning to play with your boats?"

"No. I only went on the days that the group meets."

"One thing that kept us from figuring things out as quickly as we might have was that there was no other car in the parking lot during the right time frame that led anywhere. No one who had any connections with Hustler. Mostly they were regulars who were there every day. None of them showed up on the lists of people who have been at any of the meetups lately."

Terry nodded. "I don't see how anyone from our group could be connected. It just doesn't make any sense."

"But then there is you. You live close enough to the park that you could have walked there."

"Yes," Terry shrugged. "If I wanted to lug all of my equipment there. I don't know how I would do that on foot. And I didn't. I don't understand why you would think that I had anything to do with it. Or anyone in the group."

Margie leaned in closer to him. "You knew he was grooming your kids. And even when you told him to stop, he wouldn't. You knew that he had contact with other kids. He told you guys that he was mentoring teenagers. You knew that he was up to no good, and that no matter what you said to anyone, he would just be allowed to continue. All of those kids, Terry. All of those innocent kids. Yours included. He bribed them, made them like him. You could tell them to stay away from him, and maybe they will at this age. Maybe you can scare them into listening to you. But when they're teenagers and are rebelling against you and think that they know more than their old man... what then?"

Terry's face was as white as a sheet. He licked his lips. He took a sip of the lukewarm coffee, then a few more swallows, as if trying to fill a hole inside of him.

"Predators like that... I've read the stories. I've seen how they can destroy lives. I'm not going to let that happen to my own family."

"You're the protector," Siever said.

"Yes. If I can't protect them from pedophiles and drug dealers and all of the other scumbags out there, then who will? They say it's people that you know. Your own family and friends. Parents can't be complacent and think that everybody around them has good intentions. I could see what Simon was doing. I wasn't going to let him hurt them."

"So you decided that you would meet Simon out there at the lake. A friendly little get-together. Simon wanted friends. He would have jumped at the chance to do something with one of his fellow enthusiasts. You walked over with your boat, and then you saw to it that he would never return."

Terry shook his head, in full retreat. "No. That never happened. You can't prove any of this. You have *no* evidence. I was never at the park that day."

"Because you couldn't have carried your boat all that way," Margie offered.

"They're lightweight, but they're large and awkward. You don't want to have to carry one more than a block, and it's a couple of kilometers to the park. And that's just the boat, not any of the other equipment that we take along."

Siever took a large, printed photo out of his file folder and laid it on the table in front of Terry. "That's you, isn't it?"

Terry looked down at the picture of himself early Friday morning, pulling a wheeled case on the sidewalk behind him, the skis of the boat sticking out the top. Terry's mouth opened. "Where did you get this?"

"You thought that by using the pedestrian entrance on Seventeenth Avenue you would avoid any parking lot or traffic cams."

"Where did this come from?" Terry studied it, trying to orient himself as to where it was and where the camera had been located.

Siever took out several more photos, all similar, and laid them out in front of Terry. "In case you're thinking that it's just one picture..."

Terry just sat there with his mouth open. He clearly hadn't expected there to be any evidence to show that he had gone to Elliston Park that morning with his boat to meet with Simon Hustler.

"A lot of your neighbors have security cameras now," Margie explained to him. "Mounted on their garages, up under the eaves, doorbell cameras, there are so many choices these days. It's hard to go three or four houses now without finding at least one security camera. We can follow the trail all the way from your house to the park."

"But those... those are private, you don't have access to them."

"The first thing we do is ask. If people say no—and they rarely do when they know there is a criminal stalking their neighborhood—then we can get a subpoena. But there are enough of them that we rarely go that route. We just use the ones that people agree to give us."

"I didn't... *mean* to hurt him," Terry tried, changing tack. Knowing that he was caught, that they could put him in the park, he had to move to a different explanation. "I was only there to talk to him. To explain how he needed to stay away from my kids. And anyone else's kids. Or I would turn him in. He could go to prison for what he was doing. He just laughed and said that he'd never hurt anyone. He didn't know what I was talking about."

"Maybe he didn't."

"I saw him with my kids. I know what he was doing."

"You saw him talk to them. To get down to their level and show interest in them. To buy them gifts because he liked them. You never saw him touch them inappropriately, or show them pornography, or any of those other things. You just didn't like him talking to your kids."

"Those are grooming behaviors."

"They are also steps to building a friendship."

"Not when it is a grown man and a four-year-old."

"Maybe you hadn't noticed Hustler's social awkwardness. He sent the wrong signals. His timing and judgment were off. Yes. It seemed inappropriate. But he'd never been accused of pedophilia."

"That doesn't mean that he wasn't one."

"Until there is some kind of evidence... we need to withhold judgment."

"And that's exactly what you would have told me if I had come to the police for help," Terry said, sitting back again with his arms folded. "You would have said that there was nothing you could do until I had proof that he'd hurt one of my kids. Until then, he's innocent. You wouldn't do anything about it."

Margie looked at Siever. They didn't work those cases, but Margie knew that what Terry said was true. They couldn't just arrest someone on suspicions. They couldn't arrest someone for pedophilia before they had actually broken a law. They had to wait until someone got hurt.

Only this time, the innocent victim had been Hustler.

CHAPTER SEVENTEEN

*I*t was a clear night. The sidewalks still held the warmth of the sun, but the air had cooled when the sun disappeared below the horizon. Margie bent down to make sure that the blankets around Moushoom were tucked in and that he wasn't getting cold.

"How are you doing?" she asked him. "Are you cold? Tired?"

"I am just fine, little girl," Moushoom laughed. "You worry like your mother."

Margie nodded her agreement. As a teen, she had sworn that she would never be anxious or as careful as her mother. She would do whatever she wanted to and not worry about the rest. She would be confident in herself and not worry about other people. But all of that had changed when they put Christina into her arms. Then the weight of the world landed on her shoulders, and she worried not only about Christina, but the community that she was going to grow up in. Events on a global scale. Illnesses that Christina would face, meningitis and pneumonia and appendicitis. She had known nothing about pandemics back then. But she had known that there were ills that no one could vaccinate her little baby against.

And as a mother she seemed to have become responsible for the other children in her community as well. And the elders. Her extended family. The women and children living on the streets in Winnipeg. The addicts and drunks.

And the others who were vulnerable.

Margie patted Moushoom's hand. "We'll have some hot chocolate when we get there. We filled a thermos with Tim's."

The stars twinkled overhead. In a few minutes, Christina, Stella, Margie, and Moushoom were at the "ditch," close to the edge of the embankment, looking across the city at the downtown buildings and watching the sky to the right for any changes.

At eleven o'clock, they saw the first Stampede fireworks of the night go off. Soon the sky was ablaze with color and motion. Margie poured out cups of hot chocolate for the humans and gave Stella a doggie biscuit that she'd hidden in her pocket before leaving. Stella had known it was there and kept watching her with hopeful, soulful eyes. Setting her cup where it would hopefully not get kicked over, Margie squeezed Christina to her on one side, and Moushoom on the other.

"Do you know how much you guys mean to me?"

"We know, Mom." Christina leaned over to give Margie a peck on the cheek. "We know."

ELLISTON PARK

Elliston Park is home to Elliston Lake, the second largest body of water in Calgary. There are a couple of walking loops around the lake, an off-leash dog area, playgrounds, including an accessible or inclusive playground, picnic tables, a rose garden, and a sundial. Calgary's Globalfest Fireworks competition is held in Elliston Park each year.

Home to many waterfowl, from ducks, loons, and gulls to the occasional Canada geese, the park was named after the Ellis family in 1995.

An RC boats group meets here a couple times a week, though meetups were less frequent during covid restrictions.

INDIGENOUS PEOPLES IN AND AROUND CALGARY

Calgary is built on Treaty 7 land. Treaty 7 was signed in September 1877 between the Canadian government and five First Nations: the Siksiká, Kainai, Piikani, Stoney-Nakoda, and Tsuut'ina. This Treaty granted the Government of Canada a 130,000 km2 tract of land and did not allow them to continue their traditional lifestyles. The Treaty resulted in significant hardships and suffering for those Nations, although they continue to show their strength and resilience today.

Three First Nations (Siksiká, Stoney Nakoda, and Tsuut'ina) have their territory just outside of Calgary city limits. In addition, many Indigenous people live within Calgary, representing a multitude of Nations from this continent.

Some of the Indigenous Nations mentioned in this series include:

Métis - The Métis are a constitutionally recognized Indigenous Peoples (Métis Nation) in Canada. Their culture emerged from the association of European explorers and traders with the nations already living in what would come to be called Canada. The only remaining Métis self-governing land base in Canada is located in northern Alberta, with communities known as the Métis Settlements. For some Métis, their language is a mixed language of Cree and French, called Michif. There are several variations of Michif, and it is currently spoken by fewer than 1000 people.

Siksiká Nation or Niitsitapiiks - part of the Blackfoot Confederacy. Their community lies to the east of Calgary. They speak Siksiká, an Algonquian language.

Stoney Nakoda - historically referred to as Rocky Mountain Sioux or Plains Assiniboine. Their communities lie to the west of Calgary. Composed of three Nations: The Bearspaw First Nation, Chiniki First Nation, and Wesley First Nation. The Stoney language is a variety of Dakota Siouan and is closely related to Assiniboine.

Tsuut'ina - historically referred to as Sarcee, which is considered offensive. Their community lies between and slightly to the south of the Stoney Nakoda and Calgary. Calgary is currently building a ring road through what was, until recently, Tsuut'ina land. This project has displaced a number of Tsuut'ina families.

HAZARD OF THE HILLS

A PARKS PAT MYSTERY #6

For those standing close to the edge

CHAPTER ONE

Margie studied Christina as she prepared to go out with her friends.

"Hat? Sunscreen? Bug spray?"

"Mom!" Christina gave her most exasperated-teenager groan to the word. "I don't need any of those things. It isn't like I'm going to get sunburned."

"Even with your dark skin, you can still get sunburned," Margie told her, smiling at the rich brown tone of Christina's skin, very close to Margie's own. Christina's Cree features were a little less pronounced than Margie's. Anyone looking at Margie immediately knew she was descended from one of the First Nations. Christina was most likely to be considered Indigenous, but her smaller nose and more rounded cheeks left enough doubt that people would ask rather than just assuming. "I remember going to an air show in Winnipeg once where I—"

"Was standing outside in the full sun looking at the sky for ten hours," Christina finished. Apparently, Margie had mentioned the story once or twice before. "And your skin peeled."

Margie nodded. "Exactly. You get a burn like that once, and your chances at getting skin cancer skyrocket. It isn't worth the risk. If you would at least wear a hat to keep the sun off your face…"

"No. I don't want a hat on, and I'm not going to be looking at the sky for ten hours. We'll be outside for a few minutes, and then be in one of the buildings to eat or look at exhibits. I don't need a hat and I don't need sunscreen."

Margie didn't bring up bug spray again. Christina was rarely bothered by the mosquitoes. And it was going to be a warm day. The mosquitoes wouldn't be out until the evening.

"Okay? I'm going now," Christina informed her. She leaned down slightly to give Margie a hug and kiss her forehead as if she were the child instead of Christina. "Stop worrying. I'll have my phone with me, there's security, and you raised me well, so there's nothing to fuss about. I'll be fine."

Margie knew that she probably would be, but that didn't stop her from worrying. Things could still happen. Girls could be lured and trafficked. There was, unfortunately, an increase in trafficking around the Stampede, with extra girls brought in to serve the tourists and locals looking for some Stampede side action. What if some of those traffickers were looking to increase their stables? Christina was an attractive girl of the right age. And as sophisticated as she was, there was no guarantee she would recognize the danger if she were approached by a teen boy who showed her interest.

"Who is going with you? You guys will stay together, right?"

"We're going as a group," Christina said, which didn't actually answer the question of whether they would stay together all the time. "It's just some friends from school. You don't know all of them."

"Is Tracy going?"

"Yes." Eye roll. "Tracy is going."

Tracy, a boy, not a girl, would help to deter approaches by young men, but also brought more worries.

"You won't go off on your own? It's not safe for you to just wander by yourself."

"It will be perfectly fine," Christina insisted. "I will be okay, Mom, I promise."

"Maybe I should come along. Seeing as it is Community Spirit Day, and I really should go see the Elbow River Camp. I went a couple of times when I was a little girl, but that was a long time ago."

"You are *not* coming with me."

Margie smiled and gave her daughter a squeeze. "Don't give me reason to, then. Be safe. Take all the precautions, even if you think that I'm being silly and you don't need to. Remember I'm a cop, I've seen a lot more than you."

"Yes, Mom." Christina's tone was pained. "Now I have to go. They're texting me." She flashed her phone at Margie to show her how impatient her friends were. "I'll talk to you later."

"When will you be home?"

"I don't know. It might be late. We might go to Peters' and then find a place to watch the fireworks."

Margie salivated as she remembered her own trips to the drive-in with her friends those summers she had visited her Moushoom. Peters' burgers, milkshakes in unending varieties so thick you could hardly suck them through a straw, and big baskets of fries. Back in those days, she could eat things like that without putting on weight.

"Call or text me a couple of times during the day just to touch base," she told Christina. "Then I won't call you."

"Okay, Mom. Bye."

Christina touched Margie fleetingly on the arm to soften her abrupt reply and dashed out the door. As she left, Margie saw that she was wearing sandals. If she walked in those all day, the backs of her heels were going to be raw.

Christina had promised that she would be okay. She was sure that she could control the outcomes, when all she could really control were her own choices.

ONCE CHRISTINA WAS on her way, Margie did a quick sweep through the kitchen and the rest of the house to make sure that all the dishes were in the dishwasher and clothes from the previous night were in the hamper. The house looked reasonably tidy. Christina didn't always remember to pick up after herself, but she was pretty good about it. Better, Margie was sure, than she herself had been as a teenager. She hadn't made the best choices herself, becoming pregnant with Christina when she had been barely older than her daughter was now.

The thought made her shudder.

She had thought that she was so grown up. Such an adult. She hadn't known how much growing up she would be forced to do in a short time to keep her daughter and get herself back on track.

Margie's phone vibrated in her pocket. She pulled it out, expecting to see a text from Christina, but it kept vibrating in her hand, a picture of Kaitlyn Jones, one of Margie's fellow homicide detectives, on the screen. Blond, friendly, smiling in the picture. She had made Margie feel immediately welcome in Calgary when Margie had arrived less than a year before.

Margie swiped to answer the call. "Detective Patenaude."

"Is this Detective Parks Pat?" Jones asked smartly.

Which meant that Margie's assumed specialty in solving homicides that took place in Calgary's parks was being called upon. She let out her breath. "What have we got?"

"I don't have many details yet. Body found in Edworthy Park. A woman. That's about all I know so far. Meet me there?"

"Will do," Margie agreed. "Will it be on my GPS?"

"I'm sure it will be. And the scene is actually fairly close to the south parking lot, so it shouldn't be hard for you to find once you get there. Just look for the yellow tape and people trying to see what's going on."

"Okay." Margie headed over to the door to put on her shoes. "Tell me there isn't any water at Edworthy Park."

Jones laughed. "It's on the river. But you're in luck this time. The body is not in the water."

"Thank goodness for that. I'm beginning to think that I'm going to have to invest in a life jacket as part of my on-scene uniform."

Jones chuckled at that. "See you there," she said, and hung up.

CHAPTER TWO

The route that the GPS app showed on the map of Calgary was convoluted, and Margie hoped that she wouldn't miss any exits, or she would be driving all over Calgary before she managed to find Edworthy Park. The computer voice would yell at her to perform illegal U-turns and cross medians while Margie tried to keep an eye on the screen and on the traffic and exit signs all at the same time. One thing that she wished was different about Calgary was how much area the city covered. It was not neat and compact, that was for sure. And very little of it followed the grid system that the city's forefathers had envisioned.

Margie finished braiding her hair and pinned it up into a bun.

"Okay, be nice to me," she told the GPS voice, and pulled away from the curb.

She did manage to miss a couple of turns but, thankfully, the GPS was able to compensate without making her perform any illegal turns. She did not get pulled over by a traffic cop. Explaining that she was a police detective and couldn't follow navigation directions was not how she wanted to start the case.

It was nearly half an hour before she made it to the signs designating the park. There was a steep hill down into the park with switchbacks back and forth. She was immediately surrounded by an impressive growth of trees and bushes, giving the illusion that she was out in the wilds rather than in the middle of a busy city. When she got to the bottom, she could see the series of parking lots for public parking. There was a squad car with flashing lights blocking off one access and a cop redirecting traffic away from it on foot. Margie followed the road that curved through the parking lots, aiming for that entrance.

The traffic cop bent down to talk to her when she stopped, half of his face obscured by a black mask. "Sorry, ma'am, this area is restricted."

Margie held up her police identification. "Homicide."

"Ah. Give me a sec." He moved away from the car and grabbed one of the orange A-frame barricades that also blocked the road. He pulled it to the side so that Margie could get her car past the police car, then pulled it back into place as she drove farther down the road.

Margie continued to follow the road and the waves of various law enforcement officers or park conservation officers along the way until she reached what was obviously the staging area. She stepped out of her car and was met by Detective Jones.

"Didn't take you too long," Jones observed, her eyes smiling. "I take it Edworthy Park was on your GPS?"

"Yes. Didn't lead me astray this time. Which means I'll have to be all the more careful next time…"

Jones nodded. "We're this way."

She led Margie at a quick clip to a patch of browning grass and dirt with narrow tire impressions, and there it was. Margie stayed well back from the body, looking around to see whether the forensic techs were there yet. There were a couple already geared up and waiting in the shade of the nearby trees. She made a slow circle of the body but couldn't see much other than what Jones had already mentioned. That it was a woman, and she was dead. The crumpled form was face down, limbs askew, and it was not immediately apparent what had happened to her. She wore a light jacket and long pants, so it had probably been cool when she had gone for a walk in the park and… Margie had to stop there, because she really didn't have any idea what happened next. The clothes were scuffed and had holes in them. A homeless person?

"Any idea what happened to her?" Margie asked. "Who found the body?"

"Dog walker." Jones motioned in what appeared to be a random direction, since Margie didn't see a man with a dog waiting to be interviewed. There were privacy screens up, though, and there might be a witness in one of the blind spots. "As usual. And as far as the cause of death, I would think that was pretty obvious."

Margie looked again for any sign of violence. There was no spreading pool of blood, no visible bullet or knife wound. No vomit puddles nearby indicating poison or overdose.

"I guess I haven't had enough coffee yet this morning. What's obvious?"

Jones pointed up. Margie raised her head and followed the direction of Jones's index finger. "What...?"

The hill beside them was steep, nearly a cliff. But as Margie looked at it, she realized that the stripes down the side were trails worn by bicycle tires. Margie would not have attempted to walk up or down the steep incline but, apparently, bikers used it regularly. Margie looked at the tire marks through the clearing. What amazed her was how many tire tracks and worn trails there were. It clearly wasn't just something that one daredevil had attempted, surviving the plunge to the bottom, but something that was done with regularity.

"You've got to be kidding me."

"I wish I was."

"She fell?"

"Looks that way. Went out for her evening constitutional, and..." Jones made a whistling sound.

"Ai-yi-yi! Why isn't there a fence or a barrier at the top? This is dangerous!"

"They've had fences. They gave up because they kept being pulled down by the downhill bikers."

"They should be put in jail. Or in some kind of institution. How could anyone sane even consider that?" Margie stared up the hill. "I mean seriously, is biking down there even possible?"

"I don't think I would be able to watch."

Margie took another look around, analyzing the positioning of the body once more. Not someone who had just collapsed there, but someone who had taken a tumble down the hill and landed in a heap there. The dirt and tears in her clothing not from living rough or sleeping outside, but from falling down the hill head over heels.

"How high is the hill?"

"I asked one of the CO's. Apparently, it's about 70 meters."

Margie automatically converted it in her head. Over 210 feet.

"Crap. She must have been terrified."

Jones nodded soberly.

"Well, I don't think we're going to figure out much more standing here, so let's have the experts take a look."

"Yup." Jones raised her hand high over her head, motioning for the forensic guys to come over. They looked at her for any detailed instructions she might have. "I'll leave you to it. I don't have any particular insight into people who fall over cliffs. I guess we should look for anything that she might have been holding and dropped. But I don't see anything obvious. Record everything you can, and then we'll have the death investigator take a look at the body and arrange transport."

They didn't tell her that they already knew the protocol, just nodded politely and went to work. Margie and Jones scanned the ground for anything that might have been dropped or fallen out of the pockets of the deceased. There was some litter, more likely left behind by the crazy downhill bikers, but it would all have to be gathered together for analysis anyway.

"You can't be over the police line!" A strong male voice was raised over the chatter of police radios, bystanders, and various people involved in the scene. Margie looked around one of the privacy screens to see what the commotion was about. Detective Gagnon, whom she'd not had much opportunity to work with previously, was telling off one of the bystanders, who was, in fact, properly behind the yellow police tape. Margie turned her head to frown at Jones, who was also looking at the scene with some consternation.

"You want me to confiscate that?" Gagnon demanded.

The man he was talking to had something in both hands like an electronic game. His head was down and he was working the controller in his hands. He glanced up at Gagnon, scowling, and said something back to him.

Margie wanted to go see what was going on, but if she and Jones both went over, it would look like they were questioning Gagnon's judgment or all ganging up on the bystander, neither of which was a desirable scenario.

"Go ahead," Jones said. "See if he needs a hand with anything and I'll supervise here."

Margie nodded and moved off to join Gagnon at the perimeter. "Anything I can assist with, Detective Gagnon?"

He cast an irritated glance at her, which Margie fully understood. She wouldn't want anyone trying to poke their nose in when she was handling a situation either. Only sometimes, it did help to have someone else on hand.

"This joker thinks that he doesn't have to respect the police line," Gagnon pointed out.

Margie looked at the man a few feet back of the police tape. But as she stood there, something caught her attention out the corner of her eye. She turned her head and looked up. A bird or squirrel? But the movement hadn't been an animal in the trees. It was a small box floating in the air. There was a very faint whirring coming from it that she could barely hear over the other ambient noise of the murder site.

A remote-control drone of some kind. And it was, in fact, significantly inside the police line. In a position where its camera would be able to view over the privacy screens to where the body lay. Margie looked back at the man with the controller in his hands.

"Do you want me to arrest him for obstructing an investigation?"

Gagnon's jaw clenched and he gave a curt nod. "Might as well, he won't listen to anything else."

Margie took a step toward him. "Sir, I'm putting you under—"

"I'm not doing anything!" the man protested, looking at her for a moment before looking back down at the controller in his hands, twiddling the joystick that controlled the craft's direction. "I'm not interfering. I'm back here behind the police line, just like he said. I haven't touched anything or gotten in anybody's way."

"You've been told that thing can't be over the police line. You've failed to comply. So I'm putting you under arrest. We'll impound the drone and the judge can decide whether—"

"It's here. It's here, it's not over the line anymore." The little box hovered over the man, then ducked slightly behind him, as if it were a child hiding behind his father.

"What's your name, sir?"

"Howard Ross."

"Have you got some ID?"

He looked as though he would argue. Then he bit his lip and used his controller to bring the drone down to the ground, so that he could put the controller down to go through his pockets. He pulled a wallet out of his breast pocket and dug out his driver's license for Margie to look at. He had given his correct name, and she quickly jotted down his name, address, and birth date, as well as the operator's license number in her notepad.

"Have you ever been arrested before?" she asked him.

"You can't arrest me! I'm doing what you told me to."

Margie looked at Gagnon, raising her brows. "I'm pretty sure I can," she argued. "Wouldn't you say?"

"Of course."

Margie nodded. "So, is this the first time you've been arrested?"

"I've never been arrested before. Look, all I was doing was using my drone. I didn't think there was any harm in it."

"When a peace officer gives you a command and you don't comply, you're in the wrong. Period. It doesn't really matter what you *think*."

He opened his mouth to argue, then apparently thought better of it. "Yes, ma'am."

"This is a police perimeter. You can't cross a police perimeter with a drone."

He nodded his understanding.

"I think you owe Detective Gagnon here an apology."

"I'm sorry," Ross said immediately. He turned slightly to face Gagnon directly. "I'm sorry, sir. I should have listened to what you said. I really don't want to be arrested. I wasn't trying to do anything wrong. Do you think..."

Gagnon gave him a fierce look, unblinking. Ross lowered his eyes and looked at the ground near his feet.

"I am. I'm sorry. I'm not just saying that. Please don't arrest me or confiscate my drone."

"Why don't you pick up your drone and get out of here?"

"Okay. Yes, sir. I will." Ross turned around and bent down to pick up the small drone and beat a hasty retreat.

Gagnon turned and looked at Margie.

"I hope you don't think I was interfering," Margie said. "I was just offering to help out."

"You have a teenager at home?"

"Yes," Margie was surprised that he knew. She hadn't had much to do with Gagnon at the office, and she didn't talk a lot about Christina or have pictures on her desk. She tried to keep her personal life and job from inter-mixing too much.

"I thought so. There's no one as intimidating as a mom with a teenager."

Margie laughed. "Thanks!"

"He didn't back down for me," Gagnon pointed out. "But he wasn't going to cross Mama Bear."

CHAPTER THREE

The medical examiner's van had pulled into the scene. Margie nodded to Gagnon and returned to the area behind the screens. She waved at Jones, who had noticed her return. While the techs stood to the side once more, the death investigator from the medical examiner's office leaned over the body. Margie had met him before.

"Dr. Kahn."

He looked up for a moment. "Parks Pat," he greeted, tone slightly mocking.

"That's Detective Pat to you."

He was wearing a mask and face shield, but she saw the fan of wrinkles that sprang from the corners of his eyes when he smiled at her comment.

"I suppose you're expecting me to declare cause and manner of death on the spot."

"Oh, Detective Jones has already done that," Margie said, waving a hand airily. "Accidental death caused by a fall."

"It wasn't the fall that killed her," Kahn said.

"Oh?"

Everyone nearby froze and looked at him, startled by this announcement.

"No. It was the landing that killed her."

Margie groaned. Everyone resumed their conversations, their eyeballs nearly rolling out of their heads. "That's really bad, Dr. Kahn."

"I thought you would appreciate it."

"I'm not sure *appreciate* is the right word."

He chuckled and resumed his examination of the body. Margie was hesitant to look too closely, but now that the woman had been turned over, she leaned in for a better look at the face. The fall had done a number, but she was still recognizable. Since the impact had killed her, there hadn't been any swelling. If she had survived, Margie was sure her face would have been too swollen for her own mother to recognize her.

"Do we have an identity?"

"Patience."

"Patience who?"

He ignored her. After a few minutes, he patted her pockets. He shook his head. "No wallet on her. You've looked around the area to see whether it fell somewhere close by?"

"We didn't find anything," Jones confirmed.

Kahn looked up at the hill. "Then I guess you should look at the top and follow her path down. See if she lost a wallet or purse along the way. It could be caught on a clump of leaves or a depression in the ground."

They all looked at the 70-meter climb. No one volunteered.

"Do you think it's best to go down from the top, or up from the bottom?" Jones asked Margie.

"Top down, for sure. But with a harness and rope. I'm not taking the chance of landing beside our mystery woman."

"Try the Fire Department Vertical Rescue Team," Kahn suggested. "They love stuff like this."

Margie didn't mind the idea of adding a little adventure to someone else's day. If the Fire Department would enjoy belaying down the hill, who was she to step in the way of their good time? "I'm on it."

She called the non-emergency line and explained to the phone operator what she needed. In a few minutes, she was talking to Captain Burrows, head of the Vertical Rescue Team. She smiled at the excitement in his voice when he heard that they had an actual crime scene to help out with. Not just an exercise, but not a life and death rescue either.

"We'll be there as soon as possible, detective."

"Do you need coordinates or a more accurate description of where it is?"

"Oh, trust me, I know where it is."

Margie laughed and hung up. "They'll be on their way soon," she told Jones.

"Excellent. You don't know how glad I am that no one is going to be lowering me down that hill on a rope. Do you know how long it would be before I got tripped up on a slope like that?"

Jones was a little overweight and not in the best physical shape. Unfortunately, detectives spent a little too much time at their desks and didn't get the kind of exercise that a beat cop did. She wasn't particularly clumsy that Margie had noticed, but Margie wouldn't want to be going down that hill without a safety harness either. She couldn't imagine looking down from the top of the hill, balancing on a bike, trying to work up the courage to rocket down it. It was amazing they didn't have regular calls out to the location. Maybe that said something about the common sense of most bikers. But not all of them.

She looked back at Dr. Kahn and the victim. "Was she killed instantly?" She wasn't sure she wanted to know the answer to that one. But it was something they would need to know.

"Very little blood or perimortem bruising. I would say that she probably died on impact." He was working his way around the victim's head, fingers quick and light. Margie was reminded of checking a melon for soft spots. The thought stirred a little nausea and she turned away to look around the scene.

"At least this one is clearly an accident," she offered to Jones.

"Don't jinx it."

"By saying that it's an accident?"

Jones nodded. "Yeah. You don't want it to turn out to *not* be an accident, do you?"

"No. But I don't think I can say anything now that will change it."

"Just don't bring the wrath of the universe down on you by saying we know something before the medical examiner confirms it. You know how complicated things can get when you think it's an accident but then it isn't."

Margie rolled her eyes. Yes, she had seen that on a few cases. "Okay. I'm not saying anything. Unhear it and forget all about it. We don't know anything yet. I sure hope that the medical examiner decides that it was an accident."

Jones groaned.

Margie looked at her. "Not that either?"

"No."

Margie lapsed into silence. Apparently, she was not supposed to say anything.

કજ

THEY COULD HEAR sirens off in the distance, apparently getting closer and, after a few minutes, the sirens cut off somewhere close by. Margie looked up at the top of the hill. It wasn't long before she could see tall dark figures silhouetted at the top of the hill. It made her dizzy just looking up at them.

Didn't they get dizzy looking down?

Jones waved up at them and a few of the men waved back. They stood at the top discussing things for some time, then retreated.

By the time Dr. Kahn and his assistant had removed the woman's body from the scene and were transporting her back to the van, firefighters were starting down the hill, strolling along as if they were just out for a Sunday walk. But Margie could see that they had safety harnesses attached to ropes being belayed by men up above. They worked their way down the hill slowly.

Margie gasped when she saw one of them slip and ski down the hill for a few feet on loose dirt or gravel. She could hear the sound of the skid and found herself reaching toward him as if she could hold him back. She laughed at herself, covering her mouth with her hand to prevent herself from gasping or shouting out again. But she'd heard several other gasps around her too. She wasn't the only one captivated by the sight of the strapping young men working their way down the dangerous slope.

One of the men called out and held a hand up to stop the others. Margie couldn't hear what he was saying and took a couple of steps closer, hoping that if she concentrated, she would be able to hear what he was saying.

Her phone started buzzing in her pocket. Margie answered it and heard Captain Burrows's voice.

"What do you want us to do about any evidence that we find?"

"Well... it will need to be documented." Margie stared up at the hill, where they were gathered around something. "Can they take pictures?

211

Something close up, with an object to show scale, and some shots showing context—the area it is in. We'll have to mark it all on a map of the hill afterward. Do they have gloves and evidence bags?"

"Yes, I did think that much out ahead of time. We can manage that."

"Okay. Have one person do all the collecting, he'll need to initial the evidence bags and sign an affidavit so that we maintain the chain of evidence. What did they find?"

"Couple of credit cards. No purse or wallet yet. Maybe she just had them loose in her pocket."

"Oh, well I guess you don't need to show scale for credit cards. They're all the same size."

"Got it. Thanks."

❧

Margie's phone vibrated again as the forensic techs were gathering up the last of their evidence and equipment. She instinctively looked up the hill to see whether it was Burrows again but, of course, he wasn't standing on the edge looking down at her.

She slid out her phone and looked at the face, but it wasn't Burrows this time. It was Christina.

"Hi, sweetie." Margie glanced around her. She'd hardly even been aware of the passing of time and didn't know at first whether Christina would even be at the Stampede yet. But judging by the short shadows on the ground it was noon or close to it. "How has the morning gone?"

"Really good," Christina enthused. "There were some really good bands, and we even got to talk to some of the musicians. There aren't a lot of people down here like you would expect there to be. Except with COVID, you don't know how many people to expect. But it isn't crazy crowds like I had imagined."

"That's great. What else have you done?"

"A bit of this and that. Some games and rides, a couple of exhibits. I'm going to go have lunch in the Elbow River Camp. See what's going on over there."

"That sounds great. Say *Taanishi* for me."

Christina sounded like she was smiling as she answered. "Okay. I just wanted to let you know that I was still alive and haven't been kidnapped by head hunters. We're having a good time, and everyone is fine."

"Thanks for letting me know. Call me again later."

CHAPTER FOUR

*M*argie followed Jones's car up to the top of the hill where the vertical rescue team was staged. They were met by Captain Burrows, a tall, broad-chested man in his thirties who would certainly not be out of place on one of the fundraising calendars that the fire department put out. Margie gave him a warm smile behind her mask and strove to remain professional.

"I'm so glad that we had your team available. I would not have wanted to search that slope by myself."

He nodded his agreement. "It really isn't safe. Can't believe that people would actually use it for downhill biking. Some people are crazy."

"Or suicidal," Margie agreed. "I can't imagine doing that unless you were."

"The people who do things like that don't usually think about consequences. Teenagers and young people whose brains haven't fully developed. Thrill seekers. No real concept about the kind of suffering it could bring to them or their families. Plenty of my guys are thrill seekers. It's the nature of the job. But going on a bike down that slope… that's beyond the pale."

Jones and Margie both vigorously nodded their agreement.

One of the other team members joined them, smiling in greeting. "And you must be the detectives."

"We are," Jones agreed. She nodded to the bags in his hand. "My evidence?"

"Yes. Can you walk me through what I'm supposed to do to preserve the chain?"

Jones had him seal and initial the bags and took down his name and contact information in her notepad. "I'll send you an affidavit to fill out. At some point, you could be called upon to testify, but considering that this is ninety-nine percent likely to be classified as an accident, probably not."

He nodded and handed the sealed paper bags to her.

"Did you see the name on the credit cards?" Jones asked.

"Evie Wyler." The firefighter spelled it for Jones.

"Great. Much easier to identify the body when you have a name to begin with."

They chatted for a moment, some small talk. Margie cocked her head. "Is there music?"

Burrows pointed. "It's the Wildwood Stampede Breakfast. Just over there. We've been invited to join them if you'd like to come along."

"No, we should be getting back to the office." But Margie was already salivating at the idea of a pancake breakfast. She'd had her usual coffee and toast and normally tried to stay away from big breakfasts full of greasy sausages and fake maple syrup. But she could smell the grease and syrup in the breeze and it brought back memories of Stampede breakfasts she'd had as a child when she had been visiting her Moushoom or other relatives in Calgary.

"I don't know how many opportunities we're going to have for pancake breakfasts," Jones said, looking longingly in that direction.

"Maybe... we should conduct some community interviews," Margie suggested. "People in this area must know about the hill. Evie Wyler might have come from this neighborhood. Must have if she was out walking at night. You don't drive to another part of town to go for a midnight stroll."

"Unless you're casing out houses to burgle," Jones put in.

Margie grinned. "Well, obviously."

"I think we should check it out. Keep our fingers on the pulse of the neighborhood. Identify suspects. Find out if she had friends and family in the area. Or if anyone was aware of any problems she might have been having."

"Problems?"

"Threats. Depression." Jones shrugged. "We won't know until we ask."

Margie nodded. "Really, we'd be negligent if we didn't."

"I agree."

"You call it in," Margie told her. "I'll go scout ahead."

"You can leave your cars here," Burrows advised. "There isn't much parking over there because they're using the community center parking lot for the breakfast. It's just a few blocks. That way you work off the calories walking there and back," he told her with a knowing grin.

Looking at his physique, Margie had a hard time believing that he ever had to worry about counting calories. Though, maybe that was how he had gotten into such fine shape. She should take his advice. "Okay, that sounds good," she agreed.

Jones made a quick phone call to check in as she walked to her car and locked the evidence into the trunk. She slid her phone back into her pocket. "I saw him first."

"Who?" Margie laughed. "Captain Burrows?"

"Yes."

"I talked to him before you saw him."

"Doesn't count."

Margie chuckled again as they started walking toward the vertical rescue team, who were heading down the street toward the faint music and smell of sausages. "I don't need that kind of complication in my life right now. You go right ahead."

"He's just the kind of complication that I do need in my life."

"He's all yours. With a teenager in the house, I'm really not into dating right now."

"Why does having a teenager in the house matter?"

"If she isn't totally mortified at the idea of her mother having a boyfriend or... extracurricular pursuits, then she repeats back all of the motherly advice that I ever gave her. It's one thing when she's telling me to eat a proper breakfast or to make sure I eat enough vegetables. I don't think I'm up for *that* talk from my daughter."

※

THE COMMUNITY CENTER was a little farther away than Margie would have guessed. The music was very loud and the breeze blowing in just the right direction to carry the food smells to them. Margie looked around at the long tables set up in the parking lot to eat at and the grills lined up nearby. The smells all mixed to produce that distinct *Stampede Breakfast* perfume. People were milling around, talking excitedly with one another and enjoying the band. Some wore masks, and others didn't and were quick to greet each other with friendly hugs.

"Come on over here for your breakfast," a stout woman in a plaid blue and white shirt instructed. "Free for emergency responders, of course. You can get whatever you want. Tables are set up if you want to eat there. If you want to social distance, then pick a spot on the grass."

"Thank you," Margie nodded at the woman. "This looks really great."

"It's so nice to be able to do something as a community again. I feel like we've been in prison for a year and a half and have finally been let out. It's so nice to be back to *normal*." She shrugged, looking at Margie's and Jones's masks. "Well, as normal as possible."

"Do you know an Evie Wyler?" Jones asked the woman. "I thought that she might be here." Jones faked looking around for her.

"Wyler… I'm not sure. I've seen her name on the Facebook page, but I'm not sure that I would recognize her. Charles…?"

A tall man with a bushy mustache and a straw cowboy hat turned from his grill to face her. "Yep?"

"Evie Wyler? Do you know her? These ladies were hoping…"

"Wyler. Evie. No, can't say I do. You can look around. We're only here until eleven, so she'll have to come before then if she's going to have any pancakes."

"Thanks," Jones said with a nod.

❦

MARGIE HAD BEEN to Stampede breakfasts where the pancakes were burned on the outside and raw on the inside, but the ones at the Wildwood breakfast were remarkably good. Margie and Jones and the vertical rescue team sat on the grass, but keeping social distance proved to be impossible, as all the kids wanted to talk to the cool firefighters. Plenty of the dads too. They weren't quite as interested in the lady detectives. Dressed in suits rather than uniforms, it wasn't immediately obvious what they were, or maybe there would have been more interest.

No, Margie decided. To be fair, the brave, handsome firefighters would always attract more attention than a couple of cops, even if they were homicide detectives.

A couple of men appeared to be making their rounds through the crowds. Stopping to talk to people and shaking hands or bumping elbows. They were not wearing masks and had bright-white smiles. They were wearing matching black cowboy hats, western style shirts probably from Lammles, and shiny new cowboy boots that had never met a cow patty. Tourists?

It wasn't long before they made their way over to the firefighters and police detectives on the grass.

"Vincent Skinner," the taller of the two greeted, reaching out his hand.

Margie nodded and decided to remain occupied with her plate and fork, leaving no hands free to shake. "Detective Patenaude," she introduced herself. "And Detective Jones."

"Detectives! With our city's finest?"

"Yes." Of course. What did he think she meant? She didn't add that they were on the homicide team.

"We're certainly glad that you could join us today. We're always happy to have the city's first responders at our community events."

"Just in case someone chokes," Jones suggested.

He laughed heartily. "Just in case... yes, exactly. And this is Harland Roberts, my campaign manager."

"Campaign?" Jones repeated.

"Yes! I am a mayoral candidate."

"Oh." Margie was surprised. She had been surprised by the number of election signs already up around the city. "Isn't it a bit early to be campaigning?"

"It's never too early to start getting your name out there. If I waited until September, I wouldn't have nearly enough time to meet all the constituents that I would like to."

"July just seems like an awfully long time until municipal elections in October. Aren't you afraid that people will forget your name during that time?"

He shook his head. "People need to see you out there. And that's what the big signs are for. Get my name and face firmly implanted in people's memories. Lots of exposures between now and then."

Margie supposed that a longer lead-up did give people more opportunities to get his name implanted in their minds. They said it took seven or more exposures to a brand before people were ready to purchase. The same must apply to politics.

"Well, it's good to meet you."

"I have a lot of ideas of things that will be very beneficial to Calgarians. With me as your mayor, we could move things forward in this city. Jobs, transit, improved economy." He nodded. "It's time to move out of the stagnation of the COVID lockdown into a new and brighter future!"

Jones nodded. There were murmurs from a few of the firefighters, but Margie couldn't tell whether they were moved by his speech or thought he was full of hot air. Skinner was impressive, at any rate.

Skinner looked around at them all, as if expecting them to say that they would support him, or that they must have questions to ask him about his campaign. Maybe closer to the election, people would, but they were at a Stampede breakfast, not exactly a place to talk politics and municipal development. People were there to relax and enjoy the food and the music. Across the field, children were jumping and squealing in a blow-up bouncy house.

"Have you been to the Stampede yet?" Skinner tried.

"No. I don't know if I'll get down to the grounds this year. But my daughter went today with a group of friends. It's Community Spirit Day, so cheap gate admission."

"I hope she enjoys it. Will she see the Grandstand Show?"

Margie looked down at her food to avoid rolling her eyes. If the girl couldn't or wouldn't pay full price for the gate admission, what were the chances that she could afford the limited seating at the Grandstand Show?

"No, she and her friends will probably find somewhere good to watch the fireworks. After Peters', of course."

"Ah, Peters'..." Skinner got that faraway look of a true Calgarian, remembering trips to Peters' in days gone by. Margie had to smile, despite not really liking Skinner. Could a man be all bad if he loved Peters'?

"So, do your people still have a presence this year?" Skinner asked. "Or has that all been kiboshed with all of this... *cancel Canada* stuff." Then realizing that his words might possibly be offensive he quickly added, "Not that there isn't good reason for it."

Margie stared at him, trying to form an answer that was polite and courteous as befitted a member of the Calgary Police Service, but would clearly inform him that he was treading on thin ice if he wanted votes from "her people."

"I mean," Skinner clarified, "do they still have the Indian tipi village, or whatever they call it now?"

"The Elbow River Camp. Yes, we are still trying to educate the public about our cultures."

He gave her a bland smile and started to move away, his pale campaign manager tugging at his arm, quite possibly sensing the chill coming from Margie's direction.

CHAPTER FIVE

here was a lot of work to do the day that a file was opened. Margie and Jones headed back to the office after having had their fill of Stampede pancakes and, as their stomachs tried to process the unusually large morning meal, flipped through photographs of the scene, collated data, transcribed the notes in their notebooks to electronic notes in the newly opened virtual workspace, and made sure that all departments involved had the proper coding to ensure that the forensic and pathology results would be properly routed to the workspace and their individual inboxes.

Margie had started to run background on Evie Wyler, gathering as much information as was readily available. It didn't take long to find her operator's license. Margie compared the photo with one of the accident scene photos of the victim's face to make sure it was the right person. Someone else could have lost something out of her pockets on that hill. Anyone who had gone down that hill might have left their own contributions behind.

The faces did match. Wyler's address was in Wildwood, close to the hill. Her car was probably still parked in her garage at home, as it wouldn't have made much sense to drive that distance and look for legal parking. Margie tried to imagine what Wyler had been doing. They didn't have a time of death from the medical examiner yet, so she didn't have any idea whether it had been an evening, middle-of-the-night, or early-morning stroll that had led Wyler to the top—and then bottom—of that hill. Margie had been assuming that it was dark, since that would explain a fall and her body being found early the next morning. But there was a whole range of possibilities.

Wyler had no criminal record. Not even a speeding ticket. She had made 9-1-1 and 3-1-1 calls in the past to report activities or concerns around her neighborhood. Nothing that had been flagged as a nuisance call.

She found a couple of social media accounts in the name Evie Wyler and opened the first one.

It hit her like a gut punch. She should have known that a young urban professional was unlikely to be living alone in a family neighborhood like Wildwood. Nice houses, close to the park, popular for retirees and families, but not single young men and women.

The cover image on the account showed Wyler holding a little girl of about three, both of them laughing. There were plenty of pictures of both the daughter and her husband in the feed that followed.

Margie groaned. "Wyler has a family."

Jones looked up from her work, her face pinched into a frown. "What? I checked and there was no marriage record."

"Maybe they're not married. But she has a little girl and a man in her life."

Jones swore, echoing Margie's sentiments.

"I was hoping she was single. Informing parents is bad enough. How old is the little girl?"

Margie turned her monitor for Jones to see the tiny, laughing blond.

"Oh, isn't she precious." Jones's eyes teared up, and she turned away to reach for a tissue. She dabbed at her eyes. "We'd better get over there to do the notification. Will you come?"

Margie nodded. "If you want me."

Jones glanced toward where Gagnon was sitting at his desk. "I'm sure any of the detectives would do just fine, but you have... a light touch."

"Okay. I'll come. Did the husband not file a missing person report? He got up in the morning and his wife wasn't there, and...?" She thought back to the Roscoe case, a file she had been involved in shortly after her arrival in Calgary. A high percentage of murdered women died at the hands of their husbands or intimate partners.

But Wyler's death had been an accident, not murder. If her husband had not reported her missing, there was a reason for that. Or he had reported her missing and the file simply hadn't been posted to the system yet or matched to their file for some reason. Technology didn't always work the way it was supposed to.

"I guess we'll get around to asking him that," Jones said. "Once we've done the notification."

⁂

THEY BOTH HOPPED into Jones's car and headed back out to Wildwood. It was a family-friendly area, lots of bungalows, mostly family housing. Some of them looked as if they had been built in the 60s and some were brand-new with huge, black-tinted windows.

At the community center, the band and the bouncy house were gone. All the tables and grills had been put away. Everything was tidy and clean, as if the pancake breakfast had never happened.

"It should be up here, I think," Jones said, looking at the GPS unit to identify their target. Margie scanned for the house numbers, which at least were reasonably visible during the day. Identifying house numbers after dark could be a nightmare. They found the right house and looked at it for a minute before getting out of the car. A nice house, brick or faux-brick siding, tidy gardens and lawn. Everything appeared to be freshly painted. There were no children's toys in the yard.

Jones led the way up to the front door. Everything was quiet; there was no indication that someone was anxiously looking out the window, waiting for his wife to get home or for the police to show up and help. They stood to the side of the door and rang the doorbell. In a few minutes, the man she recognized from Evie Wyler's news feed opened the door. He looked at them and shook his head slightly.

"Yes? Can I help you?"

"Calgary Police Service, sir. Are you Mr. Wyler?" Jones asked.

He laughed. "No, there is no Mr. Wyler. I'm Trevor Vance. Are you looking for Ms. Wyler? Evie?"

"Could we come in to talk?"

He looked as though he would deny them, but eventually he shrugged and stepped back from the door, allowing them in. The inside was mostly beige and darker browns. Neat and tidy. Vance bent down and picked up a stuffed rabbit, which he held in his hand, unsure of what to do with it.

"Let's have a seat," Jones suggested.

Vance gave a slight laugh as they sat down. "You're making me nervous now. What is all this about?"

"According to her driver's license, this is Ms. Wyler's residence?"

"Yes, that's right."

"And are you her partner? Nanny? What?"

"Partner, yes. I've got Ada today, but it really depends on our schedules as to which one is home to take care of her."

"It's your wife's workday today?"

He nodded.

"Where does she work?"

"From a coffee shop, most of the time."

At their quizzical looks, he explained further. "Remote work, you know, but working with the little one underfoot is distracting. She likes to work from the coffee shop, or somewhere else she can just sit and work and not be disturbed. Now that we're allowed to be in restaurants, of course. She couldn't while there were more restrictions."

"What does she do?"

"She's a teacher. Not on Zoom or somewhere they meet face-to-face, obviously, since she's in the middle of a coffee shop. But people complete online units, and she grades them, gives feedback, suggests additional resources, that sort of thing. For online accreditation."

"They don't just have the computer mark the tests?" Jones asked.

"If there is a multiple-choice section, then yes, the computer will mark that portion and just give Evie the results. But there are short answers, essays, oral reports on video, all kinds of different responses. And computers don't do very well at that kind of thing."

"Ah." Jones and Margie nodded. "So she would be at the coffee shop right now?"

"She had to go in to the physical campus today. It's in Red Deer. A bit of a drive, but she doesn't have to be there in person very often."

"So what time did she leave this morning?"

"I don't know. I slept until eight. She was gone when I got up." He looked from Margie's face to Jones's. "That's not unusual. She sometimes gets up at five, five-thirty. Goes for a walk or run. Gets started on her work early so that she will be done by early afternoon. Then she has time in the afternoon and evening for family or other things."

"Sounds like a reasonable plan," Jones agreed. "If you can get up that early."

"Me, I can't. But her body is set differently than mine. For her, sleeping in until eight would be impossible. But so is staying up until midnight."

"So you keep different schedules and don't try to match each other's rhythms."

"Yeah. When we're together, we're together. If we have different things to do, that's okay too. We're both open to the other person being independent and having a life of their own. That's what works for us."

Margie wondered if this was the new euphemism for an "open relationship." Polyamory of some flavor.

Vance looked at Jones, raising his brows. "So… I've answered your questions. Now you want to tell me what this is about? Is Evie in trouble for something? Outstanding parking tickets?" He smiled, waiting for an explanation that he was sure would be bland and unworrying.

"Mr. Vance, I'm sorry to give you this bad news, but Evie's body was found this morning. She is dead."

His mouth fell open. He looked back and forth at them, gave a little smile as if it must be a joke he was supposed to find funny. Maybe they were recording him and wanted to see if he would cry and wail, then they would tell him he had just been punked. Margie and Jones both continued to look at him steadily, waiting for it to sink in. For him to see their grave expressions and realize that no, it was not a joke. It was the end of the relationship and the start of a new life that he had not anticipated.

"My… Evie? That can't be. Are you sure it's her? Maybe someone… stole her wallet or her computer. If something had happened to her, wouldn't I know it…?"

"Some people do get premonitions," Jones offered. "But most people don't. For most people, it is quite a shock. Like for you."

"She was just here. I looked in on her before I went to bed. She was fast asleep. Everything was just fine. Normal."

"You sleep in separate rooms?" Jones asked.

"Yes. It's easier that way, with us going to bed and getting up at different times. Trust me, there's always time for intimacy whether you're sleeping in the same room or not. We just have two beds to choose from." He gave a little laugh. He'd explained this before. Their friends probably all thought they were a little weird. He had the patter memorized. It came out automatically, without the appropriate emotion.

"Well, if one of you snores, that makes a lot of sense," Margie offered.

"No, not usually. But Evie talks in her sleep. Or gets up to write or work on the computer when she can't sleep. And we're up and down at different times. Of course, there's Ada too. She still gets up the night sometimes, wet or with nightmares. So one of us can take care of her without waking the other one up."

"How do you decide which one of you takes care of her?"

"She's big enough to get out of bed herself, so she chooses which room she goes to." He hesitated. "Usually me."

"Dads are more fun at night?" Jones asked. "Big surprise."

They were both watching him carefully, waiting for it to sink in and start becoming real to him. It was easy to chatter on about Ada and their domestic life and not really think about what they had said. He could almost forget it.

Almost.

Tears gathered at the corners of Vance's eyes. "She can't be dead," he said pleadingly. "There's been some kind of mistake."

"We will need to verify her identity. At this time, a visual match has been made, comparing her face to the picture on her driver's license. But we'll need something more definitive than that. Don't worry about that part right now. What we are going to need you to talk about right now is the last time that you saw Evie, and what has happened since then."

"I just told you. I looked in on her before I went to bed. She was asleep. I went to sleep. I got up around eight when Ada got up. Had some coffee, puttered around on the computer. That's it. Played with Ada, gave her breakfast. It's summer, so she doesn't have any preschool to get to. It's just her and me today, until Mommy gets home... at two o'clock or so." He swiped at a tear on his cheek with the back of his hand. "Only..."

Only this time, Mommy wasn't ever coming home. She never would again.

CHAPTER SIX

"You said that Evie would get up early to walk or run or work. And that sometimes she got up in the middle of the night when she couldn't sleep."

"Yes."

"And you don't know what time she got up this morning or last night and left the house."

"No."

"Does she take her car or transit?"

"Her car, usually." Vance got up from his seat and walked to the back of the house, where he apparently looked through a connecting door into the garage. He returned, looking stunned. "Her car is in the garage. So she didn't go out to one of her favorite coffee shops. She just went... out for a walk?"

"Apparently." Jones waited to see what his response would be. That this was normal? Unusual behavior? That she had been anxious lately and the separate bedrooms were still quite a new arrangement?

Vance shrugged and scratched his forehead. His arms were shaking. He sat back down. "I... don't know. I have no idea what to think of this. I just thought when I got up this morning that she'd already left for work. I didn't even know there was anything wrong. I wouldn't have known until this afternoon."

"You don't talk or text during the day?"

"Well, often, yes. We send each other messages or relax for a few minutes and call to see how the other one is. But there isn't anything *set,* you know. If one of us is super busy or stressed, then we might get through the day without ever connecting with each other. And then we just try to have a nice evening together and get caught up. Even if we had gone all day without talking to each other or without getting a text from her, I wouldn't have been worried that something was wrong."

Margie made a couple of discreet notes in her notepad.

"What... happened to her?" Vance asked tentatively. "Was it a car accident or a heart attack?"

He seemed to have forgotten that the car was still in the garage. He was just looking for something that would make sense. People didn't just die without warning in his world.

"The autopsy hasn't been completed yet," Jones said. "But it looks like it was a fall. An accident."

"She fell and... hit her head, or something?" Vance asked. "Is that what you mean?"

"We won't know for sure until we get the ME's report. But please try not to obsess over that. From the preliminary information we have, it was very quick. She did not suffer."

"But... a fall. What kind of freak thing is that? People don't just die from a fall. Maybe they get a broken bone. *Maybe.*" He shook his head. "They don't die."

"I'm sorry. We'll provide you with as much information as you need later, when we have it. For now, you're just going to have to be satisfied with what we can give you. It is an active investigation and we're limited in what we can tell you."

"An active investigation. You mean you're from..."

"We are homicide detectives," Margie confirmed.

"You mean this was murder? You're investigating this as a murder?"

"No, Mr. Vance. We believe it was an accident. But each case needs to be investigated until we are satisfied that there was nothing suspicious about it. No foul play."

"There couldn't have been. No one would ever do anything to hurt Evie. She was so kind and sensitive. I don't know of anyone who didn't like her."

Jones smiled reassuringly at him. "She was well-liked? And nothing had happened lately to stress her out? Getting up late at night or early in the morning wasn't because something was on her mind? Worrying her?"

"She worried about everything." He shrugged and puffed out his cheeks, then let the air go. "She's the kind of person who always got all twisted up about injustices. People or animals or protected areas that were being threatened. She wanted to live in harmony with nature and with everyone around her. Hated hearing anything about child abuse or cruelty to animals. Always taking up a new cause."

"And what was bothering her the most recently?"

"I don't know. There was the residential school thing. That bothered her a lot. And our, uh, discussions over Ada and her diet, and whether it was okay for me to feed her meat when she was with me and we were eating out somewhere. Evie kept a vegetarian household," he explained. "And everything had to be cruelty free, but she didn't try to force other people to do the same things as she did. I'm not vegetarian, but I eat vegetarian when I'm here. But not when I go out. I figured Ada should be allowed to choose when we went out too. At least to be exposed to other foods. I told Evie that when people are deprived of a thing for their whole lives—sugar, or meat, or alcohol, or whatever—then they just go crazy when they are old enough to make their own decisions or have their own money. The kids without any self-control or adults who are immediately addicted, that's because their parents kept them from experiencing those things. If they had allowed some choice and moderation instead…"

"So you wanted to be able to raise your daughter to be an omnivore." Jones asked.

"Yes. Or to choose for herself."

As if a two- or three-year-old was old enough to make a choice like that. A child of that age would happily choose a grilled cheese diet. Or a pizza pocket diet. Preschoolers were not well-known for making wise, well-balanced decisions.

Margie didn't look up from the notes she was making in her notepad as she asked her question. Jones would be watching him carefully for his reaction. "How intense did these discussions get?"

"How intense?" Vance sounded for a moment like he didn't understand, then all at once, he did. "No, it wasn't like that. We didn't fight. There was never any violence in our relationship. Evie would never have stood for that. Neither of us were inclined that way."

"Raised voices?"

"No. Well... maybe raised voices. But no threats, no violence. Just... active debate."

Margie nodded and looked up to assess his face. No obvious tells. But she had been fooled before. People could lie well, were psychopaths, or had another reason for not feeling guilty about what they had done or the stories they were telling her. She could rely on her eyes and ears only so much.

"Was there anyone else around last night? Company over for wine?"

"No. Just Evie and me and Ada. And Ada was off to bed, of course. So it was just the two of us. Watching some TV, talking about our days, relaxing at the end of a long day."

So no witnesses.

"What was Evie's day like? What did she tell you about it?"

He thought back, licking his lips. "Umm... well..." He rubbed at the corners of his eyes again, though they didn't seem to be producing any more tears. "Pretty much the same as usual. She has her work. Sometimes she tells me about funny answers students have put on tests. Computer problems she might have been frustrated by. The meeting in Red Deer was kind of out of the blue, I hadn't known that she was going out there."

"Did she seem concerned or agitated about that?"

"No. No, I don't think so."

"Did she seem relaxed? Say or do anything out of the ordinary?"

"I really can't think of anything. You don't think that something happened and someone killed her, do you? That doesn't make any sense. She was a mom. An online teacher. Not the kind of person who attracts a lot of attention. No enemies or jealous coworkers."

"The two of you saw other people?" Margie asked. She kept her voice casual, as if this would be a normal arrangement. They were sleeping in separate rooms, after all. They might very well have other relationships, approved by the other.

But Vance's face portrayed shock. "Saw other people? Certainly not! Why would you think that?" He looked suddenly more anxious. "Was there something that made you think there was someone else? She wasn't... with another man, was she? Or in a hotel, or..." He shuddered, scaring himself with the direction of his thoughts.

"No, nothing like that," Margie assured him.

"We're just covering all the bases," Jones said blandly. As it was natural to ask how many other lovers a spouse or intimate partner might have. With the direction society was headed, it seemed like there were more and more of those "open" relationships going on than ever. Or maybe people just talked about it more, with the explosion of personal information being revealed on social media. What was a shocking secret a hundred years ago was now a social media post.

"We were committed to each other. We were exclusive. Neither of us saw anyone else."

"You didn't have any female friends that you saw occasionally?"

"Friends, yes. But not lovers. That's different."

"Did you see them with Evie, or on your own?"

"On my own. We didn't share a lot of friends. We had very different interests, weren't into the same things."

"And Evie saw people on her own. Female and male."

"I suppose so."

"And it never concerned you? You were never jealous or suspicious? She didn't seem to be keeping anything from you?"

"No. There was nothing like that. We both chose to be here, to be in this relationship. No one forced us into that. And we didn't force each other to stay. If one of us didn't want to stay together… then we would have dealt with that."

"Whose name is the house in?"

"Evie's. But that was just for convenience. So that if we needed to sell the house, she could sign everything."

Margie made a note about that. And who would get the child? Evie, presumably. The courts still favored mothers over fathers. So if Vance had wanted to terminate their relationship, but to keep the house and his daughter…

She finished her note. It wasn't murder. There was not anything to indicate that it was anything other than what it looked like. Evie had gone out for a walk. She had fallen down the hill. End of story.

Vance rubbed a hand over his face. "When can I get her cell phone back?"

CHAPTER SEVEN

*M*argie and Jones exchanged glances. While they had been able to find a few credit cards, they had not turned up a wallet or purse. No cell phone. Evie's personal effects consisted of some pocket litter and what she had been wearing when she died.

"We have not found a cell phone," Jones said. "Is it possible that she left it here by mistake? I know it is rare to go out without a cell phone these days, but she might have left it on the counter and meant to grab it or been distracted by something."

"No, I would have noticed if she had left it lying around."

Vance looked vaguely around the room. He again retreated to the back of the house to check the table or the counter beside the coffee pot, places where Evie might normally have lain her phone down and then not picked it up again. He wandered for a moment, then returned, shaking his head. He pulled out his own phone and dialed.

Everyone waited in silence, ears pricked for the ringing of Evie's cell phone, or the low rumble of a phone vibrating on a hard surface. There was no sound. Margie watched Vance's face for any changes as he held his phone to his ear, listening to the ringing on his end, as if it might all be a mistake and Evie would answer her phone and explain it all away.

Then his face fell. He paused for a moment, then pressed the end button on the call and slid his phone away.

"She must have it."

"It wasn't on her body. Maybe she dropped it," Jones suggested.

"*How* could this happen? How could something like this happen?" He stared at them, his eyes rimmed with red.

There was a small noise, and Margie turned her head to see a little angel emerging from the hall that led to the bedrooms. Mussy-haired Ada went to her father. He picked her up and held his face against her head, eyes full of tears once more. How was he going to tell this little darling that her mother was dead and would never return home again?

But he wimped out and didn't tell her right away. Maybe he needed some more time to prepare himself. A good sign. If he had been involved in Evie's death, then he would have been thinking of how to break it to Ada. He'd have a script prepared, something gentle and honest. He might have looked up on the internet how to break bad news to children.

Ada took Vance's face in her hands, one on either cheek, and rubbed her face against his.

"Daddy owie," she said. She rubbed her cheek with her hand, then put her hand back on his cheek and rubbed it. Margie could hear the scrape of his whiskers and understood. She smiled. Ada didn't like the scratchiness of Vance's whiskers.

"My sister's son said that his dad had 'dangerous sharp things' on his face," Margie told Ada. "Does your daddy too?"

"Yes." Ada gave a definite nod. "Yes, dang'rous sharp tings."

There was a lump in Margie's throat. She swallowed and tried to continue as if unaffected. They needed to be professional. Ferret out everything they could in case the significant other had any reason to want the victim dead. Do the official notification. Ask if he needed anyone to stay with him.

"Is there anything we can do for you, Mr. Vance? Is there anyone you would like us to call for you? Maybe someone who can come and sit with you and help with Ada?"

"No. I'm used to looking after my own daughter. Anyone else would just be in the way."

"You will want your loved ones around you. Are your parents in town? Siblings? Friends?"

"No. Not yet. I don't want to do this yet."

By "this," Margie assumed he meant that he couldn't accept that Evie really was dead and wasn't going to do anything that might concede that she was gone. By avoiding the truth, he could keep her with him just that little bit longer.

"I'll give you my card," Jones said. She reached into her pocket and thumbed one out. She looked at Margie, who handed her one of hers. Jones nodded and passed both of them to Vance. "There you go. That's both of us. If you need to talk, please give us a call. And we can refer you to some community resources. Grief counseling. Other supports."

"Not yet," Vance murmured. "Not yet."

AT HOME in the evening Margie was still thinking of Evie and Ada. She played some upbeat music on her iPhone and danced around the kitchen while she searched the fridge for ingredients and prepared her meal, trying to lift her spirits. She talked and sang to Stella, who sat watching her with a doggie grin, happy to have the attention, whatever the reason.

It was important not to bring all those work worries home with her. She could not fix everyone's lives or protect all the family members from feeling the effects of what had already happened. She could do her best to bring the families answers and closure, and that was all. Worrying about it at home wouldn't improve her work. The best thing would be for her to go into work the next day rested, refreshed, and ready to tackle the case again, and that meant she needed to let it all go.

She felt very virtuous making herself a vegetable stir-fry. Since Christina wasn't home, she threw the leftover chicken in as well. She considered leaving out the noodles and rice to keep her calorie intake down, but she really couldn't have stir fry without rice or noodles, so she went ahead and warmed those up as well. A run in the morning would help combat the extra calories. No reason she couldn't enjoy a little extra here and there if she were increasing her activity level.

"We'll go for a walk after supper too," she told Stella. "I can do a nice long walk today, as long as it isn't too hot."

The last couple of days, the weather had moderated a little due to the amount of smoke in the air from the BC forest fires. The temperatures had still been getting up to 29 or 30, but without the direct sun, it was much more tolerable, except for those first couple of minutes in a hot car. She had also figured out the best places to put fans in the house and it really hadn't been too bad.

But if she took a long walk, her legs might not be ready for a run in the morning. So maybe just a medium walk.

Her music stalled, a call coming through on the phone. Margie clicked her earphones to answer it without checking the caller ID first.

"Detective Patenaude."

"Your daughter," Christina snapped back, and laughed.

"Oh, hi sweetie. Sorry, I'm working hands-free and didn't know it was you. How are you doing?"

"Good. Lots of fun at the Stampede, but I'm exhausted. That's a lot of walking around. And my feet!"

"I wondered whether sandals were a good idea for all that walking around. If they're broken in, then they might be okay, but those ones were pretty new."

"Well, I guess they're broken in now. Or my feet are broken in. Ouch."

"Did you get some band-aids on them?"

"Yeah, but the straps keep rubbing against them and pulling the band-aids off. I just went to the first aid place the first time, but now I've got a box of band-aids in my backpack and I'm replacing them like every hour." Christina sighed. "The things we do to look good," she said dramatically.

Margie laughed. "Glad you're looking after them. So have you had something to eat yet? I mean other than deep-fried Twinkies and mini donuts."

"None of us are very hungry right now. Just tired. So we're going to take a break in the park, just stretch out in the shade. When we've finished digesting all of those Twinkies and donuts, we'll go to Peters'."

Margie could hardly even think of Peters' after all the other Stampede junk food without feeling a little queasy. But the teenagers had iron stomachs.

"Then we'll go find a place to watch the fireworks. I hope we can still see okay with all this smoke."

"I saw some pictures on Facebook. I think you'll be able to see just fine. It's the 'Fireworks Spectacular' tonight. Should be the best night to watch them."

"They're at eleven." Christina yawned. "Then I'll be home after that."

"Are you sure you don't need to come home and go to bed right now?" Margie teased.

"Mom! I just need a little nap, then I'll be just fine."

"Okay. You guys be careful going to sleep. Make sure your electronics are safe and out of sight and have someone stay awake to keep watch. Don't make yourselves a target."

"I promise we'll be fine," Christina reassured her.

Which didn't reassure Margie.

She sighed after the call was disconnected, then grabbed her dinner and sat down at the table to eat alone. But with the TV on and Stella at her side, she didn't feel quite as lonely.

AFTER DINNER, Margie clipped the leash onto Stella's collar. "How about that walk now? We'll get some fresh air and exercise, see if there are any squirrels or gophers, and check out all your scent posts. How does that sound?"

Stella's mouth was wide open as she panted her approval and her tail wagged back and forth so fast they didn't need a fan.

"Yes? Yes, you're ready for walkies?"

Stella gave one excited yip, then pointed her nose at the door, waiting for Margie to follow.

"All right. Let's go." Margie opened the door for both of them to step out, then locked it behind her. She let Stella pull her to the city sidewalk and start walking toward the multi-use trail along Twenty-Sixth Street.

When they reached Twenty-Sixth Street, Margie's eyes widened in wonder. She wasn't sure what to say or think. There was a teddy bear or other stuffed animal fastened to each fence post between the pathway and the road. She knew instantly what it was for. People had been setting out their own memorials of children's shoes and stuffed toys on their porches to memorialize the children who had died at the residential schools. The toys on the fence posts were clearly a continuation of this idea. They extended down the road as far as Margie could see. There were, she suspected, 215 bears, each symbolizing a grave discovered with ground-penetrating radar at the old residential school site in Kamloops.

Margie pressed her finger to the bottom of her nose for a moment, trying to quell the emotions rising up within her. It had already been an emotional day, discovering that their victim was the mother of a little girl. A sweet little angel who would grow up without her mother, and probably remember nothing about her as an adult.

"Okay. It's okay," she prompted herself. Though the raw wound she had felt each time new gravesites were acknowledged had been starting to heal, it was good to stop and acknowledge those children once more. Someone in the neighborhood—more than one someone, considering the number of toys that had been collected for the project—was mourning with Margie. She was not alone.

Despite the deniers and the people who thought that Margie should "be over it already," since she hadn't gone to a residential school herself, there were still others out there who were looking for ways to express their grief and to memorialize the deaths of the children far away from their families.

Margie tried to swallow the lump in her throat. She looked down at Stella, who was sitting beside her patiently, staring up at her and wondering what was holding her up.

"Let's walk," Margie told her lightly. They crossed the street at the crosswalk, and Margie looked for a sign explaining the memorial and who had placed it there. There was a yellow sign to the right where the line of animals started, so Margie turned right so that she could go read it.

There was no signature. No name of a school or other organization that had arranged the collection and installation of the animals. Just the words

In memory for the children found

CHAPTER EIGHT

*M*argie stayed up reading until Christina was dropped off by her friends. She entered the house quietly, then raised her brows at her mother sitting up on the couch.

"You didn't have to stay up for me, Mom," Christina whispered, as if she might wake someone else in the house up.

"I wanted to make sure that you got home safe. I know you think that I worry too much. But you don't know how much I've really dialed back. If you knew the level of worry that I *started* at, you would be really impressed."

Christina laughed. "Well, I've seen you worry, so I think I know. But I'm home safe. Nothing happened to any of us. It was a good day." She yawned widely, not bothering to cover it until she had closed her mouth again, politely patting her lips. "We had a really good time. Just—a long time."

"You'll have to tell me everything that happened."

"I will. Tomorrow. Did you know *Marianas Trench* was there? They were so good. And…" Christina yawned again. "And there was a bannock booth at the Elbow Park Camp. Mmm." She patted her stomach. "So good."

"Did you bring me some?"

"Nope." Christina's look was mischievous. "We'll have to make some."

"Oh, I see. Well, we will soon. Brush your teeth before bed."

"Yes, Mom."

Margie closed her eyes as Christina headed to the bathroom. It felt good to have everybody home.

❧

"We have a surprise," Jones announced when Margie answered her phone, not even bothering to say hello and exchange social niceties. "So you should come out to Edworthy again today. Is that okay? Are you already on your way in?"

"I was just heading out the door. And I still have it in the GPS from yesterday, so that isn't a problem. What's up? I thought we finished with the scene yesterday."

"Didn't I just tell you it was a surprise? See you when you get here." Without waiting for an answer, Jones hung up.

Margie looked at her phone for a moment, then put it down on the counter and poured her coffee into a travel mug. So much for having a leisurely coffee before work. She would drink it on the way instead. At least she had driven the route once before, so she wouldn't be as worried about not being able to find it.

Half an hour later she was blasting the wrong way down Bow Trail and looking for a way to get turned around. After forty-five minutes, she was finally pulling into the park, sweat dripping down her forehead and back, not from the heat but from the stress and embarrassment of getting lost despite the GPS and the flak she anticipated she would get from the other law enforcement officers for being so late.

There were no barricades this time. Margie got as close as she could to the staging area from the day before, and saw several vehicles pulled up on the grass. She followed their lead and drove her car out of the gravel of the parking lot. She drained the last of her coffee, very cold and bitter, and climbed out of the car.

"Here's Patenaude," someone called out.

Margie looked around and saw Cruz, a Filipino native, motioning to her, the others standing around in a loose grouping. She walked toward them.

"Sorry to be so long," she apologized. "Traffic. So what's going on? What are we doing back here today?"

"I was talking to Siever last night about the case," Cruz said, nodding in Detective Siever's direction. "We were bouncing ideas around. Got to talking about the fact that the victim didn't have a phone or wallet on her. Or keys. Jones said that you guys talked to the husband yesterday, and same thing, where is her phone? It's not at home, so where did it go?"

Margie turned and looked at the hill. It was a long way to the top. And she wasn't climbing it for another search. Not after seeing the vertical rescue team navigate it with safety harnesses the day before. She didn't need that kind of excitement.

She looked back at Cruz, who was nodding. "None of us are going back up there for a grid search," he confirmed. "Besides, what if it is somewhere you can't see or reach from the ground?" He motioned to the trees. "A purse strap could easily get caught in the branches of a tree. She's not going to hold on to it all the way down. It's going to get airborne at some point, and then... where? We don't know."

"Right. So are you hiring a pack of squirrels to search the trees, or what?"

Cruz raised one eyebrow. "That would be pretty nutty," he deadpanned.

Margie smiled, glad that she and the others on the team could talk to each other and keep things light without worrying about offending each other. Some teams were so serious that just surviving through the day was like going to battle. At least with her homicide team, she knew she could count on them to try to keep each other from getting dragged down by the gloom that came with working in dark places.

Jones walked up and handed Margie a device with a joystick.

"Are we playing video games today?" Margie asked. "That's a nice break from the job."

"This one is yours," Jones said, pointing to a drone on the ground nearby. "Flip the switch to activate it."

Margie flipped the on/off switch. The drone buzzed to life, the rotors starting to spin immediately. A screen on the controller lit up so Margie could see that it had a camera installed and ready to go. "Okay. How do I do this?"

"You'll get the hang of it really quickly. These are the sticks," Jones pointed to the two joysticks, "and those control your direction and height.

You can see your progress on the screen, and an aerial of the ground below." She pointed to each control and explained what she needed to know. It was all a little overwhelming, but Margie had seen a four-year-old flying his father's drone at a family picnic back before COVID, and she figured if a four-year-old could figure it out, she could eventually be taught how to operate one too.

In a couple of minutes, Margie had the drone in the air, and Jones ran her through a few exercises to make sure she got the hang out of how to move it around. She pointed to the hill.

"This area is yours. Everything left of that tree. You see the tall one there, with the weird branch to the right?"

"Yeah."

"So just fly this baby around, over the trees, down close to the ground, behind bushes, everywhere you can think of that the firefighters might not have been able to see when they helped out with the search yesterday. Siever, he's got one with a grabber, so that we can retrieve whatever evidence we might find, but it needs to be documented first, just like normal. All the footage is being recorded, so just fly around, get as many angles as you can if you find something interesting."

"And call Siever to pick it up."

Jones nodded. "Exactly."

CHAPTER NINE

*M*argie found that she could only operate the little craft for a certain amount of time before things started to blur and she was no longer seeing what was on the screen clearly, but just going through the motions and not absorbing what she saw.

Everyone had the same problem to one degree or another, so Margie wasn't the only one taking breaks to put down the controller and walk around looking at the ground and trees from their usual perspective for a while. Other than Siever, who seemed to have become one with his drone controller and was able not only to fly the drone much more skillfully than Margie, but to carry on conversations, walk around, and do other things while he was flying.

Margie called Christina when she was taking a break from flying.

"Hi, Mom." Christina yawned into the phone. "How's it going?"

"I hope you're not still in bed."

"No. I've been up for a long time. I was actually thinking of having a nap soon."

"I figured with how tired you were yesterday you would be asleep until noon today."

"No. I was up at eight-thirty. Something like that. I already took Stella out for a walk," she informed Margie, anticipating what she would say. "Hey, did you see the memorial over on Twenty-Sixth Street?"

"Yes, I just saw it yesterday. I was going to tell you about it, but you were so tired last night."

"Yeah, I was dead to the world in about thirty seconds. I don't think I would have remembered anything you said between the door and my bed."

"Good thing I made you brush your teeth."

"Did you? See, I don't even remember that."

Margie laughed. Christina had had that zombie look when she had walked from the bathroom to her bedroom. Already asleep on her feet. "Guess what I'm doing today?"

"Well, you don't usually sound that perky, so I'm going to say… running away from home?"

"No. I'm flying a drone."

"Really? Like Uncle Dave had at that last reunion?"

"Yep. I am now as cool as Uncle Dave."

"I wouldn't push it. You don't actually *own* a drone. I hope they didn't give you the kind that drops bombs."

"No! I don't think anyone would dare do that! These ones just record camera footage."

"That sounds like a lot of fun."

"It is."

"So who gets to *review* all of the camera footage?"

Margie groaned. "You had to say that, didn't you?"

"Sorry. Just being practical. Learned it from my mother. If you're out there recording the drone's feed all day, then it will take at least as long to watch all the footage."

And with several of them flying drones, there would be even more.

"I don't think we're going to review all of the raw footage," she told Christina, crossing her fingers and hoping it was true. "Just if we find something, they'll chop it up into stills. If we need them as evidence."

"What are you trying to find? I hope it's not a skeleton."

"No, not a skeleton. We already have the body. We're just looking for any other personal effects that might be close by."

"With a drone? Where exactly was this body?"

"I can't give you details."

"Have you found anything yet?"

"No… nothing significant. But there is still a lot of area to search."

"Well… good luck. I hope you find something. Stella says hi. When we go see Moushoom next, we should take him to see the memorial, if the weather is good. I think he'd really like to see that. To know that his friends who died aren't forgotten."

Margie nodded her agreement. "For sure. I think he would like that too."

"And bannock. Can we take him some bread? And maybe some stew? He always loves it when we take him traditional food."

It was too bad that the dining room didn't explore options from other cultures. Everything they served was so uniformly "American." None of the foods from Indigenous cultures. Margie had seen other cultures represented in the people on Moushoom's floor as well. Hispanic, Italian, Russian—they had some very different backgrounds. Maybe the kitchen staff could try a traditional recipe from one of those cultures every week, instead of always just serving bland hamburger, chicken, and meatloaf day in and day out. Margie felt bad for Moushoom when she saw the dinners they served him.

"I'll schedule some time so we can make some bannock together, okay?"

"Okay," Christina agreed. "I could probably make it myself. It's not that hard."

"Yes, if you want to. But I enjoy cooking with you."

"Me too." Her daughter's voice was warm and happy, satisfied that Margie hadn't said that bannock was too hard for her to make by herself or that she wasn't allowed to have the stove on while Margie was at work. The girl was a teenager. She could probably have made bannock herself when she was five. As she'd said, it wasn't exactly a difficult recipe.

"I'd better get back to flying. Have a good day and don't try to do too much today. After everything you did yesterday, you don't want to wear yourself out. You know you get sick when you are exhausted."

"I'm not exhausted. I slept good. And I'm not going anywhere today. Everybody is just gaming or chatting today."

"Good." Margie was glad that Christina was happy to stay home for a quiet day and she wouldn't have to worry about what Christina was up to and when she would be home. "I love you, honey. Talk to you later."

"Have a good flight."

§

IT WASN'T a surprise to anyone that it was Siever who made the only significant discovery. He had probably checked his own area and everyone else's three times over and had incredible control and attention.

"There's a purse," he announced, raising his voice above the other chatter going on around him.

Everyone crowded in close around him to look at the screen as he lowered the grapple toward the red purse, lodged in the branches of one of the trees. Margie looked at the sky, straining to see where the drone was. They were surprisingly hard to see against the trees. The drone was close to where they were gathered, just a few meters from where Evie Wyler's body had landed.

She looked back at Siever's screen again. The clawed grapple was close to the purse. He inched it closer, coaxing the hooks around the strap of the shoulder bag. The claws fell into place, and he pulled the drone up. The claws closed more tightly around the strap and, in a moment, the purse started to lift.

Margie cheered with everyone else and clapped her hands. "Detective Siever wins the prize. Nice work!"

"It was his idea too," Jones reminded everyone. "Well done, Siever."

His cheeks were a little pink and he split his focus between the screen on the controller and the drone in the sky, flying slowly home. He flew the little craft up to Detective Jones and hovered there. Jones put her hand around the strap of the purse, and he released the grapple.

"Show off," Margie laughed.

Siever brought his drone down close to the others on the ground. "Is that it, do you think? Or should we keep looking?"

"I think we've been over this area as much as we can justify," Jones said. "They won't want me using too many man-hours for something that might not even be there. This was a brilliant find. Really good work. I didn't think we were going to find anything after the number of times we have gone over this area"

"How can something bright red have been that hard to find?" Margie marveled.

"It was well-disguised by the leaves," Siever said. "I just caught a flash of something behind them. It could have been a kite or a bit of a plastic bag."

"Good eye."

Jones took a cursory look through the purse to see what it contained.

She just touched the edges of the items with her purple gloves, being careful not to smear any fingerprints or obscure any other evidence.

"Zipper was open; contents of the wallet have spilled inside the main compartment of the bag. That would be how the credit cards were lost in the fall. But… I do not see a phone."

"She had to have a phone. Where else would it have gone?" Cruz asked.

"It might have fallen out, like the credit cards. And if so, it could be anywhere."

They all looked up into the trees and the hill that they had already searched.

"Wherever it is, I don't think we're going to find it," Margie said, rubbing the back of her neck. There was only so much that they could do. Especially when they were just investigating an accident, not a murder. They couldn't put all kinds of hours and other resources into an accidental death. It didn't benefit anyone.

CHAPTER TEN

here was a briefing in the conference room once they had all returned to the office. Mac was pleased with the discovery of the purse, and gave compliments all around to the team, but especially to Siever, who blushed again at the praise.

"That was a significant find. Unfortunately, we are still left with the loss of the cell phone, which is unfortunate. Have we made a request with the service provider to give us the last known GPS location or cell tower ping?"

Jones nodded. "I've got a request in. But you know how long they can take sometimes."

"I do," Mac agreed. "And even if we get that information, it might not help us at all. Do we have progress in any other directions? How did the autopsy go?"

"Death by fall from height, blunt cardiac trauma," Jones replied.

"Which is what we expected."

Everyone nodded.

"Anything else we need to follow up on?"

Margie raised a tentative hand.

Mac nodded to her. "Patenaude?"

"I'm just… a little confused about the purse and the credit cards."

He blinked at her. "Jones said that there were cards in the main section of the purse and that the zipper was open."

"Yes, exactly."

"That explains how the credit cards fell out onto the hill."

"Yes, but what explains the purse being open and the cards spilled into the main section?"

Everyone looked around at each other. Jones started to nod, thinking about it. "The cards clearly belonged inside the wallet."

"Then who took them out? Why would Wyler take a bunch of cards out of her wallet and just leave them loose in her purse? And why would she leave the zipper unzipped? I know it's mostly men in this room, but a lot of you are married. Do your wives leave their handbags unzipped when they are out in public? With their cards, and phone in clear view? That would just be marking them as a target. You don't need to be a skilled pickpocket to grab a wallet from an open purse. Wyler was out walking at night or in the early morning with her purse gaping open? Why?"

"There's a simple enough explanation to that," Siever pointed out. "The zipper caught on a branch. Or the impact of getting caught on the tree burst it open. It probably landed with a lot of force. A car hitting a pedestrian can blast them out of their shoes. I'm sure that there would be enough force to unzip or split open a zipper."

Margie had to admit he had a point there. But it didn't answer the other question. Why were the cards outside of her wallet but inside the purse?

"How did the cards on the hill get out of the purse if it didn't open until impact?" she asked, cocking her head at Siever. "It had to be open while it was airborne."

"Hmm." Siever nodded. "You're right."

"Why would she take the cards out of her wallet?" Jones asked Margie, turning to her. "Do you ever just randomly start pulling cards out of your wallet while you're out for a walk?"

Margie laughed. "No. I take a card out to pay for something. Maybe to swipe for loyalty rewards. Umm, my health care card at the doctor's office or driver's license at a traffic stop."

"Right. The only time you take your cards out is to use them. And you don't use multiple cards in one location, except maybe loyalty card plus credit card or somewhere you have to give two forms of ID. But this was something else."

"Reorganizing them?" Cruz suggested. "Someone had put the cards away in the wrong slots."

"She wouldn't have been reorganizing them in the middle of the night," Jones countered.

"Nothing to say that she was." Cruz stared up at the ceiling, thinking it through. "She might have been doing it during the day and gotten interrupted. Kid wanted to show her a picture or fell off the couch. Or it was time to make dinner. So she just left them loose in her purse until she could get back to them and complete the project."

Margie nodded. "I suppose I could see that. Then she picks it up when she's on her way out in the dark and doesn't realize that she's left it undone."

"Either that, or someone else rifled her purse," Siever said.

Margie looked at him thoughtfully. But who would have gone through Wyler's purse? Vance, looking for evidence that she was seeing someone else? Her daughter, playing "store"? Or something more nefarious? Someone who had looked through her wallet to verify her identity. Maybe when she was already disabled or dead.

"There haven't been any indicators of foul play," Jones countered.

"This could just as easily be homicide as accident. Someone pushed her. She knew the area; it wasn't like she would just walk off a cliff because she didn't know it was there. Or that she would decide to explore a steep trail down the side of a steep hill in the middle of the night. Has the tox screen come back? Was she drunk? Under the influence of some drug? A sleeping pill? Did she really just walk off a cliff?" Siever asked.

Margie shifted uncomfortably. They had all just been going on the assumption that there was no one else involved. Wyler could have misjudged the edge, slipped, or dropped something and fallen trying to retrieve it. But was that more likely than being pushed?

"There wasn't any evidence that anyone else was there," she said.

"There were other footprints. Other people had been up there. We just can't determine who was there when. She wasn't necessarily walking alone."

"She could have been meeting someone," Margie mused.

Siever nodded. He sat back, looking satisfied that someone else had heard him.

"The husband didn't say that she walked in her sleep," Jones said, her thinking obviously off in another direction. "But people do. They can do all kinds of things while sleepwalking. Including driving a car or cooking on the stove. Or walking off a cliff."

"The husband would have noticed if she was sleepwalking when she got up, wouldn't he?" Cruz asked.

"No. I'm not sure you could tell." Gagnon had been mostly quiet until then. "And if it was at a time when she normally would have been up..."

"They didn't sleep together," Jones told him. "They had separate bedrooms."

Gagnon blinked, thinking about that. "I suppose she could have been sleepwalking, then."

"So, it's possible," Siever said a little aggressively. "But is it likely? What's more likely? That she was sleepwalking or that she met someone?"

Margie thought of the sweet little girl. Evie Wyler seemed like she had the ideal life with Vance and their little girl. She had a comfortable house to live in, good job, a partner who seemed fully committed to her and participated in the childcare. He was even the one that Ada chose to go to when she woke up from a nightmare, which suggested that he was a loving and attentive parent, not one who just did what Wyler told him to.

Would Wyler leave all of that for an illicit affair? She thought she needed more excitement in her life? She wasn't happy with her situation? Would a woman who had so much allow her head to be turned by a passing attraction to some other man?

Margie had been a cop long enough to know that it was a possibility. People didn't behave logically, they behaved emotionally. Maybe Evie Wyler wasn't the greatest mom in the world. Maybe she regretted having had a child. Maybe she wanted out of the situation she was in or wanted something else that she wasn't getting in her relationship with Vance.

Her social media posts seemed to indicate that she was happy with her family and that things were going well for her, but people didn't post the deep dark secret thoughts of their lives in public areas. Usually. They posted the superficial happy stuff, making their lives look normal and perfect, and kept the dark things hidden.

"Her phone logs may show if she was having long or frequent conversations with someone else," Margie said. "That might help sort it out. It would also show whether she had a phone call that morning that precipitated her leaving the house."

"Good thought," Mac agreed. "That will give us some more context. Maybe we should talk to a few friends and family members other than the husband, get their perspective on just what the relationship was like."

"I can reach out to some of the people on her social media," Margie said. "Since the next of kin has been notified, we can talk to other people about her death."

"When were her last posts on social media?" Siever asked. "That might help to narrow our window. And if they have a location code as well…"

"I don't think there was anything since before bed," Margie said. "I'll have to check." She made a note in her notepad.

"Location tracking," Cruz mused. "Does she share her location with any apps? Some people track their walking or running routes."

"Yes… and some people share their locations with family members or friends," Siever said, straightening up. "Does she have location sharing with her husband?"

"It might be worth taking a look at!"

"Wouldn't he have said so when he asked us about her phone?" Jones asked. "He'd be able to look at it and see where her phone was."

Siever shook his head. "He might not pay any attention to it. Some people like to watch their loved one's location, and others don't care. He might not even know he has the ability to check her location, if they happen to have a shared family account and he's never actually tried it."

"Let's find out," Margie encouraged. "Do you want me to give him a call and find out if knows if they have location sharing and to get their account information?"

"No."

Margie looked at Mac at his flat refusal.

"You get a warrant for his phone and any other electronics," Mac said, "and you go over there with it in hand. You don't give him a heads-up that you want his phone or his account information. We don't want him wiping it and deleting their accounts."

"Oh, right." It made logical sense, but Margie hadn't thought about Vance being a suspect in his wife's death. They had been thinking of it as an accident rather than a homicide, which made him a victim as well as her. But if someone had killed Evie Wyler, then the intimate partner was always the first suspect on the list.

She couldn't see him leaving little Ada asleep in bed and taking Evie Wyler to the top of the hill to have a talk with her, then pushing her over. He had come across as an honest, trustworthy, caring person. A nurturer.

He could have motive. The house was in her name and she could sue for sole custody of the child. If Wyler were having an affair, he had a lot to lose. There was a lot to be gained by disposing of his lover rather than trying to work things out and convince her to give him what he wanted. And he would be sad, devastated, the target of much sympathy from all those who knew him.

"I'll start working on a warrant," Margie offered. "Can I run it by you before we submit it? Make sure we're not missing anything?"

Mac nodded. "Of course. But if you're working on the social media follow-up, maybe someone else on the team should draft the warrant. Jones? Did you want to make the assignments?"

"Yes, sir." Jones looked at Margie. "Yes, if you could stay on the social media, I'd appreciate that. Gagnon, if you can draft the warrant. Patenaude and I can serve it once it's issued. We are both familiar to him already, so he should be more relaxed with us, more likely to hand it over without any trouble."

Margie was glad that she would still be able to be a part of serving the warrant.

Knowing where Wyler's phone had been and what had happened to it would be very helpful.

CHAPTER ELEVEN

*A*s Margie had suspected, Evie Wyler had not posted anything on social media after retiring to bed the night of her death. No early-morning shots of the sun coming up or something of interest in the neighborhood.

So they ended up at the house in Wildwood again on Sunday morning. They might even wake Vance up. He said that he usually got up around eight, so he might be up already or still be in bed. It probably depended more upon what little Ada wanted than on Vance's preferred schedule.

He came to the door in boxer shorts and a house coat, wrapping the housecoat around him and tying it up when he saw who it was. "Officers. Is there something I can do to help?"

Jones held the warrant up. "We have a warrant for your phone, sir. With the unlock code. And any electronics that belonged to your wife."

He stared at her. "What?"

"We would like to see your phone, please."

"Well…" he patted at the robe pockets and came out with his phone, but didn't immediately hand it over. "I need this, though. I can't just give it to you."

"It's evidence. You are ordered to hand it over."

He shook his head in disbelief. "You really don't know… you can't understand. I need it for my business. For everything. My life is on that phone."

"And if you dropped it in the toilet, you would find a way to replace it," Jones said unsympathetically. "We are investigating the death of your partner. One would think that you would want to help out with that."

"Of course I do. But I don't see what this could have to do with anything."

Jones put out her hand, and Vance handed it over, looking sick.

"Thank you, sir. Can you tell me whether you have any location sharing apps on the phone?"

"What? Location sharing? I don't think so."

"The ability to see where Evie was. Where her phone was. Is."

He stared at her, blinking, trying to process her words. "No, I don't think so."

Jones looked down at the phone. "Are you both on the same account? Your phone service providers?"

"Yeah. She got onto a good plan, so I switched over to it a year or two ago."

"You're on a household plan?"

"Maybe. I guess so."

"I need both of your phone numbers and your logins for your phone provider and the cloud services you use. And Evie's email address account info."

"I have her address, but I don't know her login. Her password."

"Why don't you write all of the information you know down for us," Jones suggested. "The sooner we have everything we need, the sooner you'll be able to get your phone back."

But Margie suspected he would never get the phone back. If Wyler's death was found not to be accidental, they would need it as evidence. She was starting to be swayed to Siever's thinking. Why would Wyler go out for a walk in the early morning and just walk off the edge of the hill? Drugs or alcohol? Sleepwalking? Suicide? Just tripping or stepping over the edge seemed less and less likely the more she thought about it.

It was another hour before they had all of the information they thought they needed from Vance. It was probably more than they would use, but they didn't want to have to keep going back to him multiple times and wanted the ability to be able to get into whatever of his or Wyler's accounts they could. Something in there might tell the story about what had happened to Evie Wyler.

As soon as they returned to the office, Siever was there, waiting to take the phone and see what secrets he could find.

"We should be passing it directly on to the tech unit," Jones said. "What if there is sensitive information on there that could be destroyed by us accessing it?"

"You got his unlock codes, right?"

Margie and Jones nodded.

"Then I'm not going to destroy anything. Just have a little look around. If I come across something I can't open or something that we need recovered, I'll send it over to IT recovery."

Despite her suggestion, Jones seemed to be perfectly comfortable in having Siever look at the phone. She handed it over to him without further argument. Siever cradled it in his hands like it was a small, injured animal. "Give me a few minutes and I'll figure it out."

❧

MARGIE FIGURED that a few minutes would turn into a few hours. Computer jobs always took significantly longer than she figured they would to get done what she wanted. And everybody she had dealt with on technical issues had been the same way. "Just one minute…" quickly turned into a few hours or a few days.

But Siever had some preliminary results in less than an hour.

The bullpen was quiet; it was just the three of them there on a Sunday morning. Siever hustled them into the boardroom and pointed the remote at the big screen at one end of the room. Turning it on, he quickly worked to get a few reference slides up on the screen.

"I have a few coordinates for you," he announced, looking at the screen rather than his coworkers' faces. "From the night before."

The dot on the map on the big screen showed the location of Evie Wyler's Wildwood home. She nodded. Just where they expected her to be.

"The phone is on the move just before six in the morning. Wyler is out of her house and walking down the street."

A couple of slides to show the dot getting farther away from her home.

"Between six-thirty and seven, she is hanging around a single location."

Margie wasn't good at visualizing maps when looking at the real world and, conversely, had trouble translating a flat map into the actual buildings and roads around her. Satellite imagery helped, but was still not enough to be able to fully translate between the 3D world and the 2D world.

But the big green blob on the map had to be Edworthy park, and that particular shape, the hill that they had stood at the bottom of, looking up.

"So she went there on her own, but then waited." Margie took a swig of her cold coffee. "So now we know for sure. She was meeting someone."

"I haven't gone through all of her previous activity," Siever warned. "It could be that she goes and sits there with a coffee and a journal each morning. Or something good to read. Or just her phone."

"Okay… it *appears* that she was there waiting for someone."

Siever nodded, happier with this statement. "Shortly after seven…" He changed the slide. The dot was farther inside the park. After the fall.

"So it is still out there," Margie observed. "Is this map accurate enough that we can use it to find the phone now?"

"It would be," Siever said, flipping to another slide. "If it were still there."

Margie stared at the map without any dots on it. "Wait, what?"

"Someone removed it from the scene"

"Maybe it just ran out of juice," Jones suggested.

Siever shrugged. "It's possible… but I don't think so." He flipped through a number of screenshots. "It disappeared within a few hours. Most people don't want their phones dying halfway through the day. They charge them during the night so that they are fully charged and ready to go before work in the morning. But Wyler's phone dies far too early for that." He left up the last screenshot before the phone disappeared off of the map.

Margie checked the time stamp. "That's right after we released the scene."

Siever nodded. "That's what I figured too."

And if it wasn't coincidence that it had disappeared right after they released the scene, then what?

Then someone had picked it up and shut it off or destroyed it.

CHAPTER TWELVE

"Who saw it and removed it from the scene?" Jones asked.

They all looked at each other, thinking back to the scene that day and trying to figure it out.

"The first scenario is that it was just picked up by someone random. People find dropped and lost cellphones all the time," Siever contributed.

"Right. They might have turned it in or advertised it somewhere but, since no one has identified it as Wyler's phone, no one has claimed it," Jones agreed.

"But right after we released the scene?" Margie asked. "And it was turned off, not transported somewhere else."

"Yeah. That's weird."

"It could have been damaged in the fall," Siever said. "And it just didn't die immediately. If it was wet or the battery damaged, it might have taken a few hours to short out."

"That makes sense." Jones nodded. "And if so… we should still be able to find it at the location on the map."

He nodded. "Possibly. And the other possibility is… someone was looking for it, or knew where it was, and was just waiting until we released the scene so that they could get their hands on it."

Margie had a knot in her stomach. Was that possible? Had they been working under the eye of a murderer, just waiting for the chance to wipe out any clues of his presence?

Margie rubbed the bridge of her nose. She was starting to get a headache. She really did not like where the investigation was going. It had seemed so obvious that it was an accident. To have everything turned around now…

She could accept that one of the other possibilities was more likely. She liked the idea that it might have been damaged in the fall and had survived Wyler by a few hours. Then it could still be an accident. They could go back to the park and referring to the phone's last known location, find the broken phone.

Or maybe not, if the parks service or someone else had already picked up the broken phone and tossed it in the garbage.

"Do we have pictures of the bystanders?" she asked Jones

"They might appear in a couple, but no… we were taking pictures behind the screens. We did some wider scene shots for perspective, but we didn't intentionally take pictures of all the bystanders. Most of them arrived there quite some time after the body was discovered. They were just attracted by all the activity and wanted to know what was going on."

"Most of them, probably. But people do return to the scene of the crime. They want to make sure that everything is unfolding the way they expected, that nobody suspects them, or that they're getting the kind of attention they wanted to. *If* Wyler was pushed, it's possible that the killer attended at the scene later to see how things were playing out. And it's possible that he could have seen her cell phone and removed it later." Margie shook her head. "It really seems like a long shot. How would he see the phone when we didn't? We didn't see it when we were looking for evidence at the scene, and we didn't find it when we went back with the drones."

"The drones," Jones repeated.

"The phone wasn't there anymore when we took the drones," Siever reminded them. "It was removed on Friday."

"But there *was* a drone. There was the drone that one guy was using at the scene. Gagnon was trying to get rid of him." Jones looked at Margie. "And you got him to go. Did you get his name?"

"Yeah. I wrote down all his information." Margie opened her notebook and flipped back, looking for the details. "I wanted to put a scare into him.

Make him fly straight." She chuckled at her inadvertent pun. "Make him fly straight and respect the law in the future. Here it is. Howard Ross. And I've got his address, driver's license, and birth date."

Jones grinned. "Color me impressed. I'll reach out to him. See whether we can get him to send us a copy of the pictures."

"I'll see whether I can plot the last location of the phone against the scene photos that we have," Siever offered. "In good conditions, we should be able to plot it within five to ten feet."

"Sounds great." Margie had an impulse to offer to do something that would help them to clear the case as well, but there wasn't much else she could do at the moment. It was Sunday and she should be home with her daughter, not hanging around the office any longer than she was required to be. "I think I'll head home, if no one has any objections."

She gave them all the chance, but no one spoke up. Margie nodded. "See you tomorrow, then. I'm looking forward to the morning briefing."

"See you," Jones agreed. "Maybe we'll have it solved by then."

It had been a cooler day and Stella had more energy than she had had in the recent heat. She jumped up when she heard Margie at the door and pranced around her as she walked in. Margie was happy to see her having fun. Too many days recently, Stella had just wanted to lie on the floor, panting, too hot to show any excitement.

"Hi, Mom!" Christina called out from her bedroom in the back of the house. Margie went to the doorway and looked in on her. Christina was stretched out on her bed, phone in one hand, tapping her tablet on the pillow with her other hand. Margie smiled.

"What are you up to?"

"Looking at the pictures of the fire last night. Some of my friends posted or forwarded videos of the flames and the firetrucks."

"What fire?" Margie's mind went immediately to the BC forest fires. But there was no way they had reached Calgary. Especially not the far side of Calgary. They couldn't exactly jump over the entire city to land on the other side.

"There was a fire on the train tracks night before last. Sparked by one of the train wheels, probably."

"Where, exactly?"

Christina motioned to the south. "Erin Woods. Just over there."

Margie knew where Erin Woods was. A little community a fleeing murder suspect had ended up in one day the previous year. Margie's skin prickled with goosebumps and she had a chill, remembering.

Not her best day. But they had caught him. And they would catch Wyler's killer too, if someone had caused her death.

CHAPTER THIRTEEN

oward Ross had, perhaps unsurprisingly, provided copies of his drone footage to the police when requested, so they hadn't had to chase down a warrant. Margie suspected that Jones might have had something to say about confiscating his drone so that they could get the pictures off of it themselves and to make sure that he hadn't tried to delete any evidence. He wasn't likely to want to give up his bird. Who knew when they would give it back, if ever?

Siever had already gone to work sorting out geotags so that the pictures could be arranged by the area they were taken in, giving them the ability to pinpoint the area that Wyler's phone had been in at the time of her death.

Margie and Jones sat at their desks, looking at the photos on their own computers. Margie started with the pictures that were closest to the phone. Not as helpful as it might have seemed, since all that gave her was a big tree with lots of leaves and branches. The leaves were too thick to see through, so that if the phone were in the tree branches or on the ground beneath it, she couldn't see it. She started moving outward from the tree, looking for anything else that might be helpful.

Maybe the phone had been stolen by some bird that liked shiny things. Though Margie thought that a phone would be too big and awkward for a bird to carry. Some of the ravens up north might snatch it, but most of the birds she had seen around Calgary were small and would not be able to lift something like that.

She widened the perimeter so that she should see the privacy screens, and then over them into the accident scene, including Wyler's body. She shook her head in irritation at Ross for using his toy to trespass on the scene and to scope out the dead body. There was really no excuse for that.

She remembered Siever using the grappling hook on his drone to retrieve the purse that had become lodged in the branches of the tree. What if Ross had used the same trick to retrieve a phone from the big tree? Once they had cleared the scene, he was free to go back there, and people wouldn't think there was anything strange about his flying a drone around the park once more. He was probably there often and would be invisible to the regular park users.

But why? Was he somehow connected with Wyler? Or had he just been interested in retrieving what was lodged in the branches of the tree for sport? Or out of macabre interest? Did he now own the phone of a dead woman? And if there were any evidence on it, how were they going to prove that he had it, unless he turned it over voluntarily?

There wasn't anything enlightening in the photographs of Wyler's body. She looked it over carefully, remembering everything in as much detail as possible. Was there anything out of place? Anything they had missed? Evidence on the body or nearby? Some small detail that would make a difference to the investigation?

Margie moved on to the photos taken on the other side of the tree. Not toward Wyler's body, but the interested onlookers, craning their necks for a view of a dead body. Who wouldn't be excited to go home at the end of the day and tell their loved ones around the dinner table that they had seen a dead body in the park that morning? Or to post it on their social media and get all kinds of views and responses?

Some of the faces were easier to see than others. Ball caps and cowboy hats used to shade the spectators from the sun also shielded their faces from the drone. Most of the time it was too high to get a good, identifiable view. She studied each of the people who were watching the scene. Was one of them a killer? Someone who had shown up not just by accident but because he wanted to view the aftermath, and to make sure that no one had seen or suspected him?

"Detective Jones?"

Jones turned away from her monitor to look at Margie. "Find something?"

"No. Maybe."

Jones got up and looked over Margie's shoulder for a better view. "Okay, what are you looking at?"

"You see how everyone is looking in the same direction?"

"Mostly, yes," Jones agreed, nodding.

"But what about this guy?" Margie pointed to a head that was turned at a different angle from everyone else. Black cowboy hat. Western shirt. Like many of the people who attended Stampede functions around the city, both on the Stampede grounds and off. Or even just people who enjoyed dressing up a little for Stampede when they weren't going anywhere. Margie herself had been tempted to pull out some of her traditional Métis clothing a couple of times during the week, but she wasn't sure how it would go over at work and when dealing with the public, so she had not. Cruz, a Filipino immigrant, had been wearing a different western shirt and belt buckle every day of the week. People were fine with the cowboy-themed stuff, but Margie wasn't sure they would be quite as accepting of her traditional dress. Fine for the Elbow River Camp, not so much everywhere else. There was a lot of prejudice toward the visibly Indigenous, even in times when they were supposed to be sensitive about racial bias.

"What's he looking at?" Jones mused.

Margie switched pictures to one that was pulled a little farther back, giving a bit more context.

"At the tree. Where the phone was at the time."

They both studied it. Margie zoomed in on the tree, hoping to be able to spot the phone in the branches. But she suspected she would have to be on the ground like the cowboy hat dude. Or like Ross, to have a drone that she could send closer to have a look around. It had been fun operating the drones as part of their search for Wyler's phone and the purse.

"Some of the later pictures are lower and have a better angle," Jones said, pointing to the file explorer on Margie's screen. "When you made him land his drone."

Margie started to page through the photos, looking at the spectators, keeping her eye on the man in the black hat. As the drone got lower and closer, he started to look more familiar. Who was he? Where had she seen him before?

"Oh!" She and Jones both got it at the same time.

They had seen him at the Wildwood Stampede breakfast. When they had been approached by the schmoozing Vincent Skinner, mayoral candidate, and his campaign manager.

CHAPTER FOURTEEN

"What is he doing there?" Margie demanded. She pulled out her notebook to find the notes she had made while at the breakfast to refresh herself on the names. "Harland Roberts."

"Maybe... he was just hanging around, getting ready for their appearance at the Stampede breakfast, and he was attracted by the lights and sirens, decided to go see what was going on."

"All right," Margie said slowly. "Then why wouldn't he be rubbernecking like everyone else? Trying to catch a glimpse of the body or overhear our discussions? Why is he looking over there?"

Jones nodded. "Because he saw the phone."

"And wouldn't normal Joe Public point that out to the police? Be helpful and get brownie points for helping with an investigation? Especially someone like this, so used to spinning stories for the media and getting all the attention for the campaign that he could."

"Yeah. Of course he would." Jones's lips pressed together. "It's not proof, but it's compelling. We need to know what he did with the phone. And what his connection is to Wyler. Were they lovers? Is that who she was waiting for when she was standing at the top of the hill?"

"Or is he there for Skinner, Mr. Elect-Me-Mayor? Maybe Skinner sent him to clean things up. Make sure that there wasn't anything left behind to implicate him."

Jones *hmmed* and nodded. "Can't rule that out," she agreed. "We need to find out which one of them was connected to Wyler, if one of them was. This can't be a coincidence. He didn't just happen to be there to see what was going on, and see a phone, and then not point it out to the police. And then go back and take it once the scene was released."

"We got her computer on that warrant too, didn't we?"

"Yeah. Siever's got it. Siever, you still have Wyler's computer?" Jones called across the bullpen, but walked closer to Siever's desk as she spoke to be polite.

"Better," Siever said, holding up a small, oblong box, "I've got a copy of it."

"How is that better?" Margie asked.

"Because we can play around with it all we like and not mess up the original, which forensics has. We don't have to wait for anyone else, if you know what you're looking for."

"Well," Margie looked at Jones.

"It turns out we do. We're going on the working theory that Harland Roberts or Vincent Skinner are involved in this and have some kind of connection with Wyler. Can you search that for any reference to either of them?"

"Sure, I can do that."

"I'll call the husband and ask him whether he knows either of them or if there is some way that Wyler could have run into them," Margie offered.

"And I guess I'll run background and see if there are any court cases or charges that the two of them were both involved in. See if there are any intersecting interests or favorite haunts," Jones decided, though she didn't look too excited about the prospect. Computer background was not her favorite thing, but Siever was already tied up with seeing whether there was anything on Wyler's computer to do with the case.

Margie could swap jobs with her. Jones was the primary, so she was entitled to make assignments. But Margie didn't really want to be stuck doing background all day, and Jones decided to let her do what she had volunteered for.

Margie turned back to her computer and closed the various pictures, except for the one that showed Roberts's face. She brought Vance's number up on her screen and dialed the phone.

❧

MARGIE, Jones, Siever and the others all gathered around the conference room table later for a quick bull session, making sure that everyone was up to speed on all the progress on the file.

Jones shook her head in disgust. She stretched, showing that she had been hunched over a computer keyboard for too long already. "I wasn't able to find any connections between either Skinner or Roberts and Wyler. Other than that Skinner was scheduled to campaign in the area the day that Wyler died. That's not a connection that we could use to convince a judge of anything."

"So Roberts just happened to be at our accident scene for no reason that day? I don't believe that," Margie offered. "I talked to the significant other, but he couldn't connect them either. He'd never heard of Skinner or Roberts. Wyler had never mentioned them."

"Wyler doesn't have any credit card charges to a hotel nearby or anything like that," Jones said. "I don't see any suspicious spending patterns."

They looked at Siever. The other detectives in the room quieted, waiting for his response.

"No mention of Skinner or Roberts on the computer," Siever said. "I've done a full search of all files, and neither name is ever mentioned."

Jones groaned. "So it's a dead end."

"I did get access to their phone bills through Vance's phone, though. Logged into their service provider."

Margie remembered asking Vance for the information that he had on passwords and providers in hopes that it would help them to track the location of Evie Wyler's phone. That had paid off in more ways than one.

"What did you find?" Jones asked, her voice squeaking slightly. It was clear that Siever must have found something. He wouldn't tell them that he had logged in to the phone service provider just to tell them that it was a dead end.

"There were calls and texts to a burner phone in the days before her death. Phone was registered to a fake name and address."

"Which may or may not have anything to do with Skinner," Jones said, let down.

"Before she started using that number, there was a call to Skinner's campaign office."

"What?" Jones slapped her notepad down onto the boardroom table with a crack. "We know she called Skinner?"

"We know she called Skinner's campaign office," Siever corrected precisely.

"Well it comes out to the same thing."

He shook his head. "We don't know who she talked to at the campaign office. Was it Mr. Mayor himself? I don't think so. He probably just goes by there once a week to wave to people and tell them what a great job they're doing."

"But Roberts would be there almost full time," Margie said. "So maybe when she called, it was Roberts she talked to."

There were nods around the room.

"No guarantee," Siever said, "but that would be my guess."

Margie didn't sugar coat it. "We have her calling his office, and we have him showing up at the scene of her death. But we don't have anything to show what they talked about or if he had anything to do with her death. Maybe Roberts was who she was waiting for when she died. Maybe they missed each other and he was still waiting when he heard the sirens."

"And maybe they found each other, and he took care of her," Jones said, her voice clipped. "He pushes her off the cliff, opens her purse, rifles through the content and checks her identification to see who she is. Or if she is who she says she is. Then he tosses it over as well."

It fit the evidence. It could have happened that way.

"But what started it? Why did she call the campaign office to begin with? Obviously, it wasn't because she was there to make a campaign dona-tion. She would have just sent it electronically or put a check in the mail. They wouldn't have had to have an ongoing conversation and more than one meeting for that."

"Unless she was working with a foundation that would give grants under certain circumstances, and they needed Skinner to get all his ducks in a row before she would send it. Sometimes those kinds of thing take several meetings," Gagnon suggested.

"It's possible," Jones said, but shook her head. "But I don't think she was working with anything like that. What was it her husband said she was doing?" She looked at Margie.

"Online teacher. Grading papers and such."

"Right. I don't see how that would have anything to do with Skinner's mayoral campaign."

"I don't either," Margie admitted.

It was frustrating to be able to see that there was some kind of connection there, but unable to figure out what it was.

"With her calling the campaign office, it doesn't sound like an affair," she said.

"No. I think you're right," Jones agreed. "Unless they started an affair after the first time she called, and that's why he switched to a burner."

Margie thought of little Ada. How could Wyler have done anything to hurt her? It happened, of course. Parents had affairs all the time; it didn't matter how close they were to their children. Even those who appeared to be so close to their spouses could wander.

"What about asking around at the coffee shops?" Gagnon suggested. "If that's where she often worked from, it may also be where she met up with him."

"Yes. Good idea," Jones agreed. "Oh, and while I'm thinking of it… let's do a garbage search on Roberts. If he retrieved Wyler's phone and threw it out at home, or if he threw out other evidence that connects him to this case, that would be a starting point."

Margie glanced around the room, not expecting anyone to jump in and offer to do that job. Everyone was looking away, checking their watches or phones, attempting to look as though they had somewhere else to be. Margie smiled at Jones.

"You'll help out?" Jones asked, letting out a sigh of relief.

"Sure, why not? I want to get this guy."

CHAPTER FIFTEEN

*D*espite the fact that it was a cooler day with the sun blocked by the smoke of the BC fires, sweat trickled down Margie's forehead. She used the back of her wrist to wipe it away. They had turned up the van's air conditioning as much as possible, but it didn't seem to be doing much. Probably because they also had the windows open in an effort to circulate air so that Margie and Jones wouldn't die from the stench of the garbage bags.

Margie had hoped that a guy like Harland Roberts would be a bachelor subsisting mostly on restaurant food, so that his household garbage would be mostly paper products, plastic wrap, and whatever other non-recyclables Roberts went through.

But bless his heart, he was not a bachelor, but married with two young children. Two very young children. Children still in diapers. And the diaper changers did not seem to put all the used diapers into one diaper pail bag, but into whatever garbage happened to be closest at the time, so every bag they had pulled had little—and not so little—stink bombs lurking amid the rest of the refuse.

Margie gagged. Was she ever glad that she no longer had a baby or toddler. Little children like Ada were wonderful to be around for a few minutes, until they stopped acting like angels and had explosive diarrhea.

Which happened all too often for Margie's tastes. She was so glad to have a teenager who could take care of all of her bodily functions herself.

And the food… it appeared that Roberts, and maybe Skinner too, were dressing above their class. They had looked like the rich and powerful businessmen that she associated with mayors and their offices, but Roberts didn't appear to be making enough money to take people out to fancy restaurants. There was a lot of KD, frozen burritos, and Ichiban noodles. The family threw a lot of leftovers out in the trash instead of the green bin, with only the occasional fast-food wrapper thrown in. And after sitting outside for a week or more in thirty-degree temperatures, everything was rotting and liquefying.

Jones's phone rang. She crouched there for a moment looking at the garbage, then straightened. She slowly stripped off her gloves, wiped sweat from her face, and answered the phone.

"Hey, Cruz. Tell me you have some good news."

She listened, nodding and making sounds of acknowledgment. "Okay. All right. Thanks for letting me know."

She hung up the call. Margie looked at her, eyebrows raised.

"Did he find anything? Tell me we don't have to go through any more garbage."

"Well, no one said that they had seen Roberts at the coffee shops."

Margie groaned. "So that's a dead end. And I seriously don't think that we're going to find anything in here." She looked at the heap of trash they had already been through.

"Yeah. I think this is going to be a bust too. But… one of the coffee shop employees did remember seeing Wyler."

"We already know that she frequented coffee shops to do her work. That doesn't mean anything."

"He said that he saw her there with another woman."

"Okay." Margie considered. "Is there something about this other woman that helps us?"

"I don't know. I'm thinking about it. Her job is online, on the computer. Vance said she didn't do any face-to-face tutoring, even virtually. So who was she there with?"

"A girl friend. If you know your best friend is at a coffee shop all day long, why not stop by at some point for a cup of coffee and a visit?"

"Maybe," Jones admitted. "But if that's where I went to get away from the distractions and get some work done, I'm not sure I would tell any friends where I was, for just that reason. Everyone would think it was okay to interrupt."

"So what are you thinking?"

"The witness said that the other woman seemed to be upset about something. He thought maybe Wyler was trying to pressure her into something."

"Wyler was trying to pressure someone else into something?"

Jones nodded. "I'm wondering… maybe this was blackmail. Wyler was trying to get someone to pay up. Maybe this girl was having an affair with Roberts, and that's the tie between them." Jones looked at the trash around them. "I mean… I could understand if he didn't want to come home to this. A politician with a girl on the side, that's not exactly a shocker, is it?"

"No. So would she be able to blackmail him for something like that?"

"Sure. Just because it's common, that doesn't mean that he wants everyone to know about it. If it's Skinner, he doesn't want his public to know that he's not the perfect family man. If it's Roberts, he doesn't want his boss to know that he's got a girl on the side. It's bad optics, if he gets found out. So if Skinner finds out Roberts is playing around on the side, he's gone."

"Maybe. It does seem like they're both trying really hard to appear to be something that they are not."

"Fake it 'til you make it. That's the world of politics."

"So how do we find out who has a girlfriend?"

"See if we can get the phone logs for the burner phone, to start with. See if there is another number that it calls regularly. If he had a different phone to talk to Wyler, that's probably the same one as he used to talk to his girlfriend."

"Nice. We can do that."

"We may as well go back to Vance too. See if he knows anything about this woman Wyler saw at the coffee shop. Maybe we're wrong and it's his sister, or someone else from work, or a best friend. Maybe he can tell us something. Whether we're on a wild goose chase."

Margie wiped her face. "I think we'd better get cleaned up first."

CHAPTER SIXTEEN

*V*ance did not look too impressed when he saw the women on his doorstep. Margie felt like checking the mirror again to make sure she hadn't missed a smudge or something else offensive. He should be happy that they were clean and presentable. He wouldn't have liked it if they had shown up on his doorstep half an hour earlier.

"You again." His forehead was creased. "Do you have news? Are you closing the case?"

"We're getting closer," Jones said with a bland smile. "We'll be sure to let you know our findings when we have something to report."

"Then what are you here for? You already got my phone and Evie's computer. I don't know what else to tell you. She fell down and died... it was an accident. I wasn't there. She just... I guess she just tripped and fell. Sometimes that happens. People do trip and fall."

"Can we come in to talk?" Jones asked.

He looked like he would say no, but good manners prevailed and he motioned for them to enter. "I only have a few minutes... I don't mean to brush you off, but I do still have my work to do and Ada is down for a nap. She doesn't sleep for long, so I need to use the quiet time to my best advantage."

"We shouldn't be too long," Margie assured him.

They all sat down. Jones looked around the pleasant little living room. "You have a very nice house."

"Thank you. It's very comfortable. Evie was always good at... making people comfortable. Knowing just the right touches to make a room seem friendly. Me... I have no sense of style. My idea of decorating is Ikea shelves."

Margie laughed. "There are some very nice Ikea shelves. And you know what I always loved about Ikea, besides the cool decorating ideas? That they have a kids' play place and you can just walk around and look without little ones underfoot. And then there's a restaurant at the end where you can have meatballs and a hot dog..."

Vance gave her a more genuine smile. "Date night."

Margie nodded. "And you don't have to feel guilty, because the little one has a blast too. Shopping, together time, dinner, and a happy, tired kid. It's the best."

Jones didn't have any children. She just looked at Margie and shook her head slightly, bemused. "Why not just hire a babysitter?"

"Because the play place at Ikea is *free*."

"Not if you spend hundreds of dollars on furniture you don't need."

Margie couldn't help chuckling. "Oh, believe me, you *need* the furniture."

They were all smiling. Vance was getting more relaxed. But they did want to move quickly, to get as much out of him as they could before Ada got up from her nap. She would be distracting. They wouldn't get far once she was underfoot again.

Jones began delicately. "Mr. Vance. Trevor. We've been making some inquiries at the coffee shops where Evie might have gone to do some work."

"Inquiries... about what? What could that possibly have to do with her death?"

"We're just exploring all avenues. Going where the evidence takes us." Soothing words that meant nothing.

"But she fell down a hill. What does that have to do with working in a coffee shop?"

Jones didn't try to explain it to him. He was the one who wanted them to move along. "At one of the coffee shops, they mentioned seeing Evie, and also said that she had been there with another woman."

"Another woman. Who?"

"We're hoping that you can help us out with that one."

"I don't know who she would have been there with. Someone else who hung out there to work and they got talking? It could be anyone."

"I'm thinking it was someone she knew outside of the coffee shop. Did she have a best friend that might have dropped in to see her? A sister? A client?"

"She went there to work, not to visit. But I don't know. She could have asked someone to meet her there. We didn't keep tabs on each other. She didn't tell me everyone she talked to during the day, and neither did I. We did our own things and spent time together when we were able to."

"It seems like you were more roommates than partners. Was Evie seeing someone else?"

"I told you before, no. I don't know why that is so hard to believe. We didn't have other people. Friends, yes, but not partners. Casual friendships."

"This woman was blond, a little shorter than your wife, hair in a pixie cut…" Jones offered.

Vance scowled, shaking his head. "No, I can't think of who that would be. Maybe it's just somebody who was having coffee and they got to talking. Evie was a friendly person. She liked interacting with other people. She worked on her own, but she wanted to be around other people still. Grown-up people, not two-year-olds."

"Sure, of course. So you think it was just someone she happened to meet. The witness said it seemed like Evie was trying to talk her into something."

"I don't know," Vance said blankly. He looked off into the distance. "Maybe she thought that the woman would like to take one of the classes that Evie offered. Trying to talk her into giving it a try. People are leery about trying something new."

"What kind of classes did Evie teach?" Margie asked.

She imagined some work by Shakespeare or Dickens. Maybe a whole English lit course. Or maybe she was into history. Or home decorating.

"She taught different classes at different times. But the backbone of her work was ethics."

"Ethics," Jones repeated, looking as surprised as Margie felt. She had assumed that it would be something in the arts. Something creative. What a sexist assumption. There was no reason it couldn't be math, or hard science, or ethics. "What was her background?"

"Journalism and law. Pre-law. She was taking some night classes, or online classes, through the same company as she worked for. But she wasn't sure if she was ever going to get a law degree. She really liked what she was doing. And she was very good at it. She got really high ratings from her students. I'm sure a lot of people get into this kind of teaching online thinking it's going to be simple. A walk in the park. But it was a lot of work. Like I said, it wasn't all multiple-choice tests that the computer could mark. She had to grade essays and all kinds of other projects. Her students really liked her."

"And she never saw any of them face to face?"

"No. They were all over the world. Not just local."

"And she didn't ever meet any of the local students? Maybe have a pub night at the end of the class with anyone who was in Calgary or Red Deer?"

"No."

Jones and Margie posed a few more unimportant questions, and then excused themselves, telling Vance that they were done and he could get back to his work. Which he seemed quite happy to do. He saw them out at the door, promised to let them know if he thought of anything, and they promised to let him know when there had been a resolution on the case, and they went their separate ways.

CHAPTER SEVENTEEN

*M*argie and Jones got into the car without saying anything to each other. Then before starting the engine, Jones turned to her and said what they were both thinking.

"She was teaching ethics. You don't suppose that the woman she met in the coffee shop was a student, do you?"

"One who had written an essay about someone local who had poor ethics?" Margie suggested.

Jones nodded. "Exactly what I was thinking." She pulled out her phone and dialed in, on speaker so that Margie could hear.

"Siever."

"Do you still have that copy of Wyler's computer handy?" Jones asked, knowing that he would. It was an active case; of course he still had it on his desk.

"What are we looking for?" he asked, bypassing any unnecessary discussion.

"Wyler taught ethics. We think that the meeting in the coffee shop might have been with one of her students. Someone who had written something about Skinner or Roberts."

"What meeting at the coffee shop?"

"Cruz and Gagnon were checking out the coffee shops that Wyler might have gone to in case she had been seen there with Roberts. No one saw her with *him*, but they did see her with another woman, whom she seemed to be pressuring. If this woman was a student and had written something about Skinner or Roberts, then she might have been trying to get her to report them to some authority or the media."

"There are a lot of documents on this computer," Siever warned. "And we've already searched it for mentions of Skinner or Roberts. There are no files that mention either of them by name."

"She might not have named them. Look for something about a politician or candidate. It should have been received shortly before Wyler called the campaign office. She couldn't get the student to report the guy, so she thought she would have a go at it herself."

"And written by a female student. Well, those parameters will help to narrow it down. Are you coming back here?"

Jones looked at Margie, who nodded. "Yes," she told Siever. "If we can figure out who the woman is, we might be able to pull this all together."

❦

SIEVER HADN'T FOUND the essay by the time they got downtown, but he'd made some good inroads and was reading through the files that he had filtered out.

"I could never be a teacher. All these typos and incomplete sentences..."

Margie laughed. "Luckily, you don't have to grade them. Just to find the one that made Evie Wyler reach out to her student."

"You're sure that's what happened?"

"Well... no, we can't be sure, but it's a good theory. One that we have to run down."

Siever nodded.

"Do you want to split the files between us and we can each read a few?" Jones asked.

He glanced at the file list on his screen. "No. I've just got a few left. It wouldn't be worth my time to divvy them up."

"Anything interesting so far?"

"It's an interesting topic. But I wouldn't want to spend hours reading them."

"Well... we'll just be over here, pretending that we're not waiting to see what you find," Jones said, motioning to their desks. Like he wouldn't know where to find them once he had finished his review.

Siever gave her a brief smile, then dove back into his document review.

ℰ

EVENTUALLY, Siever joined Margie and Jones with a couple of printouts. He handed them each one. "I think this is the most likely candidate. If it's not the right one, there are some other possibilities. But a local woman, in that time frame, writing about a politician… this is your best bet."

Margie took her copy and focused on it, tuning everything else out. It was the story of a hit and run driver. A woman had been killed crossing the street. But the driver would not turn himself in. The passenger had a number of reasons for not reporting him herself, including the fact that she had been drunk and high at the time. She had done her best to forget about it, to push it far away into the back of her mind.

And then the driver decided to run for office. The hit and run had never been attributed to him. As far as anyone was concerned, he had a clean record. Everyone except the passenger. But she had built a life for herself. She supported herself and did good work and service for others. If she reported it and ended up being arrested as well as the perpetrator, she would lose her child and the community would lose the other good work that she had been doing. Wasn't it better for her to remain in the community where she could continue to do good?

"Bingo," Jones said. "This has got to be it. Skinner was the hit and run driver."

"And Wyler knew that the student was local, so she tried to convince her to report it like she should."

CHAPTER EIGHTEEN

*J*ones and Margie took the chance that Kimberly Martin would be home in the evening. If she was an online student, she was probably working during the day and upgrading at night. Of course, she could be working at night and doing school during the day, but it was worth seeing whether she was home. If not, they could try to reach her in the morning.

The woman who answered the door fit the description of the woman at the coffee shop. A cute blond bob, about Margie's height and similar to her in age, though the fine smoker's wrinkles around her mouth made her look older. It was a vice that Margie was glad she had avoided.

Kimberly raised her brows, looking them over warily.

"Yeah? Can I help you?"

"Miss Martin? We're with the Calgary Police Service. Could we come in to talk, please?"

She stood there for a moment considering, then stepped back and let them into her apartment. It was small but neat. She had obviously been eating sitting in front of the computer; whether to do schoolwork or watch Netflix, Margie couldn't tell from her angle. They all sat down in the worn furniture arranged in a conversational grouping.

"What's this about?" Kimberly asked nervously.

"Have you ever met this woman?" Jones showed her a picture of Wyler, taken from her Facebook page.

"That's Evie Wyler, isn't it? She's one of my teachers."

"Yes, that's right. Did you meet with her a couple of weeks ago?"

"Yeah." Kimberly looked anxious. She shook her head. "I don't know what she's told you, but…"

"Actually, Miss Wyler hasn't told us anything. She died a few days ago."

Kimberly's eyes widened with shock. "She died? How? What happened?"

"It initially looked like an accident, but we are investigating whether it might have been homicide. We're hoping that you'll be able to help us with that."

Kimberly's mouth opened and closed. She didn't seem to be able to get the words out. Her face had gone very pale. Margie got up and, without asking, went to the little kitchenette and found a glass. She ran the cold faucet for a bit, then filled the glass. She took it over to Kimberly, who took it with a vague nod.

"Have a drink. It will help you to feel better," Margie encouraged.

Kimberly took a sip, then a longer gulp. She put the glass to the side, away from the computer. "How could she be dead?"

"When you met with Miss Wyler, I assume you talked with her about your essay," Jones said.

"How do you know about that?" Kimberly got out in a strangled voice.

"We have Miss Wyler's computer."

Kimberly breathed out a curse. She put her face in her hands, shaking her head.

"Would you like to tell us about it?"

"No! You think I want to end up dead, like her?"

"Have you been threatened?" Margie asked.

"Of course I have! Do you know what would happen to me if people found out what had happened?" Kimberly shook her head and breathed loudly into her hands, sobbing.

"You were a passenger, not the driver. You can't control what the driver does."

"He said that if I ever told anyone, they'd put me in prison too. I was… under the influence. I wasn't a credible witness. And if I said that he'd done it, they would say that I was the one behind the wheel."

"They?" Margie prodded.

"Hal and Vince." Kimberly swore again. "Why did you have to come here?"

"I know that doing the right thing is hard," Jones comforted. "But you'll feel better once everything is straightened out. I promise."

"I have a little girl. I can't go to prison. And I try to do things to help others out. I volunteer in the community. I take old people their meals. I try really hard to contribute to society."

She felt so guilty about the hit and run, she had bargained with herself, saying that she would make up for it. It wasn't the first time Margie had seen that behavior.

"Nobody has said anything about you going to prison," Jones assured her. "You need to talk about what happened. As a passenger, you are not responsible for what the driver did. You should have reported it, yes, but we can work with that."

"Hal said that I would go to prison." Kimberly was shaking. "He said if I breathed one word, I would go to prison. And then…" She sobbed, losing control. "I had to go and write that stupid essay!"

"You wanted to tell someone what had happened, didn't you?" Margie asked. "It has been such a heavy burden to bear; you hoped that it would be easier if you could tell someone else."

Kimberly nodded.

"Well, now we're here," Jones said. "Let's talk about it. Get it all off your chest."

Kimberly pulled her hands from her face and patted her pockets. Her face was wet, blotchy, and miserable. Margie had a couple of tissues ready and handed them to her. "Have another drink," she prompted.

Kimberly obediently blew her nose and drank more water, which seemed to steady her.

"When did this happen?" Jones asked. "Did you know Vince and Hal from somewhere?"

"From high school. They were buddies back then, Hal always taking Vince's crap and trying to do everything for him." Kimberly blotted the corners of her eyes. "Vince was always a bully. None of us came from money, and we kind of hung around together. The poor, unpopular kids. Vince was always trying to run some scam or another. To make money or to make the teachers think that he was such a great guy. They didn't see what he was like when it was just us. But I didn't have anyone else to hang out with, you know?"

"And this accident, did it happen during high school?" Jones asked.

So far, they didn't even have a name to put to the hit and run victim. It could have happened anywhere, any time.

"It was after school. A year or two, I guess. We didn't really hang out together anymore. Everybody had their own thing. But we thought we'd get together, have some fun. Just... relax and take a break from the rat race. From having to pretend to be something... something that we weren't."

Margie nodded encouragingly. "Take off the masks and just be yourself again. Relive those hey-days."

"We never had good times in school. It was all pretty miserable. Maybe Vince did, but the rest of us... we were just... trying to find something. Something that wasn't there. Not for us."

"So you went out together for a few drinks?" Jones suggested.

Kimberly blew her nose again. There was a tissue box nearby, and she pulled out a few more sheets. "Yeah. Drinks. Other stuff. We were all so wasted."

"Maybe you should have caught a cab or a bus."

"Not Vince. He was always so... arrogant and single-minded. He didn't *need* a cab or a bus. He could drink all night and it wouldn't affect him." Her sarcasm was biting.

"Do you remember where and when the incident happened?"

"Memorial Drive and... one of the bridges." She closed her eyes, forehead wrinkled. "I don't remember which one. In my dreams... sometimes it's one place, sometimes it's another. It was dark. I was dizzy, it's lucky I can remember anything considering how stupid drunk I was."

"And what happened?" Margie asked. "How much do you remember?"

"I remember it all. It was a red light. But Vince just blew through it. There were no other cars around, just us, so he didn't think he had to stop. But there was..." A loud sniff. Kimberly wiped her nose and pushed through, trying to get all the sickening details out. "There was a woman in the intersection. With a cart, you know, all of her stuff."

"Homeless?"

She nodded. "Yeah. Hal said..." Kimberly wiped her eyes, which were again streaming. "He said it didn't matter. No one would miss her. No one would be asking after her or care if she died. Because she was just some old bag lady. Like she didn't matter at all."

Margie wondered if her family knew what had happened to her. Whether the body had been matched to an identity, or whether she was a Jane Doe and the family had never been notified of her death.

"Okay." Jones's voice was calm and matter of fact. "Now we know what happened. Now I want to hear what happened afterward. Right after. Did they stop? Go back to see if she was okay?"

"No. I was screaming... I said we had to go back and help her. Call an ambulance. Vince was laughing. Hal said we couldn't go back. We couldn't be seen there. Vince said nobody saw us, we could still go back and report it. Pretend that we had seen someone else hit her. But Hal said... Hal said there would be a dent in the car where we had hit the woman and her cart. If the police saw that, they would know that we were the ones who had hit her."

Hal was probably the smartest of the bunch. He was still doing the same thing, warning and directing Skinner if he started to go off the rails. Trying to make sure they succeeded, because he wanted out. He wanted the life that he had been dreaming of—a nice house and car. Nice suits and prestige. A nice fat salary from the mayor.

But he knew that there was no way Vincent Skinner would make mayor if it were revealed that he was a cold-hearted killer. Calgary would elect a drunk, but not a killer.

So he had to stop anyone he thought was a liability.

"Did Hal threaten you?" Jones asked Kimberly.

She nodded. She cleared her throat, but her voice was still cracking. "He reminded me that I'd go to prison if I said anything. Said that they would both say that I was the one in the driver's seat and they had just been keeping quiet to protect me. Because they were gentlemen."

"And you said you'd stay quiet."

"Yeah. I didn't want to go to prison." She broke into fresh, racking sobs.

"Right," Jones agreed. "Now take a few deep breaths. We're going to go on and talk about Evie Wyler."

Kimberly obediently dragged in several long breaths. Margie found herself doing the same, whether to calm her own rapidly beating heart or to help comfort Kimberly, she didn't know. But it helped.

"How did she contact you?"

"She emailed me. Said that even though it wasn't a service that was included in my package, she liked to meet with the students who were local. To give them a chance to ask questions face to face and sort out anything we needed help with. But when I got there, to the coffee shop, that wasn't what it was. She started asking me about my essay. If it was true and who it was. Vince announcing that he was going to run for mayor really set me off. I was so mad that he could do something like that, pretending that he'd never done anything wrong. I was mad when I wrote that essay, or I would never..." Kimberly shook her head. "I should never have written it. I didn't want all this!" She made a motion that included her and the two detectives.

"It had to come out sooner or later," Jones said. "It was driving you crazy. You couldn't just forget it."

Kimberly nodded.

"So what did you tell Evie? Did you give her their names?"

"No... but I think she already knew. I guess it wouldn't be that hard to figure out who I went to school with. Even just picking the candidate who was closest to me in age."

"And she tried to persuade you to report the hit and run."

"Yeah. But I was too scared. I know Hal. I know he would do anything for Vince. I could never figure out why he was so devoted to Vince. I mean, it wasn't like they were anything alike. But I knew Hal would do whatever it took to protect Vince. So I wasn't going to do anything. I couldn't."

"What did Evie say about that?"

"I don't know. She was disappointed in me. But she said it wouldn't affect my mark."

"Did she tell you that she was going to contact Vince or Hal directly?" Margie asked.

Kimberly shook her head, her eyes swimming in tears. "Why would she do that? Why?"

"I guess... she thought it was the right thing to do."

CHAPTER NINETEEN

*I*t took most of the next day to verify everything they could about Kimberly's story and to get the warrants they needed but, once they had everything together, it wasn't too hard to track down Vincent Skinner. He was doing everything he could to keep the public's attention, including publishing his appearances on his campaign website and constantly live-tweeting events. So Jones and Margie went to the fundraiser and showed their police badges to get past the check-in table.

They scoped out the event, noting all the exits, as well as any security, and pinpointed both Skinner and Roberts. Since they were on opposite sides of the room initially, Margie and Jones bided their time, watching the events of the evening unfold.

Roberts went up on the stage first and, calling for everyone's attention, welcomed them and gave a little build-up to Skinner coming on-stage. After the intro, he motioned to Skinner, who joined him at the microphone, giving him hearty thanks and a perfunctory hug with a pat on his back. Roberts stood slightly to the side while Skinner made his pitch to the room. There was applause, and Skinner and Roberts started down the steps to leave the stage and schmooze with the guests. They slowed and stopped when they saw Jones and Margie waiting for them at the bottom.

Margie could see them trying to remember where they had seen the two unfamiliar women before. It was important for politicians to be able to remember faces, names, and details of their donors' lives. She smiled and motioned for them to come the rest of the way down the steps.

"We met at the Wildwood Stampede breakfast."

"Oh, of course," Skinner reached out his hand to shake with Margie, still not able to remember anything about her.

"Calgary Police Service," Margie added.

"Ah!"

She took Skinner's hand. "You're under arrest, Mr. Skinner." She swiftly handcuffed him without meeting any resistance. Skinner didn't understand what was going on.

Jones had a little more trouble with Roberts, but she was expecting it and was quick to restrain and handcuff him before he could begin to fight in earnest.

"What's going on here?" Skinner demanded. "Is this some kind of joke?" He looked at the baffled donors around him, looking for one who had arranged to make a mock arrest. Before COVID, there had been mock arrests on Law Day each year, with the arrestee having to raise money for bail, which would be given to the charity of choice, in order to be released.

But it wasn't Law Day and it wasn't a mock arrest.

Roberts's face was suffused with blood. He seemed to have a better idea of what was going on.

"You can't do this!" he growled. "What are your badge numbers? You can't just come into a private function and arrest us. Where's your warrant? Where's your cause? I want to talk to your boss!"

Margie flashed the arrest warrant at him. "Trust me, we made sure to get all our ducks in a row before coming here."

"What's going on here? What's this about?" one of the guests demanded. "I'm a lawyer. Do you really think that this is appropriate? I'm sure it could have been dealt with privately. Embarrassing a public figure could lose you your badge!"

"What area of law do you practice?" Jones asked, patting Roberts's pockets and waistband for a weapon.

"Securities," the lawyer sneered, looking down his substantial nose at her.

"Well, maybe you have a friend who is a criminal lawyer and could give these gentlemen some advice on defending a murder charge. Or rather, two murder charges."

Jones smiled at the shock on the lawyer's face.

"Murder?" Skinner repeated. "What are you talking about?"

"The murders of Kelly Forsythe,"—they'd been able to look up the name of the hit and run victim once they had the approximate date and location to work with and found that all of the details matched what Kimberly had said—"and Evie Wyler."

"Who are they? I've never heard of either one of them before."

"Let's go," Margie said, giving Skinner a little tug to get him on his way. He stumbled a little, but regained his balance again. He was reluctant to leave the event, but by the time he had reached the door had probably concluded that it was better to get out of there than for everyone to know the details of his dirty laundry. Outside, Margie pointed Skinner to one of the waiting squad cars. "You see? We could have come in with uniforms and a lot of noise. You should be grateful that Detective Jones and I figured we could make the arrests on our own."

Skinner scowled at her. "This is some kind of mistake. I'm not a murderer. I am a respected businessman."

"Well, you're actually not even that at this point." Though undoubtedly, he wished it were true. The guy hadn't been able to hold down a respectable job for more than a few months at a time. His whole campaign was smoke and mirrors. "To answer your question, Kelly Forsythe is the woman that you ran over a few years back and did not report. You were under the influence of alcohol at the time, so you might not remember it too clearly. And Evie Wyler is the ethics professor who was threatening to break the news about that death."

His jaw dropped. Margie had the uniformed officer standing by his car give Skinner a pat-down to ensure that he wasn't carrying a weapon. Though she was pretty sure that if either of them was armed, it would be Roberts. By the time he was finished and Skinner was facing Margie, he had regained his power of speech.

"Is this about Kimberly Martin? Do you have any idea of that woman's history?"

"Do I need to know more than the fact that she was there with you and saw the whole thing?"

"You should know better than to rely on the testimony of someone like her. That little tramp was higher than a kite. Any competent attorney will tear her apart on the stand."

Margie just smiled at him.

"And this other woman? Who is that? I've never even heard of her. How could I be guilty of doing anything to a woman I've never even heard of before?"

"Maybe you should ask your campaign manager about that one. I'm sure he'd be happy to give you all the details."

"Hal?" Skinner looked over at the other man, being placed in another squad car. He shook his head. "What are you talking about?"

"About the woman that he pushed off a cliff to save you having to face charges for Kelly Forsythe's death."

Skinner's face drained of color. "I don't know anything about that," he asserted. "I've never even heard of her."

Margie nodded. "I'm sure the Crown Prosecutor will be interested in anything you have to tell him about it."

CHAPTER TWENTY

*M*argie rolled her shoulders and massaged her neck before getting out of the car, trying to let go of any tension that lingered after the last few long days. She wanted to be relaxed and cheerful for Christina and able to enjoy the evening with her.

The lights were on—nearly every light in the house—so she knew that her daughter was home and not out with Tracy somewhere.

As she walked up to the front door, she could see Stella through the screen, tail waving like a flag, excited to see her. She opened the door and scratched Stella's ears as she walked in. "Who's a good girl? Hmm? Are you my good girl?"

She could tell by the smell that Christina had been cooking. She was surprised. Mostly, the two of them just warmed stuff up in the microwave or put a slice of bread in the toaster if they weren't making a meal together.

"Mmm, what smells so good?"

Christina turned to face her, smiling. "I made bannock. To take to Moushoom."

Margie felt a pang of disappointment. She had meant to make bannock with Christina. But she had been so busy with the Wyler case that she hadn't set aside the time to do it with her. She wished that Christina would have waited to do it with her. But she forced a smile.

"He is going to be so happy. You love him very much, don't you?"

Christina nodded. "I'm glad you got back early enough. We have time to go over and see him while it is still warm, right?"

Margie didn't look at the clock. "Yes. Definitely. We'll go right over so that we can catch him before bed."

"There's lots to go around, so you can have it for your supper too."

Carbs and jam might not be the best supper to lose weight on, but Margie would be sure to go for a run the next morning so that she didn't feel guilty about the indulgence. "You're the best. Thank you." She gave Christina a hug and they wrapped up the bannock.

"We'll zip over in the car today to save a bit of time."

"And the smoke has mostly cleared, so we can take Moushoom out for a walk."

"He'll like that. But most of all, he will like seeing you."

"And you," Christina pointed out.

Margie tucked a lock of hair behind Christina's ear, smiling.

MOUSHOOM HAD NOT GONE to bed yet and was eager to go out when they suggested it. Christina pushed his wheelchair up the hill and Margie held on to Stella's leash. Moushoom reached out to grab Margie's free hand. His hands, while thin, were still strong, like she remembered from when she was a girl. She squeezed his hand and smiled, walking in silence.

"You worry too much," Moushoom commented.

Margie chuckled. "Yes, I probably do."

"You need to let go to be at peace. Do your best, and then let go. We cannot control everything."

Margie had been thinking about little Ada, who would grow up without a mother. Or at least, without her first mother. Vance might find someone else he could share his life with, someone who would be happy to raise a child who hadn't come from her own body. But Ada would not remember Evie Wyler when she was grown.

That was one of those things that Margie could not control.

One of the many things she would have to just let go of.

EDWORTHY PARK

Created in 1962, Edworthy Park has been around for a while. There are picnic shelters and BBQ pits, plenty of washrooms, playgrounds, and trails. The trails are very popular for mountain bikers as well as walkers. The paved pathways join up with the Bow River Pathway and run all the way downtown to Princes Island Park and farther east all the way to Valleyview Park. It is hoped that one day a path will run from Edworthy to Haskayne Park, Glenbow Ranch Provincial Park, and through to Cochrane.

A longtime favourite for family reunions, school class trips, and throwing rocks into the river. Angel's Cafe is close to the north entrance if you're in the mood for a dinner not cooked over the campfire.

Did you enjoy this book? Reviews and recommendations are vital to making a book successful.

Please leave a review at your favorite book store or review site and share it with your friends.

Don't miss the following bonus material:
Sign up for mailing list to get a free ebook
Read a sneak preview chapter
Other books by P.D. Workman
Learn more about the author

Sign up for my mailing list at pdworkman.com and get
Gluten-Free Murder for free!

JOIN MY MAILING LIST AND

Download a sweet
mystery for free

pdworkman.com

PREVIEW OF UNLAWFUL HARVEST

ABOUT UNLAWFUL HARVEST

More Parks Pat Mysteries are on the way!

In the meantime, check out the Kenzie Kirsch Medical Thrillers, beginning with Unlawful Harvest!

CHAPTER 1

*M*acKenzie reached for the ringing phone, trying to drag herself from sleep, but her hand encountered only the empty base of the phone, the wireless handset missing.

She pried her eyes open while feeling for it on the bedside table, knocking off keys and a glass and an empty bottle and other detritus. She swore and blinked and tried to focus. Where had she left the handset and who was calling her so early in the morning? The phone rang five times and went to her voicemail. Too late to answer it. She sank back down onto her pillow and closed her eyes. Whoever it was would have to wait.

But no sooner had it gone to voicemail than it started ringing again. MacKenzie groaned. "Are you serious? Come on!"

She turned her head and squinted at the clock next to her. It was hard to see the red LED display in the bright sunlight. It was almost eleven o'clock. Certainly not too early for a caller, even one who knew that she would sleep in after a party the night before. She rubbed her temples and scanned the room for the wireless handset.

There was a man in the bed next to her, but she ignored him for the time being. He wasn't moving at the sound of the phone, so he'd probably had more to drink than she had. She slid her legs out of the bed and grabbed a silk kimono housecoat to wrap around herself. The caller was sent to voicemail a second time. MacKenzie took another look around the bedroom without spotting the phone, then went out to her living room, also bright with sunlight streaming in the big windows. Outside, the pretty Vermont scenery was covered with a fresh layer of snow, which reflected back the sunlight even more brilliantly. MacKenzie groaned and looked around. The newspaper was on the floor in a messy, well-read heap. The remains of some late-night snack were spread over the coffee table. Some of their clothing had been left there, scattered across the floor, but no phone.

It started ringing again. Now that she was out of the bedroom and away from the base, she could hear the ringing of the handset, and she kicked at the newspaper to uncover it. She bent down and scooped up the handset. She glanced at the caller ID before pressing the answer button and pressing it to her ear, but she knew very well who it was going to be.

No one else would be so annoying and call over and over again first thing in the morning. She couldn't just leave a message and wait for MacKenzie to get back to her, she had to keep calling, forcing MacKenzie to get up and answer it. Her mother didn't care how late MacKenzie might have been up the night before or how she might be feeling upon rising. It was a natural consequence of MacKenzie's own choices. MacKenzie dropped into the white couch.

"Mother."

"MacKenzie. Thank goodness I got you. Where have you been?"

Her mother had been calling for all of two minutes. Where had MacKenzie been? She could have been in the bathroom, having a shower, talking to someone else on the phone, or at some event. Granted, she didn't go to a lot of events at eleven o'clock in the morning, but it *could* happen. Mrs. Lisa Cole Kirsch had a pretty good idea where MacKenzie had been. In bed, like most any other morning.

"What is it, Mother?"

"It's Amanda. She's sick."

MacKenzie nodded to herself and scratched the back of her head. One of the things that would definitely set Lisa into a tizzy was Amanda being sick. She worried over every little cough or twinge that Amanda suffered. She had good reason, but it still made MacKenzie roll her eyes.

"What's wrong with Amanda?"

"I don't know. Maybe it's just the flu, but I'm really worried, MacKenzie. The doctors said to just wait and see, but they don't understand how frail Amanda is. They think that I'm just overreacting and being a hypochondriac. You know that I'm not just a hypochondriac."

"I know. So, how is she?"

MacKenzie had to admit that even though her mother worried about Amanda, her worry was well-justified. Amanda's health could get worse very quickly, and with the anti-rejection drugs suppressing her immune system, she was prone to picking up anything that went around.

"She's not good. She was up all night, throwing up, high fever, she's just not herself. I called an ambulance at eight o'clock. She just can't keep anything down and I don't like the way she's acting. So... weak and listless."

MacKenzie felt the first twinge of worry herself. Amanda had spent much of her life sick, but she was a fighter. She usually did her best to look like nothing was wrong, not letting on unless she was feeling really badly. She would laugh and brush it off as just a bug and smile and encourage MacKenzie to tell her about what was going on in her far-more-interesting life. MacKenzie closed her eyes, focusing on Lisa's words.

"But the doctors don't think that there's anything to worry about?"

"No, but you know... they never do. She has to be at death's door before they'll admit that there might be a problem."

"Have they given her anything or did they just send her back home again?"

"They've got her on an IV and have said that they'll keep an eye on her. But you know they don't really think there's anything wrong. They're just humoring me."

"Yeah. Do you want me to come?"

"Would you? I'm really worried."

"Okay. I'll need a few minutes to get myself together. I'll be there as soon as I can."

"Thank you, MacKenzie. I don't know what I would do without you."

The sad thing was, Lisa would do just fine without MacKenzie. Even though she said that she needed MacKenzie, MacKenzie wouldn't really be able to do anything that Lisa couldn't do herself. She'd been dealing with doctors for a lot of years, and though she didn't pick up on the medical jargon as quickly as MacKenzie did, she could hold her own very well and was stubborn as a mule when it came to Amanda's care. She would protect her baby at all costs, and Amanda would get the best of care whether MacKenzie were there or not.

But if Lisa wanted the extra comfort of having MacKenzie around, who was she to argue? She didn't have anything else going on that prevented her attendance, and even if she did, it was easy enough to beg off of any event with an excuse, especially if the excuse were that Amanda was sick. MacKenzie had used it as an excuse even when it wasn't true. Although technically, even when Amanda was feeling well, she was still sick, so it wasn't really a lie.

MacKenzie hung up the phone and put it down on the brass and glass side table. She scrubbed her eyes with her fists, and when she opened them again, Liam was standing in the front of her.

"What's up?" he asked. "Everything okay?"

He hadn't yet recovered anything more than his boxers and, for a minute, MacKenzie just let her eyes rove over the piece of eye candy, remembering the night before through a slight haze of alcohol. They had gone to the Cancer Society fundraiser, had made the rounds there and let themselves be seen, and then had returned to MacKenzie's apartment for more drinks, some real food, and private entertainment.

"MacKenzie? What's up?"

"Amanda. She's in the hospital and Mother wants me to go over there and reassure her." MacKenzie yawned.

Liam bent over to pick up the various items of clothing he had dropped the night before. "Is she okay?"

"I'm sure both Amanda and Mother will be just fine. But she sounded pretty worried, and she said that Amanda was listless, which isn't like her. A really bad flu, maybe. I hope that's all it is."

"I was going to have a shower before heading out. Do you want it?"

MacKenzie weighed the options. Amanda was in the hospital, so she would be getting the best of care. Did it really matter whether MacKenzie had to wait an extra ten minutes for Liam to shower before she got herself ready?

"Or," Liam suggested, a dimple appearing in his cheek, "we could shower together and be done twice as fast."

"I have a feeling I wouldn't be out of here very quickly if we did that," MacKenzie laughed. They could easily be another hour, and Lisa would be on the phone again, ringing insistently, demanding to know where MacKenzie was and why she wasn't at her sister's side yet.

"Okay," Liam agreed. "So, do you want it?"

"Yes. I guess so. I need to pull myself together even if I am just going to the hospital." Lisa would not want her to show up looking bedraggled. She'd expect MacKenzie to be well turned-out even if it were the middle of the night, which it wasn't.

Liam nodded agreeably. He pulled on his white shirt from the night before, but didn't put on the pants or the rest of his outfit. "Shall I make you some breakfast while you're in there so that you can get out more quickly?"

"Would you? Just a couple of pieces of toast and some juice," MacKenzie requested, heading toward the bathroom. She looked back over her shoulder at him. "And coffee."

He smiled. "I think I know by now that you don't start any morning without coffee."

"Well, I need to fortify myself with *something* this morning before facing my mother."

————

She had a quick breakfast while Liam got into the shower, but he wasn't out by the time she was finished. She poked her head into the bathroom.

"Will you be much longer?"

She could see his shadow through the shower curtain as he turned his head toward her. "Oh… I can just lock up when I leave. You can go ahead."

MacKenzie shook her head. "I don't like to leave people here when I'm not around. Sorry. Can you be quick?"

"Yeah, sure." His tone was agreeable, but clipped. He obviously didn't appreciate that she didn't trust him enough to leave him alone in her apartment. But MacKenzie had been burned in the past by people who didn't respect her privacy, and she wasn't about to leave him there without supervision. She didn't know him well enough. Just because she could go with him to an event, and maybe bring him home afterward, that didn't mean she knew enough about his essential character to leave him there alone. She valued her privacy and there were a few things around the apartment that were quite valuable. Not that she thought Liam Jackson was going to steal them. She knew where to find him if he did. But it just wasn't good policy. If she didn't notice that something was missing right away, she might never be able to track it down again.

"I'll just be two more minutes," Liam promised.

"Thanks."

She went back to the bedroom and, since she had the time and couldn't leave until he was finished, she actually went ahead and pulled her bed into some semblance of order. It didn't look as good as when the maid did it, but it was better than leaving it all rumpled. She would appreciate it when she got home later.

If Lisa could only see her now. Twenty-seven years old and actually making her own bed. On a roll, she went into the living room and picked up the newspaper, which she threw in the garbage, and her clothes, which she threw in the laundry. Liam was out of the shower but not yet out of the bathroom. She threw a random assortment of dishes into the dishwasher and had the place looking pretty tidy when Liam made an appearance, dressed, hair wet but neatly combed, and his face still stubbly, not having taken the time to shave. She stood on her tip-toes to give him a kiss. "Thanks. Sorry about having to rush you out of here. It's my sister. Mother wants me there, so I have to make sure she's okay."

Liam nodded, looking down at her and letting his fingers linger on her jaw for a moment. "That, or you got one of your girlfriends to call to break up the party so that you could get rid of me."

"Ugh. I wouldn't do that when I was still in bed."

He smiled. "Give me a call later, then. Let me know how it goes. And we'll see each other again… soon."

They didn't have anything lined up, no dates, no fundraisers, nothing on the horizon. Liam was a nice guy, good looking, and MacKenzie might add him to her regular coterie of admirers, but she hadn't made up her mind yet. She wasn't one hundred percent sure that he was her type. Whatever that was.

After seeing him out the door, she put on her coat and winter gear and headed for the hospital.

———

When she managed to find her way to Amanda's hospital room, not in the renal unit where she usually was, Amanda was asleep. Lisa sat next to the bed, watching her sleep. Not reading a book. Not looking at her schedule for the week. Just watching her sleep. MacKenzie would have gone crazy. She couldn't stand to have people staring at her.

"Hi, Mom," she said softly.

Lisa looked over at her, automatically making a motion for her to be quiet before she evaluated MacKenzie's voice and the deepness of Amanda's sleep and decided that she probably wasn't being too loud after all.

"How is she doing?" MacKenzie looked over her kid sister. Amanda was twenty years old, but when she was asleep, she looked about ten. She was shorter than MacKenzie, and MacKenzie wasn't exactly an Amazon herself. Amanda was small and elfin, and people often mistook her for a kid if they weren't paying attention. She had a beautiful face, when she was feeling well. She wasn't looking too bad. Her weight was good, her cheeks round rather than sunken like they had been when she'd been through her worst times. She had long, dark hair that got tangled if she didn't take care of it, which was hard to do when she was in a hospital bed all day, but she didn't like to cut it short so that it would be easier to take care of. She said she needed her strength, like Samson.

Amanda was pale, and that bothered MacKenzie. But if she had the flu and had been throwing up for hours, then of course she was going to be pale. It was just a virus. She would be feeling better soon.

"She's sleeping," Lisa stated the obvious. "She's been so sick all night… I'm glad she was finally able to drift off. Maybe she's on her way to feeling better."

"Probably just a bug."

"Yes. Hopefully."

There was an IV hanging, but Lisa had said that Amanda needed it to stay hydrated. It didn't necessarily mean that she was back on some treatment again.

MacKenzie pulled the other chair in the room closer to her mother's and sat down. Amanda had been given a private room, of course. There was no way she was going to be left in some hallway or emergency room curtain. Lisa would see to that.

"Do you want to go get something to eat?" MacKenzie suggested.

"Well..." Lisa's eyes flicked over to Amanda. "I don't know. I don't want to leave her alone."

"I'm here. And you haven't had anything to eat, have you? You've been with her since last night?"

"Yes, you're right."

"Well, you're not going to be any good to her if you're fainting from hunger or all angry and irritable from low blood sugar. So go. I'll be with her if she wakes up. She's not going to be alone."

"Are you sure?"

"Why don't you take advantage of the fact that I'm here, because I'm not going to be here all day. Go have something to eat."

"Okay," Lisa agreed, but she still made no movement to get up, watching Amanda with worried eyes.

"She'll be fine for now. I'll have them page you if something happens."

"Would you?" Lisa brightened at that suggestion. She could go have something to eat and still be sure that Amanda hadn't taken a turn for the worse. She clutched her purse on her lap, then nodded and got up. "Thank you so much, MacKenzie, I appreciate you coming and being here for your sister."

"And for you," MacKenzie reminded her. "Don't you try saying that I never do anything for you."

"I would never say that."

MacKenzie raised her eyebrows as her mother left. She might say it and she might not. But she would certainly imply it the next time she wanted MacKenzie to do something for her and MacKenzie had something else going on or didn't want to be there.

Lisa's heels clicked sharply as she walked away. MacKenzie watched her go. She leaned back in her chair and looked over Amanda once more. The hospital chair was far from comfortable. She was going to have to get used to it if she were going to be there for a few hours.

"I should have brought a book," she murmured to Amanda. She hadn't thought to bring anything with her. She'd just gotten herself together and headed over. And she couldn't go down to the gift shop to pick something up. Not after dismissing her mother and saying she'd stay with Amanda while Lisa was eating. MacKenzie sighed and resigned herself to just sitting there and napping while she waited either for Amanda to wake up, or for Lisa to return from lunch.

Unlawful Harvest is book #1 in the *Kenzie Kirsch Medical Thriller* series. Check it out at pdworkman.com or your favorite online retailer.

ABOUT THE AUTHOR

Award-winning and USA Today bestselling author P.D. (Pamela) Workman writes riveting mystery/suspense and young adult books dealing with mental illness, addiction, abuse, and other real-life issues. For as long as she can remember, the blank page has held an incredible allure and from a very young age she was trying to write her own books.

Workman wrote her first complete novel at the age of twelve and continued to write as a hobby for many years. She started publishing in 2013. She has won several literary awards from Library Services for Youth in Custody for her young adult fiction. She currently has over 80 published titles and can be found at pdworkman.com.

Born and raised in Alberta, Workman has been married for over 25 years and has one son.

§▲

Please visit P.D. Workman at pdworkman.com to see what else she is working on, to join her mailing list, and to link to her social networks.

§▲

If you enjoyed this book, please take the time to recommend it to other purchasers with a review or star rating and share it with your friends!

facebook.com/pdworkmanauthor

twitter.com/pdworkmanauthor

instagram.com/pdworkmanauthor

amazon.com/author/pdworkman

bookbub.com/authors/p-d-workman

goodreads.com/pdworkman

linkedin.com/in/pdworkman

pinterest.com/pdworkmanauthor

youtube.com/pdworkman

Find P.D. Workman's books at

PDWORKMAN.COM

Scan the QR code below